PENGUIN BOOKS

GOD IS A GAMER

Ravi Subramanian, an alumnus of IIM Bangalore, has spent two decades working his way up the ladder of power in the amazingly exciting and adrenaline-pumping world of global banks in India. It is but natural that his stories are set against the backdrop of the financial services industry. In 2008, his debut novel, *If God Was a Banker*, won the Golden Quill Readers' Choice Award. He won the Economist Crossword Book Award in 2012 for *The Incredible Banker* and the Crossword Book Award in 2013 for *The Bankster*. His most recent novel is *Bankerupt*. He lives in Mumbai with his wife, Dharini, and daughter, Anusha.

To know more about Ravi visit www.ravisubramanian.in or email him at info@ravisubramanian.in. To connect with him, log on to Facebook at www.facebook.com/authorravisubramanian or tweet to @subramanianravi.

# GOD

## IS A
## GAMER

## RAVI SUBRAMANIAN

PENGUIN BOOKS

PENGUIN BOOKS

Published by the Penguin Group

Penguin Books India Pvt. Ltd, 7th Floor, Infinity Tower C, DLF Cyber City,
Gurgaon 122 002, Haryana, India

Penguin Group (USA) Inc., 375 Hudson Street, New York, New York 10014, USA

Penguin Group (Canada), 90 Eglinton Avenue East, Suite 700, Toronto, Ontario,
M4P 2Y3, Canada

Penguin Books Ltd, 80 Strand, London WC2R 0RL, England

Penguin Ireland, 25 St Stephen's Green, Dublin 2, Ireland (a division of
Penguin Books Ltd)

Penguin Group (Australia), 707 Collins Street, Melbourne, Victoria 3008, Australia

Penguin Group (NZ), 67 Apollo Drive, Rosedale, Auckland 0632, New Zealand

Penguin Books (South Africa) (Pty) Ltd, Block D, Rosebank Office Park,
181 Jan Smuts Avenue, Parktown North, Johannesburg 2193, South Africa

Penguin Books Ltd, Registered Offices: 80 Strand, London WC2R 0RL, England

First published by Penguin Books India 2014

Copyright © Ravi Subramanian 2014

ISBN 9780143421399

Typeset in Minion by R. Ajith Kumar, New Delhi
Printed at Thomson Press India Ltd, New Delhi

A PENGUIN RANDOM HOUSE COMPANY

*To my father*

# Prologue

## December 2009, New York

Vijay Banga, President of MasterCard International, was anxiously pacing up and down his third-floor office in the global headquarters located in Purchase, New York.

Miles away, in Foster City, California, Joseph Saunders, the CEO of Visa International, multi-billion dollar payment processing giant and MasterCard's greatest rival, was in shock too.

The cause of their trepidation was a meeting presided over by the head of a country, a few thousand miles away. It was a routine meeting but it could shake the very foundations of their business model.

Vijay was the more amenable of the two. He knew that American corporates had elephantine egos. Joseph would not step out of his ivory tower to connect with him. Swallowing his pride, he called for his chief of staff.

'Fix a meeting with Joseph Saunders . . .' he thundered as soon as the man walked in. Vijay stared at the ceiling for just an instant and added, '. . . tomorrow evening.'

'Tomorrow?' The chief of staff was surprised. It was too short a notice.

'Yes!' Vijay nodded. 'In Washington DC. Book a suite in your name at the Hyatt Regency. I don't want the press to get wind of this.'

'What do I tell Mr Saunders?'

'You won't need to tell him anything because he won't ask.'

At 6.30 p.m. the next day, Joseph Saunders strode into the Hyatt Regency and was ushered into an executive suite on the top floor. Vijay was waiting for him. The two adversaries shook hands graciously.

'Four billion dollars is a lot of money,' Joseph began. 'Today, most of it comes to the two of us.'

'Yes. Over 20 per cent of my revenue is at stake. We need to do something.'

'We don't have a choice—they have to be stopped!' Joseph and Vijay were in agreement.

The doorbell rang. A worried Joseph turned towards the door.

'I have requested Senator Gillian Tan to join us,' volunteered Vijay. 'Someone will have to force the hand of the US government.' He peered through the viewfinder and opened the door. 'Good evening, Senator!'

Tall and handsome, with salt-and-pepper hair and a taut complexion that belied his age, Gillian possessed a personality that overwhelmed the suite. If he weren't a politician, he'd have a real shot at Hollywood.

'Fifteen minutes is all I could manage at such short notice. It better be quick, and it better be good.' His tone conveyed authority. Joseph had met Gillian in the past but not as often as Vijay seemed to have. Their camaraderie was evident.

'Two days ago, Dmitry Rutskoy . . .' Vijay started off, only to be interrupted by Tan. 'The Russian premier?'

'Yes. In his speech at the Duma, he instructed Sergei Makarov, head of Russia's finance ministry, to come up with a National Payment Card System or NPCS, which would collect fees on all credit card transactions that occur on Russian soil.'

'Why should that bother you?' Gillian knew where this was heading, but he wanted to be sure.

'For every dollar spent on a credit card in Russia, about a cent comes to the card companies. As of now, this is split between MasterCard and Visa.' Joseph butted in.

'And that would add up to. . .?' Gillian was curious to know.

'Four billion dollars. Russia is one of our largest markets. If Sergei manages to establish the NPCS, the 1 per cent payout to MasterCard and Visa will stop. We will be out of the Russian market in no time. If other countries follow Russia's lead and set up their own local payment networks, it will kill our revenues all over the world!'

'So what do you want me to do?' asked Gillian.

'Impress upon Russia to protect our interests.'

Gillian contemplated, but only for a moment. 'Send me a note. I will speak to the President.' Seeing the relief on the two faces, he rose. 'Will that be all gentlemen?'

## December 2010, United States of America

An innocuous organization shook the US government to its very core.

WikiLeaks was a small international entity that published secret and classified information, leaked by anonymous sources, online. It was threatening to release 300,000 classified documents that could severely embarrass the US government.

A furious US State Department served notice to WikiLeaks and its founder Julian Assange, labelling their activities illegal. Undeterred by this threat, in November 2010, WikiLeaks went ahead and published 251,287 US embassy cables. It took the world by storm. Journalists and newspapers in ninety countries carried extracts of the cables.

The US government struck back with a vengeance, leaving no stone unturned to alienate WikiLeaks. WikiLeaks existed to propagate its libertarian ideology and, being a not-for-profit organization, relied on grants and donations from supporters for its survival.

On 1 December, Amazon.com—which hosted the WikiLeaks website in the US—cut off access to it. Amazon's official release said that WikiLeaks had not honoured a contract but insiders caught on to the fact that Uncle Sam had called.

A week later, Vijay Banga's phone rang. He was vacationing in India.

'Hey, Vijay!'

'Morning, Gillian.'

'My team contacted your office. They were told you are on vacation.'

'Only for a few days. I'll be back after Christmas.'

'Wonderful. Unfortunately, we don't have the luxury of time.'

'Is there something you want me to do?'

'Yeah. This WikiLeaks thing. . . We don't want any American citizen donating money to WikiLeaks. We don't want MasterCard or Visa to be used as gateways to service these traitors. Please cut off all cardholders from making payments to WikiLeaks.'

'Gillian! Are you serious? What will we say if someone asks us why we did it?'

'That's not for me to figure out, is it?'

'It won't be the right thing to do, Gillian. We will get a lot of flak for it.'

'Must I remind you Vijay that the US government did not get into issues of propriety when we lobbied with the Russians for you? Even so, if you want a precedent to strengthen your case, PayPal has blocked WikiLeaks.'

Vijay didn't respond.

'You there, Vijay?'

'By when do you want this done?' Vijay was worried that this would come back to haunt him. But Gillian was too important to be denied.

'Thirty minutes? You can stretch it to forty-five if it helps.'

'Give me till tomorrow at least, Gillian.' Vijay wanted to check with his legal and compliance teams on the implications of executing something like this.

'We have to move now, Vijay. You are either with us or against us in this battle against WikiLeaks. There is no third option.'

~

By that evening, Visa and MasterCard had followed PayPal's example and blocked their customers from accessing WikiLeaks. Every WikiLeaks bank account was frozen. WikiLeaks had run dry. It was the greatest financial blockade on any company in the history of the US. The blockade crippled WikiLeaks to the extent that it began to shut down parts of its operations. Detractors baying for WikiLeaks' blood had even begun writing obituaries for Julian Assange.

And then, six months later, something rather peculiar happened. On 15 June 2011, at 4.42 a.m., WikiLeaks tweeted: *WikiLeaks now accepts anonymous bitcoin donations on 1HB5XMLmzFVj8ALj6mfBsbifRoD4miY36v.*

WikiLeaks, which was built on the concept of anonymous and non-traceable forms of information exchange, had decided to fill its coffers with untraceable digital money—bitcoins.

Unknown till then to 99.99 per cent of the world's population, bitcoins unintentionally and rather unexpectedly stepped into the spotlight. It stirred intense debates everywhere, from parliaments to coffee shops. It was being dubbed the 'currency of the future'.

In fact, this blockade of WikiLeaks by MasterCard, Visa and PayPal served as the largest shot in the arm for bitcoins. They were here to stay.

Founded in 2008 by one Satoshi Nakamoto, whose identity was a mystery, bitcoins had a rocky start. Satoshi, a libertarian, proclaimed a man's right to remain anonymous and decide what is good for him. He introduced bitcoins to give the world its first decentralized digital currency, which could be used over the Internet. The biggest benefit of bitcoins was that they could be passed on from one person to the other via just the click of a mouse, without the intervention of any bank or financial institution. It was a currency that could not be controlled by any government and whose value was completely market-driven. The price of each bitcoin, like shares in a stock market, was determined only and totally by demand and supply.

Bitcoins were stored in digital wallets on users' computers. Each bitcoin wallet was unique. No names or addresses were linked to it. Bitcoins provided the user with the much-needed anonymity which bank accounts and other forms of storing wealth didn't. Every wallet was identified by two digital keys —a public key and a private key—both being combinations of twenty-seven to thirty-four alphanumeric characters, such as *1HB5XMLmzFVj8ALj6mfBsbifRoD4miY36v*. The private key was known only to the owner of the wallet, whereas the public key could be shared with others.

If X wanted to transfer bitcoins to Y, he could easily do so by debiting his bitcoin wallet using his private key and crediting Y's wallet using Y's public key. As long as the private keys were kept safe and away from hackers on the Internet, no one could transfer or steal the bitcoins and the owners' wealth would remain safe.

Until bitcoins appeared on the scene, a currency for an anonymous, borderless world, a virtual currency was a pipe dream. Satoshi Nakamoto succeeded in making this dream come true.

Well, almost.

2011

# 1

# Washington DC

Gillian Tan picked out the Jaeger-LeCoultre from the Orbita Tourbillion watch winder, which held his collection of exquisite watches. He was running late for a senate committee meeting. A lavish breakfast was laid out for him but he had no time to eat. Quite a luxury, if he were to think back to the time when his mother struggled to make ends meet. He had lost his father when he was seven. His mother had pushed him to succeed. Day shifts in a department store and nights in a downtown pub helped her earn enough to fund his education. Scholarships saw him through to graduation. He was an extremely bright and intellectually gifted child who was obsessed with maths. His skills at mathematical analysis and research came in handy when he was drafted into the campaign management team of his dorm-mate, who went on to become the governor of Illinois. His old pal was now the President of the United States of America. Once Gillian entered politics, academics took a back seat, and the desire to excel in the powerful world of American politics took over. And to a large extent, he had succeeded in his quest.

'I gotta rush!' he yelled out to his wife, as she emerged from the kitchen with two bowls of cereal and a glass of orange juice on a tray. Three maids and two butlers to handle their daily chores yet Nikki always brought him his breakfast. Like every other marriage, theirs too had seen its highs and lows but just as it was threatening to fall apart, she had managed to pull everything back together.

'Why don't you at least drink the juice? It will keep you going till you reach the Hill.'

'Fine!' And he walked towards her. He looked at his watch again. It was ticking faster than he would have liked it to. Those idiots from the civil works department had dug up the road a mile from home. Cable work, they said. The entire road had been closed off for the last three days, forcing his motorcade to take a longish detour. His commute had increased by nine minutes.

He gulped down the juice and pushed the door open. 'Bye, I'm off,' he said and then, almost as an afterthought, added, 'honey!' Nikki rushed to his side for the customary goodbye kiss. 'Where's Gloria?' he asked. 'Still sleeping?' Their daughter had just entered her twenties. Nikki looked the other way. It seemed like she was nodding.

As he kissed Nikki on the cheek and turned to go, she asked, 'Are you meeting the President today?'

'Do I have a choice?' He frowned. 'He's agreed to see me today after the senate committee meeting.' He stepped out of the house, the frown intact.

Carl, his driver, was holding the door to the armoured Mercedes-Benz open for him. A special Mercedes was not a regular entitlement. Gillian was on the senate committee advising the government on South Asian foreign policy. The job made him a high-risk target.

Two minutes later, his entourage was zooming past the pristine landscape. His Mercedes was sandwiched between two other cars.

'We need to get there in twenty minutes, Carl,' Gillian commanded, his mind still on the meeting with the President. What was he going to tell him? More importantly, how was he going to tell him? He pulled out a few papers from the file lying next to him to focus on the task ahead. The trip metre showed 180 seconds. It seemed like an eternity. Gillian had just about starting settling into his routine, when the car screeched to a halt. The papers fell to the floor.

'Damn it, Carl! Fast doesn't mean reckless.'

'Sorry, sir.'

That's when Gillian noticed that the pilot vehicle had stopped, forcing Carl to brake. A voice piped through Carl's earphones. He whispered into the mouthpiece before turning back. 'The old road has been opened up. You think we should take that?'

Normally, Carl would not have asked but, over the last three days that they had been taking the detour, Gillian had been picking up his macchiato from a Starbucks en route. Gillian would save nine minutes if he took the old route. He nodded his approval. Carl whispered into the earphone and the motorcade moved on.

Gillian looked out of the window and then glanced back at the FedEx package lying next to him. Nikki had handed it to him on the way out. It was addressed to him but the label with the sender's address was missing. Inside was a 6-inch model of a bicycle. It looked like something one would pick up at a flea market. It was strange that someone would send it to him. His onsite security team had cleared the package for explosives or any other potentially dangerous substance. Gillian pulled out the delicately crafted cycle. He would have appreciated it much more had it not been for the intrigue surrounding the manner in which it had arrived. He brought the cycle to eye level. Was he overreacting? He wasn't sure.

The Mercedes raced along. It was approaching a stretch of the road, which had been cordoned off a few days ago. Up ahead, on the other side of the bend, parked by the side of the road, resting against a hillock, he could see a bicycle. A larger version of the miniature that he held in his hand. He looked to the right. The grassy and near perfect landscape had been somewhat damaged by the workers' digging. They seemed to have filled in the pits hurriedly and left. Very unlike the work that the subdivision contractors normally carried out. He made a mental note to take it up with the city council. That's when it suddenly, struck him—the package from nowhere, small bicycle, big bicycle, unprofessional ditches . . . It was a set-up!

'Stop!' he screamed.

Carl slammed the brakes as the first car in the convoy crossed the cycle resting against the hillock. But it was too late.

Whatever else Gillian may have said was lost in the explosion that followed as the Mercedes crossed the cycle.

The armoured Mercedes was flung high up into the air before it crashed to the ground, spun over, and came to a flaming halt on its side. Chances of finding a survivor inside it were as likely as finding Osama Bin Laden dining at the White House.

# 2

# New Delhi

The Prime Minister's Office was abuzz with activity even at 10.30 p.m. on a Friday night. The prime minister was at his desk, clearing last-minute files. He was leaving for the US that night, to be treated for Stage-1 prostate cancer, a condition that had been kept under wraps from the media. He wanted to make sure that work continued uninterrupted in his absence.

There was no great advantage in getting the surgery done in America. However, had he got himself admitted to the All-India Institute of Medical Sciences in Delhi, he would have been subjected to minute-by-minute media scrutiny.

The prime minister's principal secretary, who held the rank of a minister of state, was next to him.

'How many to go?' the prime minister asked, clearly exhausted.

'Last few papers, sir. Madam has also arrived,' the secretary said, referring to the prime minister's wife.

'Where is she?'

'In the other room, sir. The Black Cats are also on standby to accompany you to the airport,' the secretary informed him, handing over a docket from the finance ministry.

The prime minister read the letter containing the shortlist of candidates being considered to replace the incumbent governor of the Reserve Bank of India.

'When does the governor's tenure end?' he asked.

'In six months, sir.'

'So we have time.'

'Yes, sir, we do.'

'Great. Put this shortlist on hold. Tell the Hon'ble finance minister that we will take a call once I am back from the US.'

'Sir.' He nodded. 'I will make a suitable notation and return the papers.'

'Thanks,' the prime minister said, smiling at the secretary. 'And politely inform the Hon'ble finance minister that I will not be a party to him trying to install his muse in the governor's chair. I need a new shortlist.'

The secretary smiled.

The prime minister got up and walked to the door. He turned and said, 'Not a word of this in writing. Only verbal. Please make sure!'

# 3

# Mumbai

It was late by the time Swami parked his car in the basement and rode up the elevator to his sixteenth-floor apartment. A strenuous job as the head of retail banking at New York International Bank kept him away from his wonderful family—two beautiful daughters, adoring wife Kalpana, his mother and their Labrador. This was his universe. When he looked back, he had the satisfaction of seeing his family embracing the values that he had stood for every single day of the last forty-five years of his life. Swami was hardworking, sincere, committed. His team at work was fond of him and his family simply adored him.

Swami had joined NYIB as a management trainee, right after completing his MBA from IIM Ahmedabad in the late 1980s. He had worked his way up the extremely stressful corridors of power at NYIB. Luck had also played its part. In Swami's first week at the bank, Aditya Rao, the then country head, had handpicked him along with two other trainees, Sundeep and Kalpana, to kickstart the retail banking initiative. After the initial awkwardness, a whirlwind romance had ensued, and Swami had married Kalpana, the only daughter of Gujarati parents. Kalpana's career took a backseat after that as she began setting up her domestic dreamland.

Together, Aditya, Swami and Sundeep had formed a fabulous team of high-intellect, super-charged go-getters who were the envy of everyone. All had been hunky-dory until a few years later when Sundeep fell prey to the lust for power and ambition and went astray.

Womanizing, the blatant misuse of power and financial avarice caused Sundeep's downfall, that too when he was well on track to head the bank one day. It had taken all of Aditya's guile and goodwill, particularly the relationship that he enjoyed with the global CEO of NYIB, to keep Sundeep from committing professional suicide. The entire episode had brought the three of them closer. Aditya was like a parent to the other two men. He was a divorcee who lived alone. Not much was known about his family. Knowing how fiercely protective he was about his privacy, no one asked him either.

At the dining table that night, as Swami was having dinner with Kalpana, his mother walked up to him. 'Mangala had come some time ago,' she started off.

'Hmm . . .' Swami just nodded. He raised his left hand and pointed upwards.

'Yes, yes, the one on the seventeenth floor.'

'What happened?'

'She has run into some problem with your bank. Needs your help.'

'Okay?' It was more of a question than an acknowledgement.

'Seems 27,000 rupees have been taken out of her account without her knowledge.'

'And how did that happen?' Swami asked casually.

'She doesn't know.'

'How can money disappear just like that? Surely she is forgetting something.'

'I don't know.'

'Has she met the customer service guys in the branch, Amma?'

'Hmm,' Swami's mother nodded. 'She did. That's when she figured out that it had something to do with an email.'

'Email? What email?' Worry lines appeared on his forehead.

'A few days ago, she received an email from Vodafone, which said that she was entitled to a refund of two thousand rupees that she had been charged in excess. She was asked to log in to her NYIB account and enter her mobile number to accept the credit directly into her account.'

'And, like an idiot, she entered the account number and password?'

Swami's mother nodded. 'What else could she have done? Poor thing. She lives off the interest the bank pays her. For her, 2000 rupees is a lot of money. And the mail looked genuine. She showed it to me.'

'But I thought you told me once that she doesn't use Internet banking?'

'She doesn't but she had noted her password in her diary. She looked it up and keyed it in.'

'Amma!' Swami exclaimed. 'Where has she locked away her common sense? Why would anyone ask her to log in to her bank account to credit money? All you need is the account number. She should have known it was a fraud email.'

Even as he spoke, Swami's mind was working. A mail like this should have been brought to his attention immediately. That was the procedure. No one from his team had mentioned this to him yet. He wondered who all in the system knew about this.

'I don't know!' Swami's mother waved her hands furiously. 'Those fraudsters took away her money. Help her, Swami! She needs the money.'

'She is greedy,' taunted Swami, as he got up to wash his hands. 'Let me see what I can do. But for that I will have to figure out some more details. Tell her it will be a while before she sees her money again.'

# 4

# Mumbai

'Regulation Nigerian phishing scam, Swami.'

Charan Rawat, head of technology at NYIB, laid out his assessment of the emails that the bank's customers had received. Swami's neighbour was not the only one.

Swami turned to the branch banking head, who was also present in the room. 'How many complaints have we formally received till date?'

'Thirty-six.'

'When?'

'Over the last three days, Swami.'

'Why wasn't it brought to my attention? Shouldn't we have raised a red flag? Thirty-six complaints because of one phishing incident—that is not a small number!' Swami was furious.

'I saw it the day before yesterday when the first customer complaint came in, Swami.' Charan was finding it difficult to justify his negligence. 'I acted on it immediately.' He glanced at the branch banking head and shrugged.

'Clearly, that action didn't include reporting the matter to your business head,' said Swami, ridicule in his voice.

'No, Swami. That's not the case. I didn't want to trouble you for a small thing that I could handle.'

'Oh really? Thank you!' When Swami lost his temper, rationalizing was futile. 'Isn't there standard protocol to be followed in case of such phishing attacks?'

'Yes, there is,' confirmed Charan.

'And, as usual, it's been ignored,' Swami barked.

Charan's silence only confirmed Swami's fears. Had it not been for his mother's friend, he would not even have discovered this situation. He walked to the bookshelf to his right and pulled out a huge box file. He flipped a few pages and started reading: 'Clause 27 of the operations manual states that the business head, the country head and the technology teams in the regional office need to be informed . . . Attempts must be made to plug the leak within the system. An update must be sent on a daily basis to the regional executive council of the bank.' He looked up. 'Which of these has been done, Charan? Which of these?'

'I will put this in motion right away!'

'Please do!'

Swami banged the box file shut. The moment Charan left his room, Swami picked up the phone and called Malvika, the CEO of NYIB.

'Malvika, it seems like we have a problem. We are handling it but I thought it necessary to keep you informed.'

'I'm listening.' In spite of his best efforts at keeping her happy, Malvika had never really warmed up to him

'A few of our customers have been victims of a phishing attack. They received an email from an unknown sender. Owing to its uncanny resemblance to mails normally sent by Vodafone, they fell for it. They were asked to log in to their NYIB accounts by clicking on the link provided in the mail. A Trojan virus in the email tracked their key strokes. Their account numbers and passwords were recorded and used to transfer the money into another account with a nationalized bank from which it has since been moved.'

'What's the impact?'

'Well, 79 lakh rupees transferred from accounts so far. How many customers are blissfully unaware of it, we don't know. We are looking into it, Malvika. I'll have an update for you by tonight.'

'I might leave early. Call me on my mobile. We will need to involve Singapore.'

NYIB's regional office for the Asia-Pacific region was located in Singapore.

~

By the time Swami called Malvika that night, the amount siphoned off had swollen to over 1 crore rupees and the number of customer complaints had risen to fifty-eight. This was fast becoming the worst phishing scam NYIB had seen in the last five years.

# 5

# Goa

It was a lazy morning. In fact, it would be noon in a few minutes. Tanya had just woken up.

She had arrived in Goa a few days earlier as part of the organizing team for a Nasscom event. Technology and process experts from all over the world were present. A few technology services giants from India were also in attendance. The event had ended the previous night. The afterparty had stretched till 4 a.m., when the hotel officials forcefully shut it down after some guests complained about the noise.

Tanya would have slept on had it not been for the hotel attendant knocking on the door to check if she wanted the room serviced.

She looked stunning in her black hot pants and spaghetti top. Her clothes accentuated her gym-toned figure. Her brown hair was a mess but it gave her a sensuous look.

'Hope you are enjoying your stay, madam?' asked the intrusive attendant. Tanya just nodded and forced a smile.

Leon D'Souza was the name on his uniform tag. He made her bed as she silently stood by, making sure he did his job well. His frankly admiring gaze made her uncomfortable. She moved to the balcony, wrapping a stole around her shoulders.

'It's done, madam,' Leon called out from the room. 'Is there anything else you might need?'

'No, thank you.'

'If you need anything . . .' He paused, waiting for her to enter the room, and repeated, 'If you need anything at all, please call me.' He kept his visiting card on the table. As he exited the room, he looked back. A cheeky grin played on his face. 'Anything,' he emphasized as he shut the door, leaving behind a confused Tanya.

After he left, Tanya decided to indulge herself. It was the first time in days that she could afford a leisurely shower.

The phone rang. 'We are off to the beach shack for lunch, sweetheart. Coming?' One of her colleagues was on the line.

'You guys go ahead. I desperately need some rest.'

Leon's card stared at her from the table as she ordered biryani for lunch. It was a personal card—the hotel's name was missing. A naughty thought crossed her mind. She decided against trying anything stupid and impulsive while she was alone. Perhaps later, when she was expecting company.

That night, the entire gang of organizers got together in Tanya's room to drink. It started off well, but over time, the enthusiasm levels started to dip. The party was getting a bit drab when Tanya picked up her phone and called a number.

'Leon, I'm calling from room 204.'

'Yes, madam.'

'Can you come over? We might need some help.'

'What is it that you need, madam?'

'Well . . .' Tanya hesitated, 'do you think we could get some hash?'

Leon chuckled. This is Goa, madam. You will get whatever you want. Give me ten minutes.' And he hung up.

Fifteen minutes later, Leon was standing at the door. No uniform. He was off duty. He looked over her shoulder into her room. He was surprised to see so many people. Large gatherings made him nervous. The business he had come to transact was best done one on one.

'Did you get it?' Tanya asked. She took care to keep her voice low.

'My friend here will help you with it.' Leon looked to his right.

It was dark outside. Tanya craned her neck to see who it was. Someone stepped out of the shadows and walked towards them with measured steps.

Was she dreaming?

'Varun!' she exclaimed. Her grin grew wider by the second. 'You!!!' She giggled like a teen. 'I never expected to see you here.'

'Hey, Tanya,' Varun said. 'Tanya, right?'

When she nodded, he said, 'What a pleasant surprise!'

# 6

## Rio de Janeiro/Goa

A few months ago, Tanya was in Rio de Janeiro for a conference. Late one night, around 2 a.m., she was returning to her hotel after a party. She was with a colleague and the cab driver.

A few metres ahead of Hotel Le Meridien on Copacabana Beach, the car stopped just after a dark underpass. The signal had turned red. A man popped out of the darkness and held a gun to the driver's head. In Brazil, the first rule of being mugged is to give away everything you have on you. No arguments. Unfortunately, no one had mentioned this to Tanya's colleague, who started to scream. The mugger panicked, turned his attention to the back seat, opened the door, pulled Tanya's colleague out of the car, pushed her on to the pavement and started to rough her up. There was hardly anyone in sight. He snatched her necklace and handbag and was shouting for the ring on her right hand . . . That's when Tanya saw two men out for a walk evidently. Seeing them approach, the mugger fired a few shots at them but missed. He fled. Frozen with fear, Tanya hadn't moved from her seat throughout the ordeal.

The gunshots had alerted the local police, who reached the scene, rounded up everyone—Tanya, her colleague, the cab driver, the two men—and took them to the police station. One of the men was Varun. He told the cops that he had slept through the evening and got up past midnight. The room service at the hotel they were staying in had shut shop for the day so he and his friend had stepped out to grab a bite.

By the time the cops let everyone go, it was 6 a.m.

Tanya had not seen Varun since then. Until today. She was overjoyed.

Varun came up to the door and smiled at her. 'We bought more than we could smoke last night. All of us are leaving tomorrow. I mentioned it to Leon just in case anyone needed it.'

'No problem. Come on in.' For some strange reason, Tanya was relieved that Varun was not a drug dealer.

Varun politely turned down the invitation. 'There is this Nigerian gentleman who will take it from me in case you don't want it. He supplied it to me.' Tanya looked behind him. The Nigerian was waiting for them to conclude the deal. 'But you know how they are. If I give it back to him, he will only give me half the price that I paid. Isn't it criminal?'

Tanya smiled. The deal was done, the money paid to Varun, and the Nigerian packed off. Tanya and Varun decided to head to the beach to catch up on life after their Rio adventure.

'When are you headed back to Mumbai?'

'Tomorrow morning. All of us stayed back for one last party before going back to our boring jobs.'

'And I spoilt your party.'

'On the contrary, Varun, you didn't. I am so excited to see you.'

'Really?'

'Yes! Aren't you? After so long . . .'

'Yes, I am.'

And he turned. Tanya was looking at him intently. He was irresistible. She walked up to him and kissed him, flush on his lips. He stepped backwards. She persisted. Kissed him again. This time, he kissed her back. Delicately, he lowered her on to the sand. The sea water crept in under her, tickling her as it flowed back into the sea, drawing out sand from underneath. There was no one around. She wrapped her hands around him and pulled him towards her. Her tongue parted his lips even as she tore off her clothes. Her lust-filled eyes implored Varun to do the same. She was lying naked in front of him. Varun paused for a moment, considering the appropriateness of what Tanya wanted him to do. She reached out and tugged at his trousers. Varun dropped his pants and slowly pushed her back on to the sand. He lowered himself and entered her gently. She moaned. He didn't need a second invitation. He kissed her harder . . .

When they were done, the only sounds audible were the heavy breathing of two souls and the sea waves lapping passionately against the shore.

# 7

# Washington DC

Gillian Tan's assassination reverberated in the corridors of Capitol Hill. The sophisticated attack shook the Obama administration. After all, Gillian had been handpicked by Barack Obama to drive American foreign policy in South Asia.

Special Agent Adrian Scott was nervous as he paced up and down the hallway outside the meeting room on the third floor of the Edgar Hoover Building on Pennsylvania Avenue in Washington DC. It had long been home of the headquarters of the Federal Bureau of Investigation, the FBI. The Gillian Tan case was his and the White House was breathing down his neck to show results.

A young woman stepped out of the conference room and called out, 'Agent Scott, you may come in now.'

'Thank you.' Adrian straightened up, stretched his arms, freed his jacket sleeves, and tweaked the lapels of his jacket. A shrug of his shoulders, and he was ready to walk in.

His boss, Robert Brick was waiting for him in the conference room. He was standing next to the glazed window, and speaking in hushed tones with someone whom Adrian couldn't recognize because his back was towards him.

'Ah! Agent Scott.' Brick acknowledged him. Adrian nodded nervously.

The person Brick had been talking to turned towards Adrian. It was Mike Hendricks, the chief of staff of the President of America.

'Meet Mike Hendricks.'

Adrian had met him before. He nodded and extended his right hand for a handshake. He couldn't help wonder what Hendricks was doing here. He knew that Mike Hendricks and Gillian Tan would have looked through each other if they had walked past each other in a corridor. They were political adversaries vying for the President's attention all the time. His phone beeped. Quickly, he put it on silent mode.

'The President is getting edgy . . . we don't have a lot of time.' Mike looked at Adrian pointedly.

'Sir.' And after a pause, he added, 'I'm aware it's a sensitive case.'

'Good,' Mike said. 'Then we don't need to waste time on that realization. What do we know so far?'

Adrian fumbled through his papers, pulled out a docket and handed it over to him.

'Run me through it.'

'This is the chronology of events on that day, sir.'

'Hmm . . .' Mike nodded. 'I've been briefed over a dozen times on this.' He was waiting for more. 'Tell me what's not in here.'

Adrian nodded. 'It was a cycle bomb. Hidden in the saddle bag of a bicycle placed right next to the road that Gillian would take that day.'

Mike was flipping through the docket. 'I'm listening. Don't stop.'

'An 8-kg bomb. Detonated by the interruption of a beam of light.'

Mike looked up for a moment.

'Infra red,' Adrian continued. 'The beam was activated by the pilot car. And when Gillian's car crossed it, the beam detonated the precision bomb. Gillian didn't have a chance. The car is beyond recognition.'

'Wasn't it armoured? It isn't easy to bomb one of those.' Mike Hendricks tried to pick holes in the logic.

'Indeed it was,' Adrian agreed, 'but the assassins were trained. They targeted the most vulnerable part of the car.'

Mike nodded.

'The Misznay-Schardin effect—that's what they used,' Adrian continued.

'Hmm . . . a blast that expands in one direction.'

'Absolutely, sir. In such cases, a broad sheet of explosives is detonated. Unlike with traditional explosives, where the blast expands in all directions, in the case of an explosive sheet, the blast spreads perpendicular to the sheet. And if there is a hard, impenetrable object on one side, the blast deforms the explosive sheet into a projectile and propels it into the perpendicular direction on one side.

'The cycle was placed in such a manner that it rested on hard rock, while the road was on its other side. When Gillian's car triggered the blast, a copper plate attached to the explosive was projected towards the car. The bomb didn't have the precise engineering to have moulded the copper liner into the shape of a bullet but it propelled the plate at 2.5 km per second, enough to penetrate any armoured car.'

'Misznay-Schardin . . . been a while since I heard of it. Haven't seen it being used lately,' Robert muttered.

'Quite uncommon, I must confess. In fact, a bit ancient,' Adrian added, 'though there are a few groups that have been known to favour it.'

'And those would be?'

'A few defunct Hungarian militant groups. The Red Army Faction—West Germany's most prominent left-wing militant group. The last known attack was in 1998.'

'Any clues?'

Adrian shook his head. 'The road that Gillian normally travelled on was apparently blocked for repairs. I checked with the County Road Administration Board. No such work was sanctioned. The only reason the road was cordoned off and dug up was to set up the trigger mechanism. No one really saw who they were.' After a moment's pause, he added, 'The worksite was completely sanitized. No clues at the blast site. Even the cycle that was used . . . its origin untraceable.'

'How is Nikki?' Mike asked.

'She has taken it quite bravely. She has given her statement to the FBI.'

'Hmm . . . so we have nothing to report to the President.'

'We will definitely have something for you soon, sir. We are hopeful.'

'Be sensitive towards Nikki and Gloria. They are very close to the first family,' Mike instructed.

'Yes, sir. We are keeping them involved and informed of the investigation. Even when we scanned the premises for clues, we did it in Nikki Tan's presence.'

'Good. Thank you. That will be all.' When Mike Hendricks said this, Adrian got up and walked out of the room. As he opened the door, he glanced at his phone. He had overshot his time. Four missed calls. Two messages.

# 8

# Washington DC

Adrian was shivering with nervous excitement when he got out of the meeting. The case was bigger than he had imagined. Was this the career-defining case he had been waiting for all along?

He checked his mobile and returned a call. His secretary answered. 'You were trying to reach me, Mona?'

'Oh yes. It was Tony. He came looking for you. I'm connecting you now.'

'Hey, Adrian . . . Where the hell have you been?'

'In a briefing session with the President's chief of staff. Tell me someone died that you had to call me so many times.'

'No. The guy who had to die, he died a few days ago.'

'That's a terrible joke, Tony.'

'Where's your sense of humour, Adrian?'

'Fuck you, Tony. Why did you call?'

'There is something I need you to see. Sending the email to your mobile. Take a look.'

The message came in: *Cycle Job done. Confirm transfer of bitcoins.*

'What was that, Tony?'

'Since the murder, we've been watching all the agencies that could have had a vested interest in killing Gillian. British Intelligence picked up a significant increase in chatter on lines between New York and a few hubs in the Indian Ocean. This is a message they intercepted. It was being sent from a server in Latvia to a server in the Indian Ocean region. From there we lost it. So our assumption is that it's intended for someone in that region.'

'What's the connection?'

'Gillian was the President's advisor for foreign policy in the Middle East and South Asia.'

'That in itself doesn't say anything. Does it?'

'It doesn't. But it's the other visual clues that got me excited,' Tony rebutted. 'The message says cycle job. In other words, the cycle that blasted Gillian's car.'

'Okay.' Adrian sounded sceptical

'Yes. Cycle job done. The next part of the message says confirm transfer of bitcoins. Compensation for the work done? It's too much of a coincidence.'

'It's possible that what you are saying is right, Tony. Do we have a tag on the location where this mail originated?'

Tony shook his head. 'No. These guys are not idiots.'

'It's TOR again?' Adrian sounded angry.

TOR or The Onion Router was a free network for facilitating online anonymity. By directing Internet traffic through an anonymous network managed by volunteers across the world, TOR encryption made it possible for the Internet user to conceal his location and identity.

The 'onion' in TOR referred to the method of encryption, wherein any message or information transmitted over the network was encrypted and bounced over numerous nodes before reaching its final destination. Every node in the router would decrypt one level of encryption, with the final node decrypting the last level, thus delivering the data to the final destination in its intended form. No node would know the initial source or the final destination. It was almost impossible to unscramble any information sent via TOR. Newspapers called TOR the 'king of high secure, low latency Internet anonymity'.

TOR had become one of the most sophisticated tools used by criminals and drug peddlers to transact over the web. Even the sophisticated equipment and surveillance of the federal agencies was not good enough to crack the privacy that TOR provided.

After reading the email a few times, Adrian realized Tony was waiting for the next set of instructions.

'If there is any truth in what you are saying, there are too many balls in the air. It could be anything. Muslim fanatics in Af-Pak, Hindu fundamentalists in India, Sri Lankan rebels fighting the government for Tamil liberation, Iranian extremists, Iraqis owing allegiance to Saddam. It could be anything. Where do we begin?'

# 9

# Mumbai

The phishing scandal was giving Swami a migraine. By morning, over 3 crore rupees had been siphoned off from 150 customer accounts.

When Charan rang him at 5 a.m., Swami made a judgement call and shut down the online fund transfer option on NYIB's Internet banking facility. He did not see any other way of stopping the carnage. 'I am happier dealing with customer service issues arising out of the non-availability of online transfers than exposing more idiotic customers to this scam,' he told Charan. 'We don't even know how many more customers have succumbed to this and how many more fraudulent transfers like this will go through.'

From the looks of it, this time around, the phishers had got hold of the entire database of NYIB customers and spammed them with an enticing and extremely realistic offer. In the past, the phishers had used huge bait, often running into millions of dollars. Most customers would not believe it and would promptly junk the mail. This time around, the phishers promised small amounts of money and offered a believable story.

It was around 5.30 a.m. when the conversation ended. Even though he was an early riser, Swami hated being woken up before his scheduled time. Rubbing his sleepy, tired eyes, he walked up to the door to check if the newspaper had been delivered. As he picked up the *Times of India*, his pulse started racing. The lead news story on the front page read: NYIB's apathy takes customers for a ride. The article named twenty-two customers who had been cheated. Though it clarified that this was a phishing attack, it slammed NYIB's security protocol and the safety of Internet banking in general.

Swami collapsed on the sofa in the living room. He was not worried about the phishing scam as much as he was now concerned about the repercussions of the article. The Singapore office, he was sure, would look for scapegoats for the crisis. They had not even been told about it yet.

'Is everything okay?' Kalpana had also woken up by then.

Swami briefly told her everything that had happened. He pulled out his laptop and logged in.

It's always better to be the messenger when the news is bad. Else you are considered a suspect. He had to talk to Singapore before the overzealous compliance folks called them.

His phone rang. He walked to the corner of the room and picked it. 'Hi, Aditya.' Only Aditya could have called him that early.

Aditya Rao was a legend in the Indian banking industry. He was credited with pioneering the retail banking business in India, through NYIB. After working all over the world in his twenty years with NYIB, he had come back to India to set up the retail banking business. He had gone on to quit the bank and start his own BPO called eTIOS.

Sundeep Srivastava, his former protégé at NYIB, was now his right-hand man.

eTIOS had grown into one of the most respected BPO outfits in India. Seeing the success of eTIOS and the entrepreneurial skills of Aditya, several of his private equity investors had requested him to incubate a gaming company. Aditya had agreed and that was how Indiscape, the latest gaming sensation, was born. The browser-based gaming company had a website where anybody could log in and play virtual games for free.

Aditya had seen the newspaper article and called Swami. 'Hey, Swami, what happened? What is this rubbish? Your public relations team should have scuttled it. In any case, this should not have been front page news,' he rattled off.

'What can I say, Aditya? What is done is done. I'm trying to contain the damage now. I can't even get through to Madhuri. Her phone is very conveniently switched off.' Madhuri was NYIB's press relations head.

Always ready to offer advice, especially when it came to his two protégés, Aditya had only one thing to say. 'Handle this with care. Make sure you protect yourself.' Even though Swami was not directly responsible for this mishap, anything that happened in retail banking was his baby.

'Yes, Aditya. Let me call Malvika and brief her. She is one mad woman.' He hung up.

Malvika was livid. 'Swami, I can't be seen running a non-compliant bank.'

'This isn't non-compliance! Our customers are expected to be careful too. They can't be greedy and give away their account numbers and passwords to anyone.'

'Come on, Swami! Give me a better argument. How did the phishers get hold of our customer base?'

'Malvika, with so much outsourcing and sharing of data with vendors, all it would take for data to leak is an unscrupulous vendor. For all you know the data could have been stolen from Vodafone's servers. It's those of our customers, specifically the ones who have a Vodafone connection and have an auto-debit instruction recorded for their mobile bills, who seem to have been hit.'

'That won't fly, Swami. We should have anticipated that this could blow up, and escalated it as soon as the first complaint came in. As it is, wherever I go, people tell me that our Internet banking sucks because it is so slow.'

'That's a different discussion, Malvika.' Swami was getting irritated because she was not focusing on the core phishing issue.

'In any case, call Singapore and bring them into the loop. Please be ready with what we are going to say to them.'

# 10

# Mumbai

Aditya stepped into the plush new sixteenth-floor office of Indiscape Gaming Corporation. Eighteen months since it was launched, Indiscape.com had grown to become one of the most frequented gaming sites in India. As he walked in, to the right was a huge board featuring one of his quotes: 'Keep them easy and interesting. Focus on entertaining the customer. Once he likes what he is playing, revenue will come.' Above it, in bold, were the words: 'We are here to entertain.' That summed up Aditya's ethos and the operating model for his company.

The past six months had been particularly good for Indiscape. It had seen significant traction from international markets, particularly the US. A big victory had come when a game called Mafia Dons catapulted to the #10 position in the list of most popular games in America. Aditya had become the darling of the private equity community.

Indiscape operated on a free-to-use model. For the consumer, playing games on Indiscape.com was free. Revenue pumped in by advertisers kept the company going. While profitability was not huge, what excited the investors was the fact that the number of monthly active users, or MAUs, on Indiscape was high. More significantly, it was consistently high. Consumer loyalty and retention at Indiscape was best in class. All you had to do was play an Indiscape game once and you were hooked as if it were a drug.

That day, Aditya was addressing a town hall meeting for which two hundred and eighty employees from all his offices had gathered. Sundeep was there too. He managed international sales for Aditya's BPO business and had also helped him set up Indiscape.

'Friends, we have seen phenomenal growth over the last three quarters. No gaming company across the globe has moved this fast. This would not have been possible without your support. I am thankful to all of you, who have given blood and sweat to make Indiscape a part of your family. Thank you!' Aditya's speech was inspiring. He connected with his people brilliantly.

Once the question-and-answer session was done, Sundeep walked Aditya to his room. 'We had downtime for two hours yesterday.'

'Two hours! Here?'

'No, no, at eTIOS.'

'What time?'

'Between 9.14 p.m. and 11.10 p.m.'

'What happened?'

'Someone tried to hack in. DDOS attack—distributed denial of service. Our firewalls proved to be a strong enough defence. We have checked and sanitized everything now.'

Aditya pondered for a second and responded, 'Wonderful. So nothing to worry about.'

Sundeep nodded. 'Not on this front, for sure.'

'What do you mean?' Aditya looked up. 'What's bothering you, Sundeep?'

Sundeep hesitated a bit. But then there was no point. He was as much a stakeholder in the success of the business as Aditya. 'Our numbers for last month have come in.'

'And?'

'Our MAUs have dropped for the first time in the last twelve months. Some customers have logged off our network. They are not playing our games as much as they used to.'

'What do you think happened?'

'Not too sure. But it's not very worrying and the drop is not very significant. It's just that I don't like to see even a small drop. Period.'

Aditya smiled. 'I know. In any case, dig deeper. We are in the process of raising more capital and cannot afford to lose customers. They are the only hook we have for investors. We don't have much revenue to show,' he said, and after a brief pause added, 'as of now.'

'Yes, Aditya.'

'Also find out where they are going. We have their email IDs, don't we?'

'Yes, we do. In fact, a mail has gone out this morning to all customers inviting them back to Indiscape. The bait is a preview of our new game, Townsville, when it is ready. And an opportunity to sample it before the world gets to see it.'

'Task your design team. Tell them to work overnight on Townsville. It needs to be as addictive as Mafia Dons.'

'Working on it, Aditya. What about charging the existing lot to play on our website? Introducing a fee to register . . . Perhaps a monthly fee?'

'Are you joking? We're losing customers here and you're recommending that we charge them! As long as I'm around, we will never charge our customers. I want them to be our ambassadors.'

'Social media?'

'Early days yet, Sundeep. You know that as much as I do. Going on social media will impact the Indiscape brand, I feel. Our competitors have tried it, haven't they? Let's see how people respond to their games on social media and then take a call. Let's first build our brand before we look for alliances. The moment we partner with Facebook and the others, we will lose our identity. And don't forget, we don't have any revenue to pay these social media partners and advertise on their networks. Let's focus all our energy on two things: developing new, exciting games to get our MAUs up, and figuring out what made us lose our customers in the first place.'

Sundeep didn't quite agree with what Aditya had said. He didn't have a choice though; Aditya had a great track record of making the right decisions.

Aditya spent a few hours at Indiscape. As he was leaving the office and heading towards eTIOS, he stopped at the conference room and called out to Sundeep.

'Coming up?'

eTIOS' office was in the same building two floors above Indiscape. Sundeep and Aditya's cabins were next to each other there. However, when he was at Indiscape, Sundeep operated from the conference room.

As he stepped out to join Aditya, the latter asked, 'You seem too exhausted. Do you think you need help to run the business?'

'Pardon me?' He was shocked that Aditya had even suggested this.

'Do you need help in running the company? We can hire senior people to pitch in. A few days from now, Townsville goes live. And I'm worried about the success of the game if we cannot hold on to our existing pool of customers. A lot depends on this game. If it does well, we can take the company to the next level.'

'As of now, I can manage, Aditya. You know I will be the first to tell you in case I am unable to.'

'Okay!'

Aditya got into the elevator and pressed the button to go up two floors, to the eTIOS office, which was in the same building.

# 11

## Mumbai/Goa

Tanya was on her way to the Goa airport. Her flight took off in three hours.

She was in a horrible mood that morning. After the rendezvous by the beach, Varun had disappeared again. He had escorted her back to her room and walked away without a protracted goodbye. No note, no number, no promises to stay in touch. He had disappeared almost as abruptly as he had arrived, and without a trace. She had waited in the hotel lobby for almost an hour and a half, hoping to catch a glimpse of Varun, but he was nowhere to be seen.

Tanya was rudely jolted out of her thoughts by the wailing sirens of a convoy of police vans. Tanya looked out of the bus window. She counted three police vans and two fire engines, driving down the wrong side of the road. They were clearly in a hurry. Traffic had almost come to a standstill. She looked at her watch, worried she would miss the flight.

The bus stopped. A few of her colleagues got off to figure out what the problem was. To make things worse, it had even started to drizzle. Within ten minutes, her colleagues returned.

One of them explained. 'Last night, there was some rioting near Tito's Pub. Two gangs fighting over territorial rights for drug trading. Apparently, the Indian and the Nigerian gangs have clearly demarcated territories within which they operate freely. The Nigerians started selling drugs in the Indian area, which is a violation of an unwritten code of conduct. The Indians beat up some members of the Nigerian gang. The management of Tito's called the police. Everyone dispersed. But this morning, a few Nigerians retaliated. In the street violence, one Nigerian was killed.'

'Okay, but why the traffic jam?'

'The entire Nigerian community is out on the roads, protesting the murder. They are turning violent. Two police jeeps have also been torched. The cops are struggling to bring the situation under control. We should turn back.'

'Shit, that's bad,' exclaimed Tanya, 'but we have more than two hours for the flight. Let's wait it out.

Her colleague responded, 'I don't think we'll be able to make it across the blockade. And it is not safe to sit here and wait. You never know when these Nigerians will come this way and attack our bus. Let's head back.'

Everyone except Tanya agreed. She desperately wanted to reach Mumbai. Her mother would be waiting. Tanya had just completed her postgraduation abroad and signed up for specialization in her field. Her course began in another four months. It was only on her mother's insistence that had she come back to India in the intervening period.

Thankfully, by late evening, normalcy was restored. The police arrested everyone involved in the rioting, mostly Nigerians, and promised to bring the murderers to book.

When Tanya and her team learnt that the blockade had been lifted, they rushed to the airport and managed to catch the last flight out of Goa.

They arrived in Mumbai at midnight. By the time Tanya took a taxi and reached home, it was well past 1 a.m. Not wanting to wake her mother, she opened the door with her key and tiptoed into the house. The house was a mess. It seemed as though all three maids had been given the day off. She walked up to her mother's bedroom. Her mother was sprawled on the bed. Clothes in disarray, face down, motionless . . .

Fear gripped Tanya. She rushed to her mother's side. She was about to roll her over when her mother groaned, stretched in her sleep and turned. Eyes shut. Probably had one drink too many, Tanya concluded. She was relieved, but annoyed as well. Leaving her mother on the bed, she walked out. There were two plates on the dining table with crumbs of food. Two glasses of whisky. And a plate full of wasabi-flavoured nuts. Her mother loved those. A glass of whisky was never as good for her mother without wasabi-flavoured nuts.

So he'd come home. Tanya scowled and stomped off to her room.

Not that she had a problem with anyone in her mom's life. She had a problem with 'him'.

# 12

# Mumbai

The conference call with Singapore was a disaster.

Malvika conveniently laid the blame on Swami's shoulders. 'We should have had the foresight to recognize the problem when it first occurred and taken preventive steps,' she said. Swami was aghast. Rather than standing by the India businesses, she was sucking up to the global team. The *Times of India* cover story became a sore point.

'Swami, clearly someone from your team has spoken to the media. You have failed to keep your team in check,' Malvika said on the call. Swami was surprised. The media article was something Madhuri, the PR head, should have been accountable for. But Madhuri was close to Malvika. That was probably why Malvika was defending her. Whereas Swami was an orphan without a godfather.

'Give us a day, Matt. We will come back with some concrete action points,' Malvika told Matt Metzger, the regional head of retail banking. 'Until that time, please manage Peter Baron.' Matt's friendship with Peter Baron, the CEO for the region and Malvika's boss, was not lost on anyone. The two of them went back a long way.

'Let me try,' said Matt before he hung up.

Swami was very angry. The impression that Singapore would have got after the call was that Swami was the spineless head of retail banking, who had no control over his business or his team.

After he disconnected the line, Matt dialled another number.

'Peter Baron.'

'Peter, got a minute?'

'You can take two, Matt. Go on. What's on your mind?'

'India.'

'India? What about India?'

'We have a CEO of the country who has no clue of what goes on in retail banking, but believes she knows everything. And we have a head of retail banking who is just about okay but doesn't seem to share a great rapport with the CEO.'

'Put it down to my old age but I can't understand what you're getting at.'

'A leader who puts down her own people in front of her superiors can never be an inspiring leader. Malvika did just that to Swami.'

'Are you pissed off because Swami is in your direct line of control and Malvika took him apart? Is that what happened?'

'You know me better than that, Peter. I'm taking a hard look at Swami. Someone has to take responsibility for this phishing fiasco. They couldn't have done much about the scam but they could have been more responsive. Not only have we lost money in the fraud, but our brand value is at risk of much more erosion.'

'I'm listening.'

'You may want to consider looking at an alternative to Malvika in what is the biggest emerging market for us.'

'You mean . . . sack her?'

'That's an easier way of saying it. Yes.' Matt smiled.

'Can't.'

'Can't or don't want to?' Matt enjoyed these cheeky conversations with Peter.

'You heard me say can't, didn't you?'

'Purely out of academic interest, and with no intention of questioning your authority, Peter . . . why?'

'Many reasons. The most important is the fact that the woman is well-connected. Sacking her could land us in trouble.'

'But how?'

'I'll tell you over a drink sometime, Matt. It will suffice for you to know that we can't take a chance. At least not for another year.'

'By then she will fuck up the entire franchise,' Matt lamented. 'The way she was arguing her case today bordered on the ridiculous. As if the phishing scam happened in a world entirely divorced from the world she manages. Had she not been the CEO of a country like India, I would have let myself go at her.'

'I know. You're telling me all this today. I've wanted to get rid of her for almost fifteen months now. I don't have a choice.'

Matt thought for a long time.

'Matt, you there?' Peter asked.

'You said you don't have a choice. Well, you may have one now.'

# 13

# Mumbai

Five million dollars.

That is what the biggest phishing scam in the history of Indian banking cost NYIB's customers. The unwitting victims had played right into the hands of a few suspected Nigerian criminals.

Mumbai cops followed standard operating procedure. As with every other phishing scam, they raided Nigeria Wadi, a small, nondescript neighbourhood in the distant suburb of Mira Road. It was not without reason that it was called the hub for all phishing scams in India. These scams were often the handiwork of a small group of Nigerians, who stayed in cheap, one-room rented tenements, available to them at 100 dollars a month.

A few Nigerians were rounded up but had to be let off eventually because there was no proof—neither tech nor money trail—linking them to the scam. The cops had just acted on impulse and suspicion.

Even though it was not obliged to, NYIB refunded its customers every penny they lost in the scam, much to Swami's displeasure. Peter Baron had made this decision.

'Your profits are just a rounding off number for me. I don't want service issues arising out of this scam to sully the atmosphere at the annual general meeting.' There was no way the NYIB brand could be allowed to suffer in India. Malvika had agreed without a fight. Swami had tried to argue but he was bludgeoned into submission.

'Why should we refund the money and take a hit on our bottom line, Aditya? The customers must share some of this pain.' The day Peter's diktat was conveyed to NYIB, Swami met Aditya in the evening.

'Without a doubt,' Aditya agreed. 'But, Swami, in banks like ours . . .'

Swami looked up.

'. . . okay, okay, in banks like yours . . .'

Swami smiled.

'. . . it is always important to not get into a conflict with regional offices. They can kill you professionally even before you realize it. If they want to refund the 5 million dollars to customers and take a hit, it's fine. They don't really expect you to make it up from some other business. They will push you for sure. So play along and take it as it comes.'

'Aditya, would you have quietly agreed to the regional office's diktat?'

'No, I wouldn't have.' Aditya was candid.

'Then why are you asking me to do this?'

'Because those days were different. When I was head of retail banking fifteen years ago, I could have got away with murder. A lot has changed since. In those days, I could have spun the "India as an investment destination" story. A country of one billion people made global bankers salivate and put in money year after year in the hope that profits would come some day. People these days don't have the appetite for that. There is no room for dissent. Indian teams of multinationals these days are just expected to execute not think.'

Swami shook his head in disgust. He didn't want to agree with Aditya.

'You will realize this one day, Swami. The rules of the game have changed. Career longevity is more important than career enhancement. Jobs are few and there are many people chasing them. Your first priority should be to save your job. If you live, you get to fight your battle another day.'

Swami looked the other way.

'And the regional office may not be wrong. As Peter says, the profits that India gives him may not be good enough for him to fight the battle at the board level. Imagine an idiot at the annual general meeting standing up and questioning NYIB's security systems and data integrity by citing the India example. It will take the sheen off their success in other parts of the world. Remember that the pain potential India holds for them in terms of customer complaints, senior management escalations, etc. is enormous. So they are effectively shutting off all of those by paying 5 million dollars. When you look at it from their perspective, you can't argue.'

Swami couldn't say anything in response. But he was seething because his opinion in matters related to his business had been overruled.

'In any case, if the cops manage to get to the bottom of this, some of the money may be recovered. That money will come back to the bank. Part of the 5 million will be made up. So cheer up. Hopefully, your bonus will be intact this year too.'

The last part of Aditya's comment made Swami smile.

'You sure know how to make people feel good, Aditya. One must hand it to . . .'

The buzzing of Aditya's phone interrupted the conversation. He looked at his phone and back at Swami. 'It's Sundeep,' he whispered. 'Let me take this call.'

'Hi, Sundeep!' and he walked away from Swami to finish the call.

When he returned, Swami looked at him curiously. 'What happened? Hope all is well.'

'The usual. Sales pitch not going well. RAK Bank had a large budget to migrate its credit cards processes to India. We were pitching for it. Infosys and Tech Mahindra are also in the fray. I was hoping we would get it, simply because I know our competitors can't match our price. But Sundeep is not too hopeful. Let's see.'

'We had lots of fun when we were together at NYIB, Aditya. Do you think we can do something to recreate the magic?'

'I'm sure we can. The timing has to be right though.' Aditya smiled.

# 14

# New York

It was a quiet, chilly winter evening in Queens, New York.

Despite the chill, Rudra Pratap Ghosh was out in the cramped balcony of his third-floor, one-bedroom apartment. He never smoked inside the house. Sitting on a steel chair, the back of which rested against the wall, feet propped on the railing, Rudra was focused on the newspaper he was holding. His eyes were fixed on an ad he had circled.

He dialled the number.

'Hi. I'm looking for a one-bedroom or studio apartment. Your ad mentioned you wanted to lease out yours?' It was time for him to move out. He couldn't afford to stay in one place for long. Just in case!

'I wish you had called a little earlier. Gave it away cheap.'

'Cool.' Rudra hung up.

Walking back into his apartment, he pulled out a laptop. One look and he put it back in its bag and pulled out a different MacBook. He punched a few keys and, in a few moments, he was looking at Craigslist.

He shuffled through a few screens and finally stopped at one and started typing an email. His fingers paused for a moment as he considered whether to mention his background in detail. The earlier part of his educational background was stellar, the more recent one was problematic. A graduate from the Indian Statistical Institute in Kolkata, he had dedicated a good part of his life to research and application of statistics and natural sciences. Even though he was a brilliant student, he had strong ideas concerning social justice. While at the institute , he was a member of the KLO—Kamtapur Liberation Organisation—a rebel organization formed in 1995. The sole objective of KLO was to fight for the rights of the people of North East India. Wanting to carve out a separate state comprising of Cooch Behar, Jalpaiguri, Darjeeling and a few other districts of West Bengal and Assam, the KLO soon emerged as a quasi-militant organization. Assisted by ULFA and a few militant offshoots in the neighbouring countries, KLO was soon waging a war against the country for independent statehood.

Rudra was one of the top six activists of the KLO, who were trained to use firearms by the militant groups in the North East. Pakistan's Inter Services Intelligence agency was also instrumental in providing advanced weaponry training to the key resources of KLO.

Things turned hostile for Rudra after he killed a Communist Party of India (Maoist) leader at a rally in 2000. He hurriedly fled the country and flew to the US and never went back to India. That his name never cropped up in the investigation that followed the killing didn't change his mind. He was now in the US, determined to pursue statistics full time. For a person with his academic credentials, it was not difficult getting into Stanford. A couple of years later he was at it again; he led a breakaway faction of students who formed the non-violent student protest body at Stanford. This body, quite in contrast to its name and ethos, spearheaded what was the first violent protest at Stanford in years. Their demand was that the US government waive a significant portion of the near trillion-dollar student debt. As a consequence, the entire student body was banned, and several students including Rudra were thrown out of the university. The authorities were possibly scared of Rudra's increasing support base and his ability to influence the student community and garner support for whichever cause he espoused. The administration did not like an alternative power centre. After moving out of the university, the students had stayed in touch, though they had dispersed all over the country. Rudra interacted with many of them regularly through online forums that he had set up. No one knew what he did for a living.

Finding an apartment was getting tougher, and he had to be constantly on the move. If he used his real name, anyone doing a cursory search would figure out his background. Landlords don't like to give out apartments to people with a violent past. More so, to Indians with a history of violence in the US. Somewhere along the way, with help from his mentor and a few friends in seats of power, he acquired a new identity. His South American looks helped hide his true identity. Ghosh became Josh. And that's what he came to be known as. No one could have said that he was an Indian. Josh Connelly was American now.

His fingers tapped the keys again and he sent out a mail:

*Hi, I'm a 29 yo Texan man, well adjusted, clean/tidy. I do some currency trading and occasionally do freelance IT work. Mostly keep to myself, spend most of the time working, but enjoy going out and socializing from time to time. I've recently moved to the Queens area and need to find a place soon. Rent and location are both good for me. If the place is still available, please give me a number to call. Thanks, Josh.*

.Within minutes, he got a reply:

*Thanks for the interest. It would be wonderful if you could come down and meet with us. Sometime in the next two days? Cathy and I are off on vacation later this week. Many thanks, Wilbert.*

Within the next few days, Josh moved into Wilbert's two-bedroom apartment, which he shared with Stan, whom he had never met before.

# 15

# Goa

Maurice Oboyo, the Nigerian ambassador to India, was in a rage. The death of a Nigerian citizen during the Goa riots had thrust him into the limelight and he was not happy about it. Managing Nigeria's reputation as a country fraught with crime, fraud and money laundering was hard enough.

The riots following the murder of Jacob Amaku, whose badly mutilated body was found in Mapusa, had been contained by the Goa police. The situation had culminated in the arrest of 123 people, mostly Nigerian.

An upset Maurice called up Goa's chief minister for an update on the safety of Nigerians in the state. This offended the chief minister. A battle of egos ensued.

'Mr Oboyo, need I remind you that this discussion is in breach of protocol? All communication with the states of the Indian Union should be through the Ministry of External Affairs. I would not like to discuss anything regarding matters of state security with you.' The chief minister was trying hard to stay polite.

'A citizen of my country is brutally murdered. Your cops have no clue who killed him. You then have over a hundred of my countrymen arrested. And you want me to follow protocol, Mr Chief Minister?' Maurice yelled into the phone.

'Yes, Ambassador. That's exactly what I'd like you to do.'

'Fine! But let me also warn you that if the police does not stop arresting Nigerians and evicting them from their homes, thousands of Indians living in Nigeria will be thrown out on the streets. It will be up to you to explain the fallout.'

'I will inform the central government of your intent, Mr Oboyo.' The chief minister did not lose his cool. 'Will that be all, Ambassador?'

Maurice slammed the phone down.

The chief minster called his aide and handed him a recording of the conversation. In no time, the Nigerian counsel's threat was being broadcast all over television and social media.

'While I empathize with the Nigerian counsel, I also must remind him that the law will take its own course. We do not have anything against Nigerians but we have to maintain law and order. And if we have to arrest Nigerians or, for that matter, people of any other nationality, to maintain peace, we will.' The chief minister went on record on television. The Indian public loved the drama that was being played out.

This episode embarrassed the Nigerian government immensely. Diplomatic channels of communication were opened up directly from Nigeria, Maurice Oboyo was immediately recalled, an apology was issued, and all efforts were made to assuage the sentiments of the Goans. The Nigerian government even offered to compensate the damage that the riots had caused in Goa.

The issue was amicably settled. Once the paperwork was completed, 122 of the 123 people arrested during the riots were released.

All but one.

# 16

# Mumbai

Malvika woke up feeling very happy that Sunday morning. She looked forward to catching up on her sleep over the weekends. As the CEO of a bank, her social engagements kept her sleep deprived every day of the week. She looked around. The room was still dark. She had drawn the black-out curtains before going to sleep. On a working day, she would have left them slightly open, to allow light to creep in. But not on a Sunday morning. She glanced at her phone, to see the time. It was 9.42 a.m. That's when she saw the missed calls. Five from the same number. Why was he calling her on a Sunday?

She walked to the bathroom and stood below the shower. She did that every day, the moment she got out of bed. It was a habit which had stayed with her since childhood. As the shower jet hit her body, she shivered involuntarily. She was stressed out. The happy mood had disappeared. The missed calls worried her.

She wrapped a towel around herself and came out of the bathroom. The screen on her phone was flashing. The ringer was turned off. It was the same number. She picked up phone and accepted the call.

'Morning, Malvika. How have you been?' A voice came through as soon as she answered.

'Morning, Peter! Sorry, I missed your calls. The phone was in silent mode.' Irrespective of the level one was at in any organization, the excuses for not taking a call remained the same.

'I want to meet you.' After a pause, he added, 'Today.'

'Today?'

'Yes. Today. I'm in Mumbai.'

'What? Why didn't you tell us you were visiting?'

'I'm on my way to the Maldives for a short vacation. I thought of this as an opportunity to meet you and took a detour. If you're free, can we meet at the Intercontinental near the international airport?'

'Oh!' Malvika was taken aback. The CEO of a region visiting without advance notice. Something wasn't right. Flights from Singapore didn't stop over in Mumbai. It was a very clumsy attempt at lying.

'Of course, Peter. When do you want me to come?'

'Whenever you get the time. My flight out is only at 10.30 p.m.'

'I'll be there in an hour.'

'Great! See you then.' Peter hung up.

An hour later, a worried Malvika's Mercedes pulled into the parking lot of the Intercontinental. Peter was waiting for her in the lobby. As she stepped in, he welcomed her warmly, with a generous hug. This was not normal. Peter was not a naturally warm person. Malvika chided herself for reading too much into it and followed him into the coffee shop.

A few pleasantries later, Peter came to the point.

'I wanted to convey something to you in person, Malvika. That's why I decided to make this trip to India.'

Malvika leaned forward. She was trying to act calm but there was a tornado building up inside her.

Peter guessed her state of mind but didn't empathize with her.

After what seemed like an eternity, he exclaimed, 'Congratulations, Malvika!'

Malvika blinked and sat upright, her arms dropping to her sides. 'What for?' She looked very surprised.

'The group has decided to elevate you and make you chairman of the group in India. All the group companies will report to you, Malvika!'

'What?'

'Yes, Malvika. Congratulations! You are the NYIB group chairman in India.'

'You can't be serious, Peter. You really can't be!'

'I thought you'd be happy to hear this.'

'Thrilled, Peter. Really?' Malvika rolled her eyes as she said this. 'Is this a promotion or a kick-up?'

'What do you mean?'

'Every NYIB business in India reports to its corresponding head in Singapore. A CEO here has less power than his or her counterparts in Indian banks. One expects a chairman to have adequate powers to run businesses the way she wants. And to top it all, it's a position that doesn't even exist right now.'

'After all that you have done in India, Malvika, we need to give you something larger. What better than the head of all businesses in India?'

Malvika shook her head. She didn't believe a word of what Peter was saying. 'How much of this decision is etched in stone?'

Peter's expression changed. When he realized that Malvika had seen through the charade, he became serious. 'I must confess this is a decision taken at the board level in Singapore. They will announce it the day after. I wanted to tell you in person. After five years as CEO of the Indian franchise, I'm afraid this is the only career option they have for you.'

'Who is replacing me?'

'Yet to be decided. Of course, you will be among the first to know.'

Malvika was confused about what had just transpired. She was just being shunted out of her position into a parking slot. What should she make of it? A part of her thought that she should take it and relax. But there was another part of her that was in violent disagreement. Even after she bid adieu to Peter and left the hotel, the fog of confusion did not lift.

# 17

# Mumbai

The announcement finally came. Malvika was now the chairman of the New York International Banking group in India.

Along with it came another surprise. Matt Metzger was to be the next CEO.

Apart from Malvika, there was one person who was not too pleased with this development. Swami had harboured hopes of taking over from Malvika. In fact, when he had returned to head retail banking in India, Peter Baron's predecessor had promised that he would be made CEO after Malvika. But, in corporates, successors are not bound to honour commitments made before their time. What made it worse for Swami was that as head of retail banking he functionally reported to Matt, and they had not hit it off well. Things could only get worse with Matt moving to India.

The breaking point was not too far. It came within the first few days of the new CEO taking over.

As part of his regular orientation, Matt met with the various business teams, including retail banking. After a day-long session, Swami left Matt in the conference room and walked back to his cabin. Matt wanted to attend to some urgent emails. After fifteen minutes, Swami went back to check on him. His secretary was in the room, talking on her cell phone, but Matt was nowhere to be seen.

She covered the phone with her hand, looked at Swami, and mouthed, 'He's just gone around the corner.' She went back to her call and stepped out of the room, leaving Swami alone. Swami didn't quite understand what she had said and was about to walk out when he noticed that one of the papers in the pile, which Matt had been perusing earlier in the day, had his name on top. Curiosity got the better of him and he walked to the table to see what it was. His heart sank. He pulled out his iPhone and took a picture of the page and walked out of the room.

'Bitch!' he exclaimed when he met Aditya that evening and showed him the picture. It was Swami's confidential report that Malvika had submitted as part of Matt's takeover process. She had been extremely critical of Swami, to the extent that she had accused him of insubordination and incompetence. No one had ever written anything like that about him.

'This kills my career in this organization, Aditya. Is this what one gets for loyalty?'

'Hold it! Hold it, Swami. Relax. We will figure a way out.'

'There is no way out, Aditya. I don't know what her problem with me is. I really don't.'

'Perhaps she felt threatened by your intellect? She was insecure and saw you as a threat. She knew that you had been promised the CEO's job after her. That would have only added to her discomfort.'

'I have no clue Aditya but one thing is certain. I will make sure that Malvika is history. I will expose her inefficiencies to the senior management. I will do that 100 per cent.'

'You think they don't know? Why else do you think she is being made the chairman? They can't keep her here. They can't sack her. So they did the next best thing. Kicked her upstairs. At least she will be out of the way for a couple of years, by which time Peter Baron's tenure as regional CEO will come to an end. Someone else will come and deal with the problem of how to remove her from the chairman's post.'

'Whatever! They don't have a right to do this to me.'

'Forget it, Swami. Such things happen. You just have to bide your time. If you become too negative now, people will brand you a negative influence when it is time for the tide to change.'

'I feel like quitting, Aditya. Just showing these guys the middle finger . . .'

'Even if you have to quit, Swami, it's important to quit on a high. That's when the world will respect you.'

Swami didn't say anything. He just stared out of the window.

'As for Malvika, I will speak to her. She is not a bad person. We go back a long way. I'll try and find out what is bothering her. I suspect she made you the fall guy for the phishing scam. Which is quite natural for someone who is insecure about . . .' His phone buzzed, interrupting the conversation.

He looked at the phone and then at Swami.

'0832? Where is that?' He took the call. 'Hello,' he said, softly. 'Dad!'

# 18

# Mumbai

Aditya's past had finally made its way into his present. No one knew of this aspect of his life.

He got up hurriedly and reached for the keys to his Mercedes.

'What happened? Who was it?' asked Swami. The uncharacteristically manic look on Aditya's face worried him.

'Come with me.' It was all Aditya could say at the time. There was a quiver in his voice.

Swami got into the car. Aditya drove out of his Bandra residence and turned towards South Mumbai. It was late at night, the traffic signals were switched off, and Aditya was speeding.

'Want me to drive?' asked Swami. Aditya didn't respond.

He drove straight to Malabar Hill via narrow alleys until he stopped outside a huge gate. Swami looked at him in surprise. He recognized the building but didn't ask any questions.

Aditya was out of the car in a jiffy. He looked at Swami and asked, 'Are you staying in the car or coming with me?'

Grudgingly, Swami got out of the car. He didn't want to go in. But he didn't want to leave Aditya alone in that state either.

Aditya ran into the building. Swami had a tough time keeping pace. The elevator was on the sixth floor. Rather than wait for it to come down Aditya dashed up the stairs. He stopped in front of a door and rang the bell.

'Oh my god! Aditya! Why are you panting like this?'

'I need your help, Malvika.' Aditya paused to catch his breath.

Malvika reached out and patted his shoulder. 'Calm down, come in. Tell me what happened.' They had been peers for a long time.

When Aditya finished what he had to say, Malvika dialled a number.

~

Aditya took an early morning flight to Goa. By 5.45 a.m., he was in Goa airport. By 6.30 a.m., he was in Goa Central Prison, seated in front of the jailor, who had been hurriedly summoned at that hour. Along with Aditya was a team of lawyers from Kudremukh & Co., to assist him with the legal proceedings.

When he returned from Goa that evening, Varun was with him. Varun was one of the 123 people arrested by the Goa police in connection with the Nigerian riots. The police were happy keeping him in jail till they got a call from the chief minister's office, who in turn had been called by the finance minister.

'You should have reached out to me earlier,' Aditya said on the flight back.

'I knew you would come to pluck me out of hell, whenever I called. But I wanted to try to do it myself. When it became too much to bear, I called you.' Varun looked away, out of the window of the aeroplane the moment he said this.

# 19

# New York

Josh pulled out a Coke can from the refrigerator and walked back to his room. On the way, he looked at Stan and smiled. Ever since he had moved in, he had barely spoken to Stan. In his line of business, familiarity caused complications. He never went out unless it was absolutely unavoidable. He usually ordered in food. He would get the door only if he were expecting something.

The laptop was on the table, plugged into the charger. He pulled the wire and walked back to his bed. He had just settled down when he heard the apartment door open and someone walk down the steps. His antennae tingled but he didn't get up. The footsteps returned in sixty seconds, followed by the sound of the door closing. Through the gap under the door, Josh noticed a shadow linger outside his room for a few seconds. Moments later an envelope was pushed in through the gap.

'Thanks!' he yelled. He looked at the envelope and smiled. It was a green envelope, thick, cloth-lined, designed to carry important papers or, for that matter, anything heavier than a few pages but light enough to be contained in an envelope. Delivered by US Post, it said.

He slit it open and carefully pulled out its contents. A few bills— decoy paper, basically. A flier advertising a downtown designer store—again useless stuff. He opened the envelope wide and looked in. Deep down, at the bottom, was a small plastic pouch, 2 inches by 3 inches. He pulled it out, opened it and smelled the contents. Breathing in the aroma, he shut his eyes for an instant. He loved it.

He walked to his cupboard, opened a built-in safe and deposited the packet. It was enough to last him a week. He thought for a moment and snapped the safe shut. It would be better to order the replenishment stock now itself.

He walked back to his laptop and punched in a few keys. In no time, he was on the TOR network. Using TOR protocols, he logged into the website. A page that looked strikingly similar to the Amazon e-commerce website opened up on his screen. Two words flashed: Cotton Trail.

Cotton Trail was the best thing to have happened to him and others like him in the past six months. Cotton Trail was a marketplace for all kinds of narcotics, prostitution, banned substances, even paedophilia. Anonymous retailers peddled their wares on Cotton Trail. You could buy any item, which was illegal or banned in the real world. You could choose from a range of suppliers for the product and order, just like you would while ordering books from Amazon.com. Cotton Trail even had a sophisticated supplier-rating mechanism to help buyers choose vendors. The goods were supplied all over the world via mail. Compared to couriers, regular post was subject to less scrutiny.

Josh ordered the drugs that he wanted and selected the checkout option. A window popped up with instructions he had to follow. He knew them by heart now. The most important one was: *If the package falls in the hands of law enforcers, deny that you ordered this. Our systems are secure. No one can prove that it was you who placed the order.*

The logic was simple. In case of discovery, the ownership and the genuineness of the transaction could be tracked back to the buyer only under two circumstances. The electronic transaction trail could lead back to the computer which was used to place the order. Or, the payment could somehow be tracked back to him. Nothing else could prove his involvement.

Cotton Trail was accessible only through TOR, hence the encryption effectively concealed the identity of the buyer's computer. And Cotton Trail only accepted payments in bitcoins, thus preventing any access to the identity of the consumer.

Josh paid for his order with bitcoins and logged out.

While the TOR network and payment via bitcoins maintained anonymity for clients, there was a weak link in the process. The buyer never knew who the supplier was or where he operated from but the seller often knew who the buyer was, unless the goods were ordered to a mailbox, in which case identification was tougher though not impossible. There was a lurking fear that in the eventuality of any of the suppliers getting caught, the buyers would be exposed. But this risk was nothing compared to the overall experience of encountering a drug dealer in the dark and dangerous alleys of the city. Cotton Trail was far safer and easier albeit a bit more expensive compared to other alternatives.

As Josh was logging off from his system, a notification caught his attention. It was about a mail he had received. This time, it was from someone who wanted to meet to discuss a job that had to be done. The time and place for the meeting were mentioned.

Josh confirmed that he would be there and logged out.

# 20

# Mumbai

It was a double whammy for Aditya. Townsville, Indiscape's new game, had just been released. And Aditya's long lost son had returned. Life was on the upswing.

When he met Varun in Goa, it was after twenty years of separation. He had last seen Varun as a ten-year old whose voice hadn't even cracked yet.

Aditya had always been fiercely protective of his personal life. Everyone knew he had gone through a terrible divorce and now lived alone. No one had met his ex-wife and certainly no one knew that a son existed. Sundeep and Swami were both shocked.

It took Varun a few days to settle down and get used to life with Aditya. His time in jail had traumatized him. Aditya made sure that he got everything he needed.

'It's a long story,' Aditya told them when Sundeep and Swami came over to visit. 'I had given up everything at that time. My family, my wife, my fortune—everything in an instant. I used to be a brash and angry man. I travelled on work for twenty days a month. And when I got back home, I just wanted peace. A time and a place where I could relax and recharge. My family wanted just the opposite. They wanted to be around me and enjoy the ten days that I'd be with them. This clash of priorities led to terrible arguments and created a void between us. My wife and I couldn't stand the sight of each other any more. Varun was around ten years old then. I realize the value of a family now but back then, I only cared about my career. My wife found someone who gave her the attention I didn't and took Varun with her. It was an expensive divorce. Her lawyers in America took away everything. I could have got custody of my son—my wife was happy to squeeze me dry and let me have him in return—but I didn't push for it. I had no clue where I was headed. I was almost broke. I wasn't sure I could provide for him, give him the life he deserved. In his own interest, I let him stay with his mom. It was a very tough decision. Probably the toughest I have made in my life. At least his daily life would have gone on comfortably. But despite having the right intentions, I was not ready for what the courts had in store for me. My wife was willing to take custody of our son but on the condition that I wouldn't interfere in their lives. The courts ruled in her favour. This shattered me . . .'

Aditya started to cry. Sundeep and Swami had never seen him in such a state.

'. . . and I left them, without ever looking back. I have few regrets in life; this is one of them.'

He went silent. His eyes were fixed on the floor. He was unable to look up. 'She died of cancer three years ago. No one even bothered to inform me. Varun was at Stanford then. Now he is all alone!' He lamented, 'I wish I had looked back. Life would have been different. We are all chasing illusory pleasures. Our real wealth is not in our bank accounts.'

'Since we've known you, you've been very generous in all your relationships. Perhaps this is an opportunity from God to correct the mistakes of the past,' said Sundeep.

~

Once Varun was emotionally up and running, Aditya wanted to introduce him to his world. He organized a small party at the Taj Lands End for all his friends and acquaintances, most of them bankers who owed him their careers.

Aditya was taking Varun around to meet everyone. It was a

proud moment for him. His invitees were discreet enough not to ask embarrassing questions.

That's when he saw Malvika entering the banquet hall with a companion. He tapped Varun on the shoulder and pulled him towards the door. Malvika had used her contacts and helped pull Varun out of prison, Aditya wanted to express his gratitude.

The moment Varun turned to meet Malvika, he smiled. He thanked her profusely. She smiled, hugged him and gave him a peck on the cheek. After exchanging pleasantries, she walked around to meet the others. As soon as Malvika and Aditya turned, Varun hustled over to Malvika's companion and pulled her aside.

'What are you doing here? Why are you hell-bent on chasing me?'

'Do you think it's appropriate for you to speak in such a manner to someone who is your father's guest and . . .'

'And what?'

' . . . and whose mother helped you get out of jail?'

Varun said, 'You can't be serious.'

'I'm always serious. Even when I'm chasing you.' Tanya was grinning from ear to ear. 'It's a small world, dude. Now that I know you didn't run away from me, but were in jail . . . give me a call.' She gave him her number before walking off briskly towards her mother.

The party got over well past midnight. All the guests had left. But Aditya was worried.

Sundeep hadn't showed up.

# 21

# Mumbai

Aditya walked into his eighteenth-floor office early that morning, first in, like most other days. Indiscape and eTIOS operated from different floors of the same building. Indiscape's was a newer, sportier, more open office that made liberal use of glass. Aditya had two lavish cabins, one on each floor.

He had tried calling Sundeep a few times but his phone was switched off. Natasha, Sundeep's wife, was away in Delhi, visiting her parents.

After depositing his bag in his cabin, by force of habit, he walked towards the washroom. The light in Sundeep's room was on. Assuming that he had forgotten to switch it off, Aditya ignored it and walked straight into the loo.

And froze in his tracks.

'Sundeep?' he exclaimed, going from shock to worry in a second. Sundeep was sitting on the floor, his hair in a mess, his eyes puffy and red. 'What the hell are you doing?'

Sundeep didn't respond. He just sat there, staring into space.

Aditya was getting really worried. He shook Sundeep by the shoulders. 'Is everything all right?' Sundeep had had a drinking problem in the past but Aditya couldn't smell booze on his breath.

'Everything is a mess, Aditya. I don't know what is going on.'

'What do you mean?'

'It's been a week since we launched Townsville. The game has just not taken off. I was here analysing the MAUs all night. As of yesterday, we only have 23,000. Mafia Dons had over two hundred thousand MAUs in the first week itself. At its peak, it had over twenty-five million! Townsville is a disaster.'

The numbers were indeed ominous. Twenty-three thousand MAUs meant a washout. Sustaining the game online with such a paltry user base was impossible. Keeping it alive would cost more than what the game would rake in through advertising revenue. Advertisers would start pulling their ads and revenues would plummet. They would have tough questions to answer.

Whatever the reason though, Aditya couldn't let Sundeep continue in such a state.

'Go home, Sundeep. Get some rest and come back. We will figure out what to do. I'm sure we will find a way out.'

'I don't know Aditya. It's never been like this. First the RAK Bank deal goes out of our hands and now this Townsville disaster. I don't know what's going wrong.'

'It's life, Sundeep. Shit happens. We just have to figure out a way of cleaning it up and moving on.'

Sundeep nodded. He turned and walked to his room. Each step he took was a tired one. He picked up his bag and said, 'I'll be back by noon. I've called all the game designers. We will figure a way out of this mess, Aditya.'

Aditya smiled. 'We will, Sundeep.'

And when Sundeep was out of earshot, Aditya muttered, 'We have to.'

# 22

# USA

America was forgetting Gillian Tan. From front page news, he had been relegated to page 7. TV channels had stopped covering the tragedy. A man who may have been murdered in his quest to serve his nation was quickly losing the nation's attention.

A close aide of the President had been blown up in broad daylight and the Feds' investigation was going nowhere. The FBI chief was cutting a sorry figure in front of the President.

No terrorist organization claimed responsibility for the attack. The assassins had disappeared into thin air. The FBI unsuccessfully followed up the lead of the courier package which Gillian was carrying with him in his car. After three weeks, they were exactly where they had started.

During an emergency meeting of the officers handling the case, Adrian was called in for a debriefing. Neither Adrian nor Tony had much to add.

'It's been only four weeks since I got the case, Robert. Give me some more time. We're getting closer.' Adrian argued.

Robert was very categorical. 'Two weeks are all you have, gentlemen. If I don't get results, you can kiss this case goodbye. Mike Hendricks is breathing down my neck on this one, and I don't want the President to think that we cannot find the people who assassinated one of his closest aides.'

If Adrian couldn't figure it out quickly, he'd have to make way for someone else.

# 23

# Mumbai

Sundeep returned that afternoon. He looked as much a zombie as he had when he left in the morning. The imminent collapse of the game was too much for him to bear. The future of Indiscape was riding on Townsville. Investors had pumped in huge sums of money, wagering on the game's success. It was also about pride. Indiscape was now one of the world's top ten gaming companies. That would change if they couldn't resurrect Townsville.

Varun was in Aditya's room when Sundeep walked in.

'Hey, Varun, how was the party last night?' Sundeep asked, trying very hard to smile.

'Good, sir. You were missed. I know very few people here and you are one of them.'

'I know, I know. I was stuck in office last night. And, by the way, I'm Sundeep. I'm not as old as your father, so don't call me sir!'

'Yes, of course!'

Sundeep looked at Aditya. 'I'll just check if the game designers are here. We can meet them and decide on a plan of action.'

'Call me once they are in the conference room,' said Aditya.

Sundeep nodded. He looked at Varun. 'Why don't you join in too?'

Half an hour later Aditya walked into the conference room with Varun, and took his position at the head of the table while Varun retreated to a corner.

Aditya went straight to the heart of the matter. 'Townsville has not got the traction we had hoped for. We have invested a lot of money in this game. It's a make-or-break game for Indiscape. Twenty-three thousand MAUs is hardly a number. What do you think happened?'

'People are still playing Mafia Dons. We were hoping that they would give Townsville a try and migrate to it but they haven't,' Sundeep volunteered. 'We had put up teasers for the game on the Indiscape.com home page, Aditya, inviting people to try it. Most of the MAUs have come via plug-ins on our home page, so far and some via Google Ads. We significantly overestimated the conversion from our home page.'

Aditya thought for a moment. 'Do you think there could be a problem with the game design and construct?'

'Prelaunch research reports were positive.'

'Do we know how many people clicked on the game teaser on the home page?'

'Sixty-two thousand.'

'Hmm . . .' Aditya paused. 'Look, even if all of them converted to MAUs, it still would have been less than the 200,000 that Mafia Dons had in the first week.'

'True.' Sundeep nodded. It was fast turning out to be a conversation between Aditya and Sundeep, with the others listening in.

'Which means your hook is not working. Sixty-two thousand clicks on your teaser on the home page is too low a number. You need to get that up. Get more customers to see your game. If they experience your game, they will continue playing it. If they don't even experience it, how will they become sticky and active users?'

'I agree: promotions are a problem. We need to diagnose which aspect of it has not worked,' confessed Sundeep.

'Let's increase our advertising spends. Let's be visible all over the net.'

Sundeep looked at him, a bit worried. 'Aditya, we had a budget of 25 million dollars for this game, of which 18 million dollars have been spent on game design, special effects, execution and hosting. We have already committed over 4 million dollars in spends to various online portals across the world. We hardly have anything left.'

'Well, 4 million dollars is not getting us anything in our campaign.'

'For Mafia Dons, our budget was 5 million dollars for everything,' Sundeep commented.

'That's because when Mafia Dons was launched, you had no competition. An online game was a novelty. People were excited. Advertising online was cheap compared to today,' Varun spoke up from his corner. Everyone turned towards him. 'Isn't it obvious? Things have changed. I've played Mafia Dons. I was hooked to it from the first second.'

'Varun . . .' Sundeep began, 'it's not all black and white.' He wasn't too pleased with Varun's unsolicited intervention.

'True, sir, but games are played by instinct. One has to touch that nerve in the gamer. The hook. Promotions and ads must be placed where the customers are. On sites that customers visit. I've been on the net over the last few days. I haven't seen a single ad for Townsville except when I access Indiscape.com to play Mafia Dons.'

'What are you trying to say, Varun?' Sundeep was beginning to sound irritated.

'Hold it! Hold it! Hold it!' Aditya interrupted the two of them. He didn't want them to battle it out in front of the entire group. He turned to the designers and said, 'I think there is a consensus that it's not about the game design. We will meet you guys once we have some clarity on what we want to do.'

After the last person had left, he turned to Varun, 'You need to be careful about what you say and in front of whom.'

'I'm sorry but I thought you were seeking opinions. I will keep my mouth shut.'

'It's okay. What were you saying?'

# 24

# Mumbai

'I think you're stuck in a time warp,' began Varun. Diplomacy was clearly not his forte.

Offended, Sundeep turned towards Aditya. He was dying to retort but was unsure. The last thing he wanted to do was antagonize Aditya by taking on Varun. Aditya didn't seem bothered by Varun's tone. He encouraged dissent. 'Dissent fuels debate,' he always said. Even when he ran NYIB.

'What do you mean?' Aditya asked.

'You are investing millions of dollars in creating world-class games. Every gamer who plays Mafia Dons is a fan of Indiscape. They will do whatever you tell them to. Call it control, call it influence, doesn't matter. But I'm sorry to say that Townsville is hardly a game that a Mafia Dons player will play. It's too soft. No guns, no blood, no gore. Technically, it may be a fabulous game but it does not draw an instinctive response from the gamer. The target markets for these two games are completely different. And yet you hope that the guy who visits Indiscape.com to play Mafia Dons will experiment with Townsville and get hooked. Even these 23,000 MAUs will dwindle quickly.'

Sundeep started to get defensive. 'We are advertising on all the popular websites and in newspapers. We are doing everything to draw in new customers who have not explored Indiscape or Mafia Dons. Next week, our television ads are starting. What else can we do? We have explored and continue to explore every avenue!'

'Dad, I don't know how you guys operate in India. I am speaking as a user. The gaming community in the US is extremely mature. Gaming started many years ago with easy-to-play arcade games like Pacman and Pong.'

'We know what arcade games are, Varun.'

'I guess you do.' Varun smiled sheepishly, realizing his mistake. He continued, 'Once war and strategy games came in, gaming became more hardcore. Gaming consoles became more powerful. And games got more complicated. That's why Mafia Dons became such a hit.'

'It was a good game,' Sundeep muttered. He had a look of disgust on his face but he couldn't do much about it because Aditya had tuned in and was focusing on every word Varun was saying.

'But all that is changing. Complicated games are being developed for companies like Sony PlayStation and Nintendo. If you want to reach out to gamers and succeed in the business, stand-alone is not the way to go. You need to tie in with Sony or Nintendo and build games for them.'

'It's been our policy from the beginning to not form a tie-up with these biggies. Sony or Nintendo will take over 70 per cent of the revenue from the games which will severely compromise our position and reduce our margin.' Sundeep was arguing now.

'Fair enough but imagine if Mafia Dons were available on Sony PSP or on Nintendo devices. Your reach in the UK, the US and Japan would be ten times what it is today. Right now you receive the entire ad revenue from the games—that too is a bad strategy. Had you joined hands with these guys, you may have got only 40 per cent of the revenues from advertisements, but it would have been from a much larger pie. At the end of the day you would have ended up with significantly higher revenues and even better branding. How long will you keep pushing people to come to Indiscape.com and play games? To my mind, that's a dying proposition.'

'We don't want to give away proprietary control of the games, Varun. Sony and Nintendo will start influencing our creativity and we don't want that. We want to retain our creative licence.' Aditya didn't have an iota of doubt about this.

'If that is the case, there is only one option for you.'

'Aditya,' Sundeep was getting restless, 'this is a waste of time. The designers are waiting. We need to tell them what we want them to do.' Sundeep was irritated and tired and in no mood to listen to some kid telling them what to do about a multi-million dollar business.

'Wait, Sundeep!' And Aditya turned towards Varun. 'What were you saying? Only one option? What option?'

'If you can't get your customers to come to you, there is only one option and that is to go to where the customer is . . . social media.'

'Rubbish,' Aditya said. He didn't believe in social media. 'You mean Facebook?'

'Yes.' Varun was categorical. 'I've always wondered why only one gaming company advertises on Facebook and no one else does.'

Aditya and Sundeep both knew that Zynga, the world's leading gaming company, was the only one promoting its wares on Facebook. Zynga had met with a fair bit of success on account of its social media blitz but the sceptics outnumbered those who were positive about the role of social media in Zynga's success.

'That's because it's a useless piece of shit. And will die a natural death.' Sundeep was quick to seize the initiative. He and Aditya had had multiple discussions about this in the past and right now, though he himself had made the case for advertising on social media in the past, he parroted Aditya's viewpoint.

'I don't think so. A game, in the format that you have currently developed, will be useless on Facebook.'

'What do you mean?'

'If you have a stand-alone game on Facebook, like the ones that are there now, it will not be effective.'

'Then how . . .?' Aditya was curious.

'By the end of last year, Facebook had 600 million users against 350 million the year before. When each of those 600 million accesses Facebook, he is technically sitting with a gaming console in front—

his or her computer. Just imagine . . . if you were able to put a great game like Townsville on the screen in front of them and say, Come dude . . . now PLAY! That's what Zynga did with Farmville. It was not a flash in the pan for them. It was a well-thought out strategy.'

'Keep talking,' Aditya said.

'You can continue to give your customers the games for free but build them on Facebook. Let the players play them once they log in to Facebook. Make them shareable. Make it mandatory to invite their friends to play for them to move across levels in the game. Let them compete with real friends, compare their scores. Automatically post status messages when people complete a particular level. Let it come on the newsfeeds. Whenever anyone logs into Facebook, he should not miss it. It should set him thinking that if he is not playing the game he is missing out on the fun that his friends are having. The ultimate ethos for games to succeed today is . . . click click click. Simple tasks. Something for everyone. Shareable.'

'Isn't that too much of a hard sell? Customers may hate us for spamming their newsfeeds.'

'As of now, customers don't have an option. They aren't going to turn away from Facebook because you spam them. They are just beginning to get the hang of Facebook. This will work for the next few years. And Dad, there is no point being so moralistic in this. You are not doing anything illegal. If you don't do this, someone else is going to wake up to the potential of Facebook and do it. It's got to be us, Dad!'

Aditya looked at Sundeep, whose look of irritation hadn't changed for a minute.

'Dad!' Varun interrupted. 'We must start monetizing the games. Get customers in for free, but sell them tokens, which can be used in the games. Get them to pay as they progress. Sell them cheats, which they can use to short-circuit the game levels. There are a number of things we can do once we go social.'

'How do you know so much about gaming?' Aditya asked.

'A customer knows more about your product than you can ever

imagine. I'm a hardcore gamer. I know more about gaming than all your designers.' Varun's overconfidence bordered on arrogance. 'And . . .'

'And?' Aditya asked.

'During my postgraduation, for three months, I interned with Zynga in their finance department. I worked closely with their CFO. This approach towards social media in gaming is part of their long-term plans. Anything that goes viral, for them, is a revenue spinner. That's the reason they locked on to Facebook early on and signed an exclusive deal with them for two years. No other gaming company can advertise on Facebook till Zynga is with them.'

Sundeep was frowning. 'Yes, I'm aware of Zynga being in bed with Facebook. But why are we discussing this if we can't even think of execution?'

'Because we might just have a window of opportunity. Facebook is extremely pissed at the way Zynga is behaving. They have become too big for their boots. Facebook wants to throw them out but it's too much money to give up. If they can find someone willing to pay even 75 per cent of what Zynga pays them, they will annul their contract with Zynga. That "someone" could be us.'

Aditya looked pensive. Varun had contrarian views but he seemed to have the knowledge and the drive. If he learnt some tact, he could lead Indiscape into the future. Ironically, he sounded like the Sundeep of yesteryears.

# 25

# New York

Josh reached Midland Café, dressed very casually. A white tee and blue jeans helped him blend in with the evening crowd. Not too many people were in the café at the time. He sat down at a designated table and waited for a while. A few people walked in and out. He waited. Since he was not much of a coffee drinker nothing there appealed to him.

Finally a steward appeared.

'What can I get for you, Mr Connelly?'

Josh was startled. How did the guy know his name?

'It's Mr Connelly, right?' The steward smiled. Josh nodded. The steward pointed to a table in the corner where a middle-aged man was sitting. A large tweed coat enveloped his slim frame and a hat covered his sandy hair. He'd been sitting in the café for twenty minutes but Josh hadn't realized that the man was waiting for him.

The man patted the seat next to him. Josh got up and walked to the table. Without waiting for further invitation, he pulled the chair back and sat.

'Josh Connelly. Technology whiz. Admin at Cotton Trail. All-round hacker. Welcome!'

Josh saw his face when the man looked up and removed the hat. He was at least sixty years old. Fair with freckled skin. His build didn't seem to be American. European maybe. South African, possibly. Josh was trying to form an opinion when the man asked him, 'How do you manage to do all this?'

'I can see you have done your homework on me. That too, impeccably,' Josh commented.

'Well, one has to. Especially when you are looking for someone to run a job for you.'

'A job?'

'Yeah. I'll give you the details later . . . but we will need a team for that.'

'Team? What are you talking about?'

'A team of twenty people. Young. People your age would be better. Not mine, for sure. People you can trust with your life. Or know from your past exploits. Possibly illegal immigrants, who have no records. No tracks. No history. Members from your student body days at Stanford would also do.'

'What are they expected to do?' Josh was surprised that he knew every detail about him.

'How long will it take you to put this team together?'

'Where is the job?'

'New York City.'

'A month.'

'Too long.'

'What do you have in mind?'

The old man looked at his watch. He was old-school, the kind who looked at their watches to confirm the date. 'Two weeks?'

'Tough. If you want me to put together a reliable team, I need time.'

'Time is something I don't have.'

'Give me three weeks at least. Anything less than that and I can't do it.'

The old man laughed. 'Anything is possible if the price is right.'

'What is to be done?'

'Okay, three weeks it is. Here's the deal. Three Saturdays from now, I will meet you here at ten thirty before the café opens. You and your entire team. You will be told what to do once we meet. Tell all of them to carry large backpacks.'

'What's in it for me?'

'Each of those guys keeps 5 per cent of what they manage to get away with. You get to keep 10 per cent of the total amount.'

'What numbers are we talking of here?'

'Does half a million dollars for you sound good?'

Josh looked at him with a fair bit of apprehension. 'How do I trust you?'

'Well, 100,000 bitcoins will be transferred to you before EOD, today. Each bitcoin is worth two dollars. Will that be enough for you to trust me?'

Josh got up. 'I'll email you my bitcoin public key on TOR mail.'

'See you in three weeks.'

# 26

# Mumbai

Malvika had just returned home after a long session with the corporate banking team. It was Matt's way of driving the agenda with his people—hold full-day reviews. He hadn't invited Malvika for the session though. She had gotten wind of it at the last minute and gate crashed.

Matt had made no effort to conceal his displeasure. Throughout the session, he blatantly ignored her and avoided taking her advice on anything. This had become a daily affair at NYIB. Malvika's importance was fast getting eroded and that was clearly affecting her. These days Matt had the regional office's confidence.

The past few days had been terrible for her—she couldn't sleep without a shot of whisky and sleeping pills.

That day she was looking forward to the evening. She always looked forward to the time she spent with him. Malvika wanted to soak in the large tub in her apartment and drive away the negativity. She took care to ensure that she was at her best whenever she met him.

～

Around the same time, Varun's phone rang. He looked at it, smiled, and took the call.

'Hi, Varun!'

'Hey, Tanya, wassup?'

'Where are you?'

'I can be wherever you want me to be.'

'Shut up,' she said, even as she smiled to herself. 'Will you come with me?'

'Where?'

'It's mom's birthday next weekend. Saturday. I need to buy her a gift.'

'Ha! You want me to drive you to the mall so you can shop for your mom?'

'How cruel do you think I am? I just thought I would get to spend time with you while I do some boring work,' Tanya replied.

'I'll come, sweetheart!'

'Great! I'll see you at the Taj Hotel shopping arcade in an hour.'

Little less than an hour later, Varun drove into the portico of the Taj Mahal Hotel at the Gateway of India. As he handed his car keys to the valet, he spotted Tanya in the lobby.

He gave her a generous hug. She reciprocated. 'What do you propose to buy for your mom?'

'There is a Louis Vuitton store down on the right. I thought an LV bag would be a great gift for her. It's got style and class.'

'Cool.'

Varun slipped his hand into hers. She turned to look at him, smiled and squeezed his hand back. 'Want a coffee before we go shopping?' he asked her and she nodded.

The two of them headed towards the poolside coffee shop.

'What were you doing when I called you?'

'Dad has launched a new game. Was taking stock of that.'

'New game?'

'Uh-huh. Townsville. Indiscape is betting big on it. Let's see how it shapes up. It hasn't taken off so I'm helping him bring in a few changes. I was on a conference call with the folks at Facebook. We are negotiating a deal with them.'

'What deal?'

'After going back and forth, I've finally convinced dad and Sundeep to get on to social media and look to build an exclusive alliance. The folks from Facebook are coming next week to meet us. Was just doing some background work for that.'

'Cool.'

They headed for the LV store. After a lot of looking and trying, Tanya finally picked out a bag.

~

At her home in Malabar Hill, Malvika stepped out of the tub, dried herself, and looked at the clock. It was 7 p.m. She had to meet him in an hour. From her eclectic collection in the closet, she pulled out a bright orange saree. It took her five minutes to wrap it around herself. Another fifteen minutes to apply her make-up and she was ready to go.

She always called him before she left. Just to make sure that he was free. The phone kept ringing but he didn't pick up. She tried a couple of times, after which she decided to wait for him to call back. He would see her calls at some point.

She switched on the TV and sat down on the lounger, aimlessly surfing channels. She landed on UTV where Mini Menon was anchoring a show called *Eavesdropping*. It brought out news from the grapevine. Rumours, which could neither be confirmed nor denied. She loved that programme and let it play. Five minutes and fifteen glances at the phone later, she was about to switch off the TV when Mini announced: 'D.V. Subba Rao is said to be in the running for the post of governor of the Reserve Bank of India.'

Malvika sat up with a jerk. What the hell? How could this happen. Her face went red in anger. This was not going according to the script she had written. Would all the compromises she had made be in vain? Had he been playing her all along?

She had to confront him.

# 27

# Mumbai

Varun was dressed in a formal suit when he came down for breakfast. Aditya was waiting for him.

'Looking good, Son.'

'Thanks, Dad. Is Sundeep uncle joining us?'

'He hasn't said so. I think he will come there directly.'

'Cool. Let me quickly grab a bite before we leave. I seriously hope something works out today.'

'Yes. Same here. Sundeep is not happy about it though.'

'I know, Dad. But you know what? Facebook is the future for gaming.'

Aditya nodded.

They left after breakfast. Office was just a twenty-minute drive from home. The meeting with the Facebook team was at 11 a.m. Two hours to go.

Sundeep came in at 10 a.m. He didn't look his normal energetic self.

'Sundeep,' Aditya called out when he saw him walking to his cabin.

'Yes, Aditya?'

'I know you are upset.' Aditya walked up to him and put his arm around him.

'No, Aditya, it's just that I don't agree with what you and, more specifically, Varun want to do.'

'Sundeep, you and I, we go back a long way so I can tell you this.

Varun is back in my life and I don't want to lose him. I marginalized him from my life in the past. I want to make up for that. He wants to try something new, I am letting him. If you ask me whether I am 100 per cent confident, I'm not. But our methods haven't worked either. I believe that the youth of today are more in sync with current trends than you or I. I need you to help me in this. You need to support Varun.'

'Aditya, I will do whatever you tell me to. Varun is as dear to me as he is to you.'

'Thanks, Sundeep.'

The discussion ended in an uneasy truce. Aditya was sceptical about Sundeep and Varun finding common ground.

The delegation from Facebook Singapore comprised four people, all of Chinese origin. After exchanging a few pleasantries, Varun stood up and made a dramatic presentation to them. 'A thorough integration of the game with Facebook. It should seem like an app from Facebook. Users should not only be able to play the game on Facebook but invite their friends too. We need to build an entire community of Indiscape players.'

The Facebook team listened intently. Facebook had annual revenues of around 2 billion dollars, of which 90 per cent came from the US and Europe. Asia was a blip in the ocean. Of the 100 million dollars that Asia contributed, about 75 million dollars came from advertising revenues. Facebook in Asia was desperate to gain ground. The icing on the cake for the team would be that the replacement client for Zynga came from this region.

At the end of the presentation, the regional director of Facebook looked at Aditya and asked, 'So what do you expect us to do?'

'Gentlemen!' Varun interrupted, not letting Aditya answer. 'We have given you a broad picture of what we want you to do. Before we get down to the specifics, let me tell you what we will do for you,' and brought up a slide on screen.

'One, we will make our games exclusively available on Facebook for a period of one year from the time they are launched. A user will have to have a Facebook account to play our games. Two, we will make sure all links on our portal, which has over 1 million hits a day, point to the Facebook page, where the game can be played. The login ids of each of our users will be automatically converted to a Facebook account. We have most of the details one needs to create a Facebook account. The customer will just have to click and fill in additional details and, lo and behold, his account will be activated. Remember, we have over 30 million users logged on to Mafia Dons, of which we have 25 million MAUs. If any of them are not Facebook users, we will insist that they become users.'

Sundeep was shocked. He looked at Aditya. He was about to speak when Aditya whispered, 'Hold on!' Sundeep got up and walked to Aditya. 'Placing all our eggs in the Facebook basket might screw us badly. We should partner with them without signing away exclusive rights,' he whispered.

'We aren't signing anything away today, are we? We'll chat once these guys leave.'

Varun carried on, oblivious to the consternation he was causing. ' . . . and three, we will make sure that our advertising campaign is Facebook-friendly. Not only that, we will share a predetermined percentage of all our revenues arising out of advertising prior to, during, or after the games, with Facebook. These are our terms, gentlemen, please let us know if you want to proceed.'

The four Facebook representatives went into a huddle to discuss the offer. Aditya could hear strains of Mandarin. Finally the regional director looked up. 'Can you please share with us the financials that are at stake here?'

'Give us fifteen minutes, gentlemen.' Varun walked out, followed by Aditya and Sundeep. The latter hadn't uttered a word during the meeting.

# 28

# Mumbai

After about ten minutes, Aditya returned with Varun and Sundeep. Varun walked to the head of the table. He thrust a pen drive into the USB port of the computer and opened a PowerPoint file. It had only one slide with three bullet points.

1. Advertising worth 20 million dollars on Facebook at a 50 per cent discount on rack rates.
2. Exclusive gaming contract on Facebook for twelve months. No other gaming company should advertise on Facebook for this period.
3. 30 per cent of the revenue from customers who play the game (if we start charging customers) will be passed on to Facebook. Facebook, in turn, will provide advertising worth the same amount for free. For instance, if Indiscape collects 20 million dollars from customers during a year, it will pass on 6 million dollars to Facebook. In return, Facebook will provide advertising worth 6 million dollars to Indiscape for free. At rates agreed in #1 above.

'If this is acceptable, sir, Indiscape commits a 25-million-dollar income to Facebook in year one,' Varun added.

Aditya and Sundeep said nothing.

Varun continued, 'This comprises 10 million dollars from direct advertising and 15 million from revenue sharing. In three years, I expect this sum to cumulatively go up to 125 million dollars.'

The Facebook people promised to respond after conferring with their colleagues.

'We are in a fairly advanced stage of testing a game called Townsville,' Varun continued, 'and if you do view our proposal positively, we would like to stop spending on other channels and focus on yours alone.'

The regional director shook hands with the three of them and left, followed by his team.

'Are you out of your mind?' Sundeep yelled the moment the Facebook reps were out of earshot.

Varun smirked. This irritated Sundeep even more.

'Uncle,' Varun said, 'including development charges, we are already over 20 million dollars down on this game with no users to show for it.'

'How does that justify this kind of an extravagance?'

'First, it is not an extravagance. We will be able to reach 600 million customers in one go. I'm willing to wager that customers who are hooked on to Facebook will try out anything new on it. Today all our users play for free. We run an extremely popular but unprofitable enterprise. The moment we go back to our advertisers and tell them that they will now have access to 600 million customers—a number Facebook expects will rise to 1 billion in the next two years—they'll start banging on our doors, cash in hand. That's when we increase ad rates. That will take care of a large part of our 10-million-dollar payout to Facebook.' He paused.

'And second, we need to convert our games from completely free games to premium games. We will charge our customers a small amount to move from one level to the other. Townsville has fifty levels. We should ask the game designers to increase it to seventy-five. I project that this will net us another 25 million dollars in revenue. And once we have 20 million dollars worth advertising space on Facebook, we will not only advertise Townsville but also Mafia Dons and all our old games. We will relaunch them by making them

Facebook-friendly. Look at the revenue opportunity there. And by accessing that market with an exclusive contract with Facebook, you are effectively barring the competition from benefiting from social media for at least one year. By the time they wake up, we'll be well on our way to being one of the top gaming companies in the world.'

It was beginning to dawn on both Sundeep and Aditya that they had become victims of their own rigid beliefs. Unwilling to change the way they went about their business, they had refused to look at emerging trends. The world around them was changing. They could either adapt or perish. What Varun had brought to the table was a fresh approach. Had Sundeep or Aditya looked at the business from the point of view of consumers, who were largely the youth of the world, they would probably have arrived at the same conclusion as Varun. It's not often that a novice beats seasoned bankers at strategy. But this was not strategy. It was a simple case of having ears to the ground.

That evening, the regional director called Aditya and asked for a written proposal. Within a few days, the deal was signed.

# 29

# New York

The furrows on Josh's forehead ran deep that morning. He had carefully put together the twenty-member team, most of them from the student body that he had led. However, at the last minute, one of them backed out.

Josh was pacing up and down his room at 4 a.m. when he had a brainwave. His flatmate Stan was an illegal immigrant from Mexico and he did not have a steady income. It would not be too difficult to convince him to be a part of the team. He had not asked Stan earlier because he didn't want him to know about the job. But now, he didn't have choice. Once Stan was convinced, his team was set. It was execution time.

On Saturday morning, the old man and Josh arrived at Midland Café at almost the same time.

'The team is in place. No blood. No gore. No murders. No guns. Non-negotiable.'

'Yes, I remember,' the old man confirmed.

'Will you now tell me what you want them to do?' Josh asked.

The old man bent down to pick up a bag that lay at his feet. Rummaging inside, he pulled out a leather folder, opened it and laid it out in front of Josh. He pulled out key cards for Hotel Grand from the folder and extended them towards Josh. 'Here,' he said.

Josh was both surprised and curious. 'What am I supposed to do with these?'

Seeing his apprehension, the old man explained, 'These are not hotel room keys, Mr Connelly. These cards have been coded with the details of five different international credit cards. They can be used to withdraw cash from ATMs. The PIN is written on the backs of the cards.'

Josh turned the card around.

'These twenty people will be split into ten two-member teams. Each team will be given five cards. They will go to ATMs across New York and withdraw cash using these cards. Each withdrawal will be exactly 2000 dollars. Five cards per team, makes it 10,000 dollars per ATM. They will need to cover as many ATMs as they can. They have till 4 p.m.'

'Won't the cards run out of cash? The accounts might get fully tapped out, right? What happens then? ATM cards might not work endlessly.'

'The ATMs will dispense cash endlessly. It's been taken care of. Half an hour ago, our team hacked into the banking systems of these cards and raised the withdrawal limits on each of these cards to 1.5 million dollars. You won't have a problem. We need to get in before the bank discovers the leakage and plugs it.'

'You actually did that?' Josh smiled. He looked at the cards again, then at the old man. 'What do we do with the cash?'

'That's why we have you. Collect the cash from your teams. Wait for instructions. We will tell you what to do. Remember, the faster you move, the more cash you collect. I don't need to remind you that 10 per cent of the total collection is yours. And each of the individuals in the team get 5 per cent of what they collect.'

'Is that all?' asked Josh, as he got up to give instructions to his team.

'Raid the Manhattan ATMs first. They normally dispense notes of higher denominations. It'll be easier for you to carry around. And . . . ' he paused.

'And?'

'Please advise your team to steer clear of the CCTV cameras in the ATMs. When they enter the ATM lobby or get close to the kiosk, instruct them to draw up their hoodies. We don't want the cameras to catch them in the act. If anyone gets caught, there will be no one to take responsibility. They will be on their own.'

Josh nodded and got up. As he was walking towards the exit he froze. Seated in the corner, quietly engaged in reading a copy of the local magazine, was someone he knew. Josh pulled up his hoodie, covered his face and hurriedly exited the café. His team was waiting for him.

Thirty minutes later, all the ten teams had been briefed and they set out to raid the ATMs in New York City.

# 30

# Mumbai

The who's who of the Indian banking industry attended Malvika's birthday party at the Four Seasons on Saturday. CEOs, business leaders, regulators, bureaucrats, opinion-makers, page 3 people were all in attendance. Until the morning of the birthday, Tanya had kept the party a secret. But then she had to reveal it to Malvika so she could dress up for it.

Malvika had not been herself lately because of the changes at NYIB and Tanya hoped the party would lift her spirits.

Aditya was among the first to arrive. Varun was already there, helping Tanya.

'Looking gorgeous as ever, Malvika!' He said, and she blushed as she gave him a big hug.

A steady stream of visitors followed. Swami and Sundeep walked in together without their wives at about 10 p.m. Sundeep walked up to Tanya and complimented her, 'Looking nice.' She smiled. 'I'm sure your mom is going to be jealous of you.' He looked at Varun and asked, 'Don't you agree, Varun?'

'Of course!'

'And my my, is that a Birkin?' Sundeep asked. He recognized the Hermes handbag that Tanya was carrying. Tanya blushed, a bit embarrassed.

Swami sought out Aditya. 'I need to talk to you.'

Aditya walked with him to the terrace adjacent to the banquet hall. It was empty.

'It's Matt. He says he wants to be closely involved in the running of retail banking. He claims that it's a business which is getting a lot of attention in the regional office, all for the wrong reasons, and he wants to be hands on,' Swami complained.

'What's wrong with that? He is your boss. He has every right to be involved in what you do.'

'I know that, Aditya. The problem is he doesn't want a head of retail banking.'

Aditya's expression changed. 'What do you mean?'

'He doesn't want another head of retail banking. He wants to take on that role himself. Manage business directly.'

'Rubbish. Where will he have the time? He is the CEO of the bank.'

Suddenly, Swami grabbed Aditya by his shoulder and pushed him slightly to his left. 'Watch out,' Swami said and Aditya glanced to his right. The terrace parapet wasn't high or broad enough. Inadvertently, Aditya had strayed too close to it. Once Aditya had moved, Swami continued. 'He wants me out. He didn't say it in as many words. Said he needs to find me another job. Asked me what I preferred. All this happened today, Aditya. I was too shocked to even respond!'

'But why would he do that?'

'Because of this woman. This bitch Malvika. She has coloured his opinion.'

'Watch your language, Swami. You are at a party thrown for her.'

'I always thought that I would get the top job after Malvika. Not only did that not happen, but she also screwed me over in her handover report to Matt. My career in this bank is finished. I will never forgive her.'

'It's okay, Swami. Forget about it. Let's talk about it later. There are others here who will try to prey on your emotions.' He tried to subtly gesture that someone was approaching.

'I don't care about her, Aditya. I came here because you were going to be here.'

'Who was going to be where, Swami?' A female voice.

Swami turned. Malvika was walking towards them. 'Hi, Malvika. Happy birthday,' he managed to say.

'That's not coming from your heart, is it Swami?' Malvika ridiculed him.

Swami didn't respond. Clarifications caused complications. He had learnt that from Aditya.

'Never mind,' Malvika said and walked on to meet someone else. As she was walking away, she turned towards Aditya and smiled. 'I hope you haven't forgotten our plan, Aditya. Remember, we have to take these guys out tonight?' Aditya just smiled and nodded in response.

He watched a beaming Malvika walk towards the entrance of the banquet hall to welcome the governor of the Reserve Bank of India who had just entered. The governor was walking towards Malvika when he saw Matt. He stopped and turned.

'Hey, Matt!'

Matt saw him, waved and approached him.

Aditya was watching this. 'These bureaucrats are so snooty when you meet them in office but socially they are the friendliest of all people.'

'I know, Aditya.' Swami grinned. The sight of Malvika being snubbed by the governor had brought a smile on his face.

Malvika's face had turned red with embarrassment. Hadn't this been the story of her life ever since Matt Metzger had come into it? Everyone in her team and even outside the bank, people who mattered, had stopped giving her importance. The press that had once loved her had stopped carrying articles about her. So much so that when the newspapers had carried news of Matt's appointment, they didn't even mention her name.

'Serves her right,' Swami muttered. 'Natural justice.'

The party went on for a long time. At fifteen minutes to midnight there was a flurry of activity. A few uniformed men walked in, looked around and took positions outside the room. Within minutes, the finance minister made an appearance. Tanya's reaction indicated that he was not expected. How had he landed up there? Aditya looked really perplexed as well.

Malvika volunteered. 'I invited him. When you told me about the party this morning, I called him. He said he'd be in Mumbai and would try and drop in for ten minutes.'

Tanya frowned. 'You should at least have mentioned this to me, Mom.'

'It's okay, Tanu. Why make a fuss over such a small issue?' She walked to the entrance to welcome the minister and hugged him warmly.

'Can I chat with you privately for a few minutes, Mr Minister?' Malvika requested. Both of them walked out to the open terrace, where Aditya and Swami had stood just moments ago. The terrace was on one side of the hall, separated by a thick curtain.

A couple of minutes later, a steward walked up to Tanya with a tray bearing a glass of whisky for Malvika and a few snacks. She had asked for one just before the minister had arrived. The steward looked at Tanya and then at Varun, who took the tray from him. At that very instant, the governor of the RBI walked up to Tanya. He complimented her and thanked her for a lovely evening. That conversation lasted for a couple of minutes after which Tanya turned her attention back to Varun. She took the tray from him and walked up to the terrace. Varun drew the curtain back just a bit so Tanya could walk onto the terrace. She went up to Malvika and the minister, who were engrossed in a very animated discussion. Varun was with her. The discussion stopped the moment the curtains were drawn. Varun offered the whisky to Malvika and looked at the minister. 'What can I get for you, sir?'

Malvika didn't wait for the minister to respond. She picked up some snacks from the tray and gave instructions. Varun and Tanya nodded and left, leaving the two behind. Another five minutes passed. No signs of the discussion ending.

'What is she up to?' an irritated Aditya asked, walking up to

Tanya. 'I think you should tell them that the guests are waiting for her to cut the cake.'

Just then the minister came back into the hall, went straight to the RBI governor, exchanged a few words, and left the party. He looked agitated. The hectic activity, which had had the room aflutter following his re-entry from the terrace, died down almost immediately.

The emcee for the evening announced that the countdown to the birthday was about to begin. Swami's phone buzzed. He ignored the call and put the phone on silent mode. Someone from the office was trying to reach him.

Everyone was looking around for Malvika. Tanya walked to the terrace and came back within seconds. Malvika was not on the terrace.

Suddenly, the lights went off and music blared.

'Hey! What's that?' exclaimed Varun.

It was pitch dark in the room. The countdown began: Ten, Nine, Eight, Seven, Six, Five, Four, Three, Two, One . . . Happy birthday to you! Happy birthday to you, dear Malvika! Happy birthday to you . . .

The song began playing on the audio system. A few of the lights were switched on but most stayed dim for effect. The spotlight was trained on the French doors that led to the terrace. Everyone was waiting for the curtains to part and for Malvika to step in.

Instead, the doors to the hall were thrown open and the hotel's general manager stepped in looking flustered. He spotted Tanya and walked up to her. 'You need to come with me, ma'am.'

'What happened, Mr Krishna?'

'Please come with me. I will tell you on the way.'

Tanya turned towards the crowd, searching. Varun ran up to her, stopping only to grab her Birkin handbag.

Krishna led them into a waiting elevator. In no time, they were in the hotel lobby. Contrary to what he had promised, he did not offer any explanation. Quietly, he led them outside. And stopped.

Tanya was stunned by the sight in front of her.

Lying on the pavement, face down, blood pooling around her, was the lifeless body of Malvika. The fall from the thirty-fourth floor had knocked the life out of one of the most powerful women in India.

Tanya turned towards Varun. She hid her face in his shirt and started to sob uncontrollably. He hugged her tightly.

# 31

# Mumbai

Malvika's body was swiftly placed in a van by the hotel authorities and taken to Lilavati Hospital in Bandra, a ten-minute drive away. Tanya was in the van. Varun had tried to get in as well but there was no space. He ran to his car and rushed to Lilavati so he could be there before Tanya reached.

Aditya followed in his car with Sundeep and Swami, driving at breakneck speed. There was pin-drop silence in the car as Aditya drove at breakneck speed. The only time Swami had seen him drive like that was when Varun had called for help from a jail in Goa.

The cops had just arrived at the hotel. They had been called even before the general manager had informed Tanya and others about the mishap. They wanted to talk to everyone in the room and piece together the sequence of events before letting them go.

The silence in Aditya's car was shattered by the ringing of Swami's phone. He looked at the screen. 'Why is he calling at this hour?' he muttered under his breath. As he cancelled the call he saw sixteen missed calls from the same number. 'What the hell?' He called back.

'What happened?' He thundered into the phone. 'Sixteen calls?'

As the guy on the phone spoke Swami's face turned pale. It was as if he'd just seen a ghost. Sundeep had turned back and was looking at him, wondering what was going on as Swami's face went through a million transformations.

'What?' Swami howled into the phone. 'Are you serious? How did this happen?'

The car crossed the Bandra–Worli Sea Link, speeding behind the hotel van.

'What action have we taken?'

Swami was silent for a long time, listening intently.

Then, 'Hmm. This does not sound good. Let me call you back.'

The moment he disconnected, Sundeep asked, 'What happened?'

'Some of our cards have been compromised,' Swami said. And, after a pause, 'This one is really bad.'

'Compromised?'

'Yes, Sundeep. Fraud prediction system picked up five cards on which there have been multiple cash withdrawals overseas.'

'How much has been withdrawn?'

'Roughly 5 million dollars.'

'What?' Sundeep was shocked. 'That's huge.'

'There's more. When they checked the cards on the system, they found that the withdrawal limits on these cards had been raised to insane levels just a couple of hours before the fraud. That shows that either the system was hacked or someone on the inside did the job. The technology teams think it's a sophisticated hacking job.'

Sundeep's face went pale. He was finding it difficult to say what was on his mind. He glanced at Aditya who was looking straight ahead of him. He seemed to be in a trance. He hadn't heard a word of what Swami had said.

'Aditya!' Sundeep called out.

No response. He looked carefully at Aditya's face. His eyes were open, tears streaming down his cheeks. He was driving instinctually. Sundeep was worried that he might crash the car.

'Aditya,' he said again. He reached out grabbed his shoulder and shook him. 'Aditya! Are you okay?' The sudden jerk brought Aditya out of the trance he had been in. He braked abruptly, and the car screeched to a halt on the roadside. He sat in his seat, head in his hands, for a long time. Finally, when Sundeep said, 'Aditya, we might have a problem,' he looked up.

Realizing that he had not heard a word of what Swami had said, the latter repeated everything.

A worried Aditya turned to Swami, fear and stress writ large on his face. 'What are you saying?'

'Yes, Aditya, I can't believe it myself.'

Aditya looked at Sundeep, 'But NYIB's card operations are outsourced to eTIOS!'

# 32

# USA

The audacity of the ATM heist had shocked the Feds. They immediately activated the Economic Crime Investigation Unit. An operation of this kind and scale was unprecedented in the United States.

The FBI would have preferred to keep the incident under wraps till they got to the bottom of it. However, NYIB in India had gone public with it so the FBI had to make a statement. It didn't take them long to figure out the modus operandi but they had no clue whatsoever about the people behind this operation. The surveillance videos from the ATM cameras had not thrown any light on the perpetrators. The only thing the FBI could make out was that they were carrying backpacks and their heads were covered.

Later in the day, the FBI issued a press statement:

*Five million dollars were stolen two days ago from 520 ATMs in New York in what is one of the biggest ATM frauds in the history of the United States of America. The perpetrators hacked into the card processing systems of a service provider of New York International Bank in India. They skimmed off the personal data of the users and also raised the allowed limits on these cards exponentially. This stolen data was used to create a fraudulent card by encoding the same user data onto a hotel key card with a magnetic strip. These cards were used by a team of mules at various ATMs across the city of New York to withdraw unlimited amounts of cash. These operations are called Unlimited Operations.*

The release went on to document the various steps that the FBI was taking to make financial products fraud-proof. 'The FBI's Economic Crimes Investigation Unit is working on the case. We are following some leads and expect to nab the culprits soon.' The spokeswoman reading the statement signed off with these words.

Tony was reading a copy of the statement on the FBI website, when Adrian walked in. 'Did you see this?' he asked, picking up a large slice of his pizza. He usually had a giant pepperoni for lunch. That's when he was on a diet. 'Crazy bunch of geniuses!'

'You wish you were one of them, don't you?' Adrian chided him.

'Why do these things happen only in good old America?'

'It's easy?'

'Huh?'

'You heard me. It's easy to do it here.'

'Crap. We are the most technologically advanced nation in the world. Aren't we?'

'We love to call ourselves that. But what the world doesn't know is that America is wildly behind the times in terms of transactional security. The magnetic strip, which is used on cards, is fifty-year-old technology. The strip contains the card holder's information and is easy to copy or steal. When you take it to any store, the store owner can just swipe the card on a data skimmer and transfer the entire data. Once you have the data, you can use a magnetic card writer—the kind hotels use to imprint code on magnetic room keys—and transform any card—old credit card, hotel key, driving licence, what have you—into an active card, by just imprinting this data on to it. You can buy a card writer for less than 200 dollars. Once the new card is activated using a PIN, it can be used on any ATM to potentially withdraw unlimited sums of money.'

'How do they get the PIN?' Tony asked, baffled.

'Typically, when these cards are issued, they come with a PIN.

But when the thieves are the ones creating the fraudulent cards, the PIN is hardly protection.'

'But how could they have managed to withdraw 2.5 million dollars? And if these things are so easy, why don't they happen every day?'

'The risk always exists, Tony. However, going by the report that FBI has put out, the guys not only stole card information but also hacked into the card systems of the bank and altered the withdrawal limits on the cards. It's not easy to break through the firewalls of these financial service giants . . . Unless they have a weak link—a service provider, who has access not only to their systems, but is also internally compromised. By hacking into the service provider's systems the perpetrators could have gotten access to the bank's data.'

'What if someone on the inside is helping them?' Tony asked, reaching for the last slice of the pizza.

Adrian's phone rang. It was Robert Brick.

'I thought you were competent agents when I gave you guys the Gillian Tan case to investigate,' he hollered the moment Adrian took the call.

'We are trying, Robert. Every possible angle is being investigated in detail.'

'Fuck you, Adrian! You guys are a bunch of incompetent fools. Now that I have built this halo around you, I can't even go and tell the President that you guys have made no progress; I will look like an idiot,' he screamed into the phone and cut it abruptly.

Pressure from higher-ups to get to the bottom of the Tan case was mounting by the day.

# 33

# Mumbai

Malvika's death was front-page news in all the mainline dailies and financial papers. Even though it happened late at night, almost all the papers carried the gory details the next morning itself. Images of her body splattered on the pavement were on every newspaper, every website. TV channels were a step ahead. Minute-by-minute details of what allegedly transpired were pieced together from the accounts of the people who had attended the party. The fact that it happened in the presence of so many people added spice to the story.

People began to speculate. Was it a failed love affair? A career setback? Problems with the daughter? Stress in the family? And so forth . . . Tanya was extremely distressed by all this rumour-mongering.

'Could we get a court injunction to stop people from writing about her?' she asked Aditya, in a fit of desperation.

'I know it is difficult, Tanya. But the more we tell them not to do something, the more they will. That's the paparazzi for you.'

Tanya had tears in her eyes. 'Why are they doing this to mom? Her body has not even been released from the hospital and the slander has begun.'

Aditya put his arms around her to console her.

Malvika's cremation took place that evening. Attendees included the finance minister, the RBI governor, as well as NYIB's rank and file. Peter Baron flew in too.

A couple of days later, a squad from the Mumbai crime branch came calling at Tanya's house. They had with them a copy of the six-page long post mortem report. Tanya had seen the report earlier but hadn't understood anything, except the last few lines.

> *Death caused due to excessive bleeding and internal haemorrhage. All injuries found on the body are consistent with fall from a height. Victim was in a state of inebriation at the time of death, as indicated by high alcohol content in blood. Preliminary toxicology tests do not indicate foul play.*

'If we go by this report, Miss Tanya, it's a clear case of suicide.'

Tanya refused to believe the report. She tried telling the crime branch personnel but to no avail. The cops had made up their minds.

# 34

# USA

*Immediate action: convert 1 million dollars into bitcoins and transfer them to the wallet, details of which are being sent to you separately. Send 1 million dollars through a trusted personal courier. Procure two Rolex Submariners—they don't cost more than 500,000 dollars. Wear one on person and leave the other in the check-in baggage. Other 500,000 dollars to be carried on person. In 500-dollar bills. We will advise you on how to remit the balance.*

Josh was a relieved man when he read this message. He had been awaiting instructions since the ATM heist. He was nervous—5 million dollars in 20-, 50-, 100- and 200-dollar bills was a lot of paper to be lying around in a room. He had bundled the money in two large suitcases a day after the heist. The backpacks were also crowding his room. He had not disposed of them yet.

The mail was crisp. To the point. All on TOR mail. He read the mail three times to make sure he understood it.

Josh was quite familiar with the process of converting cash into bitcoins, which had emerged as a darling of the underworld over the last two years. The dark internet. Money launderers.

Josh was the admin on Cotton Trail, which only accepted payments through bitcoins. A customer placing an order on Cotton Trail would pay in advance by transferring the required amount of bitcoins into Cotton Trail's wallet. Cotton Trail would wait till the goods were delivered, which took roughly five days, and then transfer the merchant's dues into his bitcoin wallet after retaining 15 per cent as its commission for facilitating the transaction. At any given point in time, Cotton Trail had bitcoins worth five days' sales in its wallet. Given that the daily trade on Cotton Trail was over 1.5 million dollars, the escrow, at any point in time, had bitcoins equivalent to in excess of 7.5 million dollars.

Josh had access to Cotton Trail's bitcoin wallet. For a minute, he considered transferring the bitcoin holdings of Cotton Trail to the perpetrators of the ATM heist but dropped the idea. Such transactions could be made only after seeking the concurrence of the entire group. He decided to ask. It was better that way.

That was the easier leg of the instruction. As per the instruction, he had to send 1 million dollars in liquid cashable objects through his mule. The address that was sent to him was in Santo Domingo in the Dominican Republic. He couldn't trust anyone with the money. On the other hand, he couldn't travel himself. If he did, where would he leave the cash that was stuffed in his room? He was in a fix.

That's when he decided to take a punt. He walked up to his roommate. 'Stan?'

'Yeah?'

'You free this week?'

'For what?'

'I need you to go to Santo Domingo. Obviously not for free.'

'What's the deal?'

'Ten thousand dollars to deliver cash and back.'

Stan agreed. He had just got travel documents made through an agent he had contacted on Cotton Trail.

After talking to Stan, Josh sent a message to the Boss: *Delivery boy will be on his way in three days. Money will reach you by the weekend.*

# 35

# Mumbai

Once news of the breach into NYIB's card operating system managed by eTIOS became public, other banks started to panic. Almost all the banks in the country had outsourced some process or the other to eTIOS.

It was a huge challenge for Aditya to logically explain to the banks that the breach was not eTIOS' fault but the handiwork of an international criminal gang. Not many bought the story. Sundeep too had his hands full, helping Aditya disseminate the right information.

Swami called Aditya that evening. 'Matt wants us to dump eTIOS and annul our contract with you.'

'What?' Aditya was shocked. Of all his clients, NYIB had been with him right from the beginning. Running eTIOS without NYIB as the anchor client was unimaginable.

'Yes. These guys are all short-term thinkers. They want to tangibly demonstrate to the world that they are taking action against the service provider. And the only action he can take against you is termination.'

'It's not our fault, Swami, you know that. The hackers could have gotten into the systems of any bank, any BPO, any service provider!'

'You're preaching to the choir, Aditya. I'm just telling you what Matt said. I've asked him to hold on till the investigation is complete, at least. Hopefully, by then we will know what went wrong.'

'True.'

'Just got a bit worked up at the way he said it. These expats just don't understand how we operate in India. Relationships don't mean anything to them, Aditya.'

'What an asshole!' Aditya seldom got flustered but that day he couldn't bottle it in. It was the fag end of the day by the time he was done meeting the chiefs of four banks. He had tried to convince them that eTIOS was a safe organization to work with. They hadn't been completely convinced though they had agreed to wait for now.

In the interim, Varun had taken complete charge at Indiscape. The last two weeks had seen good traction for Townsville. The game had been taken off their website and made available exclusively on Facebook. Customer interest was encouraging. Work had now begun in earnest on porting all their other games to Facebook. Indiscape was rolling again. Varun had made a tremendous impact. The deal with Facebook could be the game changer after all.

# 36

# Washington DC

Adrian and Tony were in a downtown pub that night. Adrian had already downed six pints of beer. He was in a very sombre mood, reflecting on his past. He didn't have a family. He had gotten divorced long ago for reasons he didn't even remember clearly any more. Now, his only love was his job, his investigations, his cases. Nothing else mattered. And all that had come to a stuttering halt. For the first time in his life, he had been called incompetent. His commitment to his job had been questioned. His self-esteem was down in the dumps.

When he ordered his seventh beer, Tony stopped him. 'Adrian, let's go.'

'Don't want to. We are losers, Tony. When I got the Gillian Tan case, I thought I finally had an assignment where I would make a difference. Now we run the risk of this being taken away from us.'

'Nobody will take it away from you, Adrian. Come, let's go.' Tony helped him up. He dropped a 100-dollar bill on the table and gestured to the waiter, who nodded.

'Where are you taking me?' Adrian asked.

'We're going to my place. I'm driving. You're too drunk.' He supported Adrian as he stumbled towards the door. They crossed a television playing late-night news. Images of the CEO of a bank in India who was talking about the safety measures the bank was putting in place to prevent a repeat of the 5-million-dollar heist were flashing on the screen.

'Some stupid bank. Couldn't protect customer data. All banks are the same, Tony. Here or India, the story is the same,' he slurred.

Tony didn't respond. He just held him by his hand and tried to lead him outside.

The image transitioned to a map of New York, showing the ATMs where the heist had taken place. Adrian stopped and stared at the TV.

'Let's go, Adrian!' Tony tried to pull him.

'No, wait!' Something had caught his attention. 'Hold on a sec!'

Tony looked at the TV too. He couldn't make out anything. He was about to pull Adrian again when Adrian turned to him. Though his eyes were still red, the effect of six pints had seemingly disappeared. 'Will you take me to Edgar Hoover right now?' The slur had gone.

'Now? You want to go to the FBI headquarters in this state?'

'Can you take me there?'

'We'll go tomorrow, Adrian, what say?' Tony led Adrian out of the bar.

'Don't you worry, my friend. I will be okay.'

Tony just threw up his hands. 'Whatever!'

In no time, they were hurtling through the streets of Washington DC, towards the Edgar Hoover Building, the headquarters of the FBI. There, Tony swiped his card and walked in. Adrian followed. They quietly walked into the elevator and straight to the office on the sixteenth floor. Adrian was completely sober now.

'Tony, can you get me a list of the ATMs?' Seeing the blank look on Tony's face, he added, 'The ATMs that were raided, Tony!'

'What do you want to do with them? We are not dealing with the ATM case.'

'I know. Just trust me and don't ask any questions. I need this information right now.'

It didn't take Tony long to pull it out of the system. List in hand, Adrian walked up to the wall, pulled off a giant map of New York and placed it on the floor. For the next hour, he plotted the ATMs one by one on the map with a marker. Tony was getting restless.

'Just a couple of minutes,' said Adrian, not lifting his eyes off the map.

Once he was done, he looked up. 'I need to call the Prick.' And without waiting for Tony to respond, he called Robert Brick.

A surprised Robert picked up the call the moment he saw it was from the FBI headquarters.

'Robert, it's Adrian.'

'Are you out of your mind? It's an hour past midnight! You better have a damn good reason for calling.'

Adrian quickly told him why he had called.

Robert was aghast. 'I'm coming over. Wait for me.'

# 37

# New York

It was 2 a.m. when Josh was woken up by the persistent ringing of his phone. He looked at the screen sleepily. It showed a private number. He took the call.

'How long should I wait for you to pick up the phone?'

The tone jolted Josh out of sleep. 'Who the fuck is this?'

'Your guy hasn't reached with the money. Where is he?'

'What? I don't understand . . . what you are saying!'

'Which part of what I said did you not get?' Ferocious grunt. 'Go, find him!'

Josh was sitting upright on his bed in the middle of the night, wondering what could have gone wrong. He had sent Stan with the million dollars. The checkers at the airports at JFK and Santo Domingo had been bought, so it was unlikely that Stan had been caught.

Where the hell was Stan?

And where the hell was the money?

# 38

# Washington DC

Robert Brick reached Edgar Hoover in less than an hour. Adrian was waiting for him outside his room.

'You better be sure of what you are saying. I detest being woken up at night.'

'Okay, here goes. The ATM heist seems to be the work of Islamic militants.'

Robert was not impressed. 'You told me that already. Which group is it?'

'Not sure. Could be Al Qaeda or Lashkar-e-Taiba or even a local faction . . . can't say. It needs to be investigated.'

'Then what makes you say with such conviction that it's Islamic terrorists?' He walked back to his chair, sat down and sighed. 'Five minutes is all you have, Adrian.'

Adrian dug into his bag and pulled out a large map of New York. He cleared a space by pushing away everything that was kept on Robert's table and placed the map on the glass. Not for a moment did he look apologetic for the mess he had created.

'Here, Robert . . . they strike first at the ATM outside Coney Island Hospital. The second strike is at an ATM twenty feet from there.'

'We know that.'

'For the next fifteen minutes, one by one, all the ATMs along this route from the hospital to the Coney Island rail yard are visited by the gang.' Adrian drew a line from Coney Island Hospital to the rail yard along Shore parkway . . . a straight line.

He looked up. Robert was looking at him, perplexed. 'But Robert, fifteen minutes after the perps go down this route, an ATM near the Waldbaum's on Ocean Avenue comes up on the target list. We could have assumed it was the same team but there is a problem. Waldbaum's is over a couple of miles from the rail yard where the first trail has already reached. Clearly, this is a second team in operation. While the first team progresses along the yard's periphery, this second team goes on to rob the ATMs along Ocean Avenue.' With a pen he traced the path on the paper. 'This is trail number two,' he said.

'Another fourteen minutes, and the first ATM on another route appears on the horizon. Next to Sheepshead Bay. Along E16th Street straight down to Graves End, Neck Road, Barbara Reign School and further down . . .' Adrian drew a line tracing the path of the ATMs on the E16 that were looted by the gang.

In front of them, on the map, were three distinct lines. 'Now we know that there were three teams, looting different ATMs in sequence, on three different trails.' Adrian divulged more as he progressed with his revelations. One by one, he drew six trails of the ATMs looted in Brooklyn.

'Six lines. Six trails. Six teams.'

Robert nodded. 'Apart from this, there are two distinct trails in Manhattan and two in the Bronx. A total of ten teams. The trail of looting in Manhattan started forty minutes after the first ATM in Coney Island Hospital was hit. The one in the Bronx, meanwhile, started thirty minutes after Coney Island.'

'What are you trying to prove, Adrian?'

'Two things. The entire operation was run out of here . . .' He circled a small area on the map. Robert looked at the map and then at Adrian.

'The teams that went to the Bronx and Manhattan were the first to leave from here,' Adrian explained, pointing at the circle on the map. 'It took them thirty minutes across the GWB to the Bronx and forty minutes to Manhattan. The moment they reached, the Bronx and Manhattan legs of the unlimited operation started. After dispatching the teams to Manhattan, the operations in Brooklyn and Queens would have started. The first team started down this path ...' He pointed to the line he had drawn, joining Coney Island Hospital to the rail yard route. 'The second team went down Shore Avenue and Waldbaum's. The third went down E16 and so on.'

'I understood it the first time you explained,' Robert said testily.

'If you pull back these six lines, extrapolate them backwards, you will find that they all meet right here,' Adrian said, pointing at the circle on the map. 'Right here, at the cluster near Tete-e-Tete in the Brighton beach area. Near Coney Island Avenue. I'm assuming the operation has something to do with someone in this neighbourhood.' He tapped repeatedly at the circle he had drawn on the map. 'Here. It has to be here.'

'And who do you think is behind all this?'

'This cluster is dominated by Asians. Indians, Pakistanis and a few other ethnic groups from southeast Asia. Several Muslim fundamentalist organizations are known to have roots here.'

Robert sat back in his chair and pondered. 'I hear you, Adrian, but security camera footage from the ATMs tells a different story. The perps' faces are not visible but one can clearly make out that most of them are white people, not brown.'

'That doesn't count for much,' Adrian argued. 'Many Muslim jihadis in America these days are white. Almost 21 per cent are born in America. Not much of a distinction between whites and non-whites, we must confess. A blonde woman in a business suit is as likely to be a criminal as a Muslim woman in a black headscarf.'

There was merit in Adrian's hypothesis. Why hadn't his team thought of it? Robert's face betrayed no emotion. 'You have made little or no progress on the Gillian Tan case. As a result, I am disinclined to accept this theory of yours. But, given the promise and drive you have otherwise demonstrated, I'm willing to put my neck on the line. But not for long. A week is all you have to get to the bottom of this. If you are able to make progress, you get to stay on as lead investigator. Else I take this case from you and you can get the fuck out. Got it?'

'Yes, Robert. Thank you!' Adrian gleefully accepted the offer.

'Better get moving. You don't have much time.'

After Robert left, Tony confronted Adrian. 'While I admire your impeccable logic, Adrian, it doesn't add up. Something is missing from the plot.'

Adrian looked up. Tony normally never questioned him, but there was an intense look on his face now. He wanted to believe everything Adrian had said but something was stopping him.

'What?'

'Why would a terrorist organization or a religious fundamentalist group do something like this for 5 million dollars? It's a drop in the ocean for them. One would imagine they would rather strike big.'

'This is running through my mind too, Tony. Maybe, just maybe . . . this was a dry run for something larger, something more sinister.'

'I hope not.' Tony sighed as he walked to the coffee machine. His caffeine-deprived body was demanding espresso.

# 39

# Mumbai

'Breaking news coming in!' the anchor on Times Now screamed even as a red band flashed on the bottom of the screen. Written in bold on the band were the words: 'Sensational disclosures in the Malvika suicide case'.

The anchor rattled on: 'Malvika Sehgal jumped to her death from the top of Hotel Four Seasons in Mumbai a few days ago. Does her suicide have anything to do with her career aspirations? Are stress and ambition driving people from corporate India to end their lives? We take you now to our political correspondent, Karuna Rawat, who is standing outside the Prime Minister's Office at 7 Race Course Road . . . Karuna, can you hear me?'

'Yes, Sonia, go ahead,' Karuna yelled.

'Okay, Karuna, what is the latest development in the Malvika suicide case?'

'Sonia, something sensational has just come to light. Malvika had been recommended for the post of governor of the Reserve Bank of India. Had the recommendation been accepted, she would have taken over from Y.V. Reddy when his term ended this September. We have a copy of the recommendation note here . . .'

The camera zoomed in on the paper Karuna was holding in her hand. It was a note from the finance minister to the prime minister. Malvika's name was the first in the list of candidates for the governor's position.

'Sources in the PMO have told us, Sonia, that the prime minister was not happy with the recommendations and had sent the note back. Apparently someone very senior in the finance ministry was pushing for Malvika's appointment. It is too early to even speculate if this had anything to do with the Malvika Sehgal suicide case. One thing we are sure of though . . . this is one story that refuses to die down!'

'Thanks, Karuna, this really is a sensational disclosure. Stay with us, we will continue this discussion after a short commercial break.'

The moment the commercials came on, Sonia asked Karuna, 'What's the story, babe? Who is this "someone very senior" that you mentioned?'

'Who do you think?'

'Don't know. No clue.'

'The finance minister, babe, the finance minister.'

'Are you serious?'

'What do you think? She was having a scene with the minister.'

'Who is your source?'

'The principal secretary, who retired yesterday. He told me that the prime minister had returned the recommendation letter, saying he wouldn't be party to the finance minister making his muse the RBI governor. She was sleeping with the minister!'

'Tell me you are joking!'

'You know me. I don't joke about such matters.'

'You don't joke at all, bitch.' And they laughed.

Sonia's face had lit up. This was the scandal of the decade. The CEO of a bank has an affair with the finance minister. The minister recommends her for the post of the RBI governor. The PMO shoots down the idea. The CEO lands up dead. Could there be a bigger story on national TV? Then again, it was too big for her. She couldn't take a call on running it by herself. She had to run it past the chief news editor.

# 40

# Mumbai

The NYIB deal with eTIOS was hanging by a thin thread.

Ever since Swami had told Aditya about Matt's intention to pull out, Aditya had been fretting. A lot depended on whether NYIB continued with them, from the perspective of credibility as well as revenues. Aditya and a few private equity funds had invested heavily in the games at Indiscape. Any adverse hit on revenues at eTIOS would hurt him very badly. His mind was all over the place as he got into the car.

'Dad, you okay?' asked Varun as he drove. Aditya was in the back seat with Sundeep.

'Just tired. Let's get home fast. I need to get some sleep.'

They dropped Sundeep off and headed home.

'Dad,' Varun said, 'don't worry. It will all fall into place.'

'It looks like it's falling apart.'

'It won't dad. It will all be fine.' And he paused. After driving for a few minutes in silence, he asked, 'Will it impact us very badly if NYIB decides to take its business elsewhere?'

'Look, Varun, we are not a small company. We are one of the largest in this space. So NYIB taking its business elsewhere will not impact us in the long run. It will, however, put pressure on our finances in the short run, particularly given the investments we have made in Indiscape. We have to watch out for that. But more than that, it's a question of our reputation. There is no insurance for reputation. If NYIB pulls out, we will have serious credibility issues. That worries me more than anything else.'

'I just wish I knew someone there. Some contact who could make it easier for us. Don't know why, I just hate seeing you and Sundeep uncle so worried about it,' Varun said. Aditya could feel the pain in his voice. The last few months had brought father and son closer.

'How's Townsville shaping up?' Aditya asked.

'It's looking good, Dad. The Facebook promos have really helped us scale up. We will know the response in a few days. Click through rates have been quite good so far. Hope people like the game and stay on and play. I've called for a stock taking meeting with the game designers at nine.'

Tonight?

'Yes, Dad.'

~

Like any other gaming office, Indiscape too came alive at night.

For someone who had just taken over the gaming business, Varun was quite a revelation. He had a contagious energy. He was able to get people to rally around him. Sundeep was still trying to run the place like a multinational bank—processes, approvals, conference calls, presentations . . . everything that the younger employees despised. Varun was outgoing, inclusive and communicative. Growing up fatherless in the West had made him mature beyond his years.

At the meeting, the Townsville director presented the latest activation numbers. In three days, they had had over 100,000 hits and over 47,000 people had actually started playing the game. It was a great beginning, far better than the 23,000 figure at the time of the earlier launch.

Varun looked at the director and said, 'I told dad that social networks are like a great cocktail party—it's great to see all your friends there but its true worth is in the ties that don't exist today.

The key driver of social networking is people you don't know but want to meet. They are the friends of your friends. They are the people you wouldn't have imagined meeting. If you can strengthen these potential ties, you will have won the battle for revenue.'

Everyone in the room nodded.

'The activation is on track. What does the design team have to say?'

A few guys belonging to the denims-and-hoodies club walked up to the head of the table. One of them plugged a pen drive into the computer and brought up a presentation on the large screen. 'Seventy-five levels have been already built into the game. By the time users complete those levels, we will be ready with the next seventy-five.'

Varun had a serious problem with this. It would take the design team at least three weeks, possibly longer, to build the next seventy-five levels. He had not even seen what those levels would entail. Someone should have made sure that those who wanted to play would not be constrained because some idiot decided to launch Townsville with seventy-five levels and not one hundred and fifty. If customers completed the levels and moved on to some other game, bringing them back to Townsville would be extremely difficult. Almost like acquiring a new customer.

'What is the plan for the next seventy-five levels? We agreed that work would begin on that last week, didn't we?' he asked, calmly.

'We are working on an innovative design. It will be out of the world, I promise you,' the head of the team stated.

'What will be innovative about it?'

'It will be a riot of colours and fabulous graphics. People will be able to take town planning, designing and living to an entirely new level.'

'Does it have any potential to get revenues? Anything for which people will have to buy virtual coins? Or pay real money? Is there anything that makes money for us while we incentivize them to move from one level to the other?'

The guys at the head of the table looked at each other. Varun looked at the director.

'Actually, sir, your dad is strictly against charging customers to play our games. He believes that revenue should come from advertising, not from selling virtual coins, level pass through cheats, and so on to customers.'

'I'm aware of that but that discussion was licked when we decided to advertise on Facebook. We have to make it worthwhile—for us, for Facebook, and for the consumer, in that order.'

'We will put out minds together and come up with an innovative plan. Give us a week, Varun.'

'Fuck your innovation!' Varun yelled. 'Look at games on other gaming sites. Look at the most popular ones. You are not smarter than them. Copy. Shamelessly. We are throwing millions into promoting them. Cut the time to market. Tell me what's working in the market and let's do the same thing on a grander scale. This is the last time I want to hear someone say innovation.' After a long pause for effect, he added, 'I'll be back at 10 a.m. tomorrow. I want to see the plan for the next seventy-five levels and revenue generation by then.'

That night, every person in the Indiscape senior management was busy playing games created by competing companies and paying close attention to them to see if they could incorporate similar concepts into Townsville. Varun's obsession with making it big had begun to burn everyone.

The next morning, when Varun met with his groggy-eyed team of creative gaming executives, two decisions were made:

1. The gaming roadmap for the next seventy-five levels would be unabashedly copied from Farmville, a game created by the competition. Copyright laws on gaming were weak.
2. Customers would be given three easy levels from the beginning of the game. They would bump the drop rate

for every third level, from the fourth level onwards—i.e. bump the drop rate for the fourth, seventh, tenth, thirteenth level so on. Drop rates indicated the statistical probability of a customer failing a particular level. Bumping the drop rates would make the customer get stuck at a particular level and hence make him restless. He would then be willing to pay his way through levels. The customer could buy virtual coins with real money to pay for cheating his way through levels.

But there was one hitch.

'We don't have enough programmers to put this into motion,' confided the programme director.

Varun didn't betray any signs of worry. 'Let's hire them then. And while we are at it, let's steal them from the competition.'

# 41

# Washington DC

'Get the video feeds. They will be the starting points for our investigation,' Adrian commanded.

'We have the video feeds from the ATMs. They don't show anything!'

'Not the ATMs, Tony. Get the feeds from the Coney Island Avenue street cameras. Then let's examine the feeds from the security cameras at all the ATMs again. Layering one on another might give us something to work on.'

Tony walked out of Adrian's room. He was back in ninety seconds.

'The feeds from all the cameras around the Coney Island Avenue bridge will come to us by tomorrow. The DOT will share them with us,' he said, referring to the Department of Transportation.

'Ask them to get off their fat asses and get some work done. Why should it take so long to share feed?'

'They said that they can show us right now but we'd have to go down to their Traffic Management Centre in Long Island, Queens.'

Adrian looked at the ceiling, scanning from end to end. He turned to Tony. 'Let's go. We don't have time to waste.'

'It's a four-hour drive, Adrian.'

'Tell them to keep the office open. We will be there in four hours, max.'

He got into his car. Tony followed.

# 42

# New York

Josh activated all his underground channels. He spoke with everyone who had been a part of the ATM heist, to check if they knew the whereabouts of his roommate. No one did. Stan was his guy. No one had ever met him before.

Josh figured it was about time for the next phone call, when the phone rang.

'Did you find the rogue?'

'No. I am trying. Every fifth person in New York is hunting for him.'

'You are an idiot. Do you actually think he is in New York, waiting for you to find him? We need our money. How long do you think it will take?'

'I need some time. I will get back to you as soon as I have some information. You need to trust me.'

'We made that mistake once. We won't make it again.'

'I don't have a choice.' Josh sounded helpless.

'You have one. Find the money. Twenty-four hours is all you have. Get the money. Don't make us come for you.'

'I don't understand . . .'

'Twenty-four hours.' The call ended with a click.

Josh's hand went up to his forehead. He was sweating, despite the chill.

He didn't have much time.

# 43

# New York

Franklin Duster, the officer on duty at DOT met Tony and Adrian in the lobby and led them up to the control room. In front of them was a maze of screens tracking live feed from cameras at various locations across New York City. 'There are three cameras around Coney Island Avenue,' Duster said as he brought up one of them on screen. The feed was from the day of the heist. Adrian and Tony watched the entire feed from 9.30 a.m. till 10.40 a.m., the time when the first withdrawal was made from the Coney Island ATM. It did not throw up anything of significance.

The second camera was out of order. 'Several cameras are not functional at any given point in time,' Franklin Duster explained. They moved on to the third one.

For the first 58 minutes, which they fast forwarded and watched in 20 minutes, they couldn't zero in on anything of interest. Finally they got lucky.

At 10.28 a.m., on the day of the heist, three men, two of whom were wearing hoodies and carrying backpacks, walked past the camera. No face shots. Only their backs were visible. Tony hurriedly dug into his bag and pulled out a whole pack of pictures. He sifted through them swiftly, dropping a few in the process. 'Wait, wait!' He was yelling.

Duster paused the video.

'He is one of the guys,' screamed Tony, pointing at one of the three, who was carrying a backpack and was closest to the camera.

'Look at his hoody. Maroon patterned. I remember seeing a similar pattern in one of the ATM camera feeds.'

'Are you sure?' Adrian asked. He knew that Tony's greatest strength was his elephantine memory. Tony pulled out a picture from his pile and showed it to Adrian. It was a screen shot of the image captured by the ATM camera. The pattern on the hoody one of the guys was wearing in the picture matched the pattern on the hoody in the feed they were watching. Adrian nodded. He noted the time on the camera and they moved on. 'Looks like we are getting there,' he commented before the camera started rolling.

Both of them looked back at the screen. Duster began to roll the frames.

'Hold it! Can you go back a few frames?' Tony was staring very intently at the screen. Duster paused the camera and rewound the tape for ten seconds. 'Stop! Play it now,' Tony instructed.

About two seconds later, Tony yelled. 'STOPPP!' And then continued in intermittent bursts, 'Stop! Stop! Stop! Stop! Stop!'

'What the hell are you doing, Tony?' Adrian was getting irritated.

'Look here,' Tony pointed to the right-hand corner of the screen where a tall man wearing a tweed coat and a hat stood, covering his face. Duster replayed the video in slow motion. The three guys, who were on the left corner of the screen, did not stop but one of them subtly nodded at the man in the tweed coat. The latter didn't respond but one could make out a stiffening in his stance, just in time with the nod.

'Who is this guy?' Tony asked as Adrian noted the time mentioned on the frame and told Duster to move ahead. 'Why did he suddenly stiffen? I have a strong feeling he knows something about what's going on.'

For the next few minutes, they didn't notice anything that would help them move any further. And then something happened.

Two men, heads covered, carrying backpacks, came out and walked into a waiting cab. Adrian asked Duster to freeze the frame. He took out the pictures of the ATM video grabs and compared whatever they could make out with the images on screen. The pattern on the hoodie on one matched with the images captured in one of the ATMs in Manhattan. The shape of the patch on the elbow matched perfectly. They were on the right track.

'Can we get the registration number of the cab?' Adrian asked. 'Might help. We might also get some info on who those guys were.'

'It is likely to be a fake,' Tony responded.

Nonetheless, Adrian took down the number. One by one they spotted the ten groups of perpetrators leaving the location. Four by cab and the rest on foot. But in none of the sightings were they able to get a clear shot of any of their faces.

Overall, the cameras were a big disappointment for Adrian. The only fact that they could establish was that their initial assumption was correct. The crime was hatched in the neighbourhood. They had been able to visually confirm that all the ten groups were in the neighbourhood just before the ATM heist began.

Adrian stood up. 'Let's go.' he said.

Duster got up too.

'Thanks, Franklin, for doing this at such short notice.' Tony started to follow Adrian, then suddenly swivelled back to look at the screen again. Duster hadn't switched it off. The feed was still playing. 'Adrian, take a look at this!'

Adrian turned.

Tony pointed at the screen with his index finger. 'Same guy, isn't it?' he whispered.

It was indeed the same tweed coat, hat and invisible face. But this time, he was with a woman. A woman wearing a floral dress and stylish hat, and carrying a designer handbag.

Tony replayed the feed.

The woman gave the man a quick hug and walked towards Coney Island Bridge, where she went out of the camera's range. The old man turned and walked back in the direction he had come from.

'Play it from the top,' Adrian instructed. Tony rewound the

video and cued it to when the man and woman just were about to enter the frame.

'Stop!' Adrian yelled the moment the man's face became visible. 'Can we get a larger image?'

'Yes. The resolution is good. I can zoom in.'

Adrian looked on as Duster zoomed in. He was a dusky old man, sporting a moustache and glasses. 'Can we get a facial scan, please?'

Duster nodded.

Tony pressed play on the remote and the video moved forward. In ten seconds, the woman's face appeared on the screen too. Adrian raised his hand. Tony paused.

'I can zoom this one too. You will get a better image,' Duster volunteered.

Adrian looked at the image of the woman in the floral dress in shock.

'Should I zoom in?' Duster asked. He was at the console now.

'Not necessary,' Adrian said, as he turned towards Tony. 'Let's go. There is one person who can give us the answers.' He looked pale.

# 44

# Washington DC

Josh was sweating when he logged off. How was he going to do this? He had agreed to the ATM heist only because, as a handler, he had done one of the tasks earlier. As a student leader, he had experience in handling groups of people and mobilizing teams. To top that, the money he had been offered was phenomenal. He made good money as the admin of cotton trail, but half a million for a day's work was easy money. Delivering the goods to Santo Domingo, however, was never a part of the original deal. How he had got sucked into the entire thing was a mystery to him.

For a long time, he sat there wondering what his next step should be. What if he picked up the remaining money and disappeared? Would they be able to track him down? What would happen if they did?

The idea went out of the window faster than it occurred to him. These guys would be watching his every move. He had only one option: figure out a way to get the money. And he had only twenty-four hours to find it if he didn't want to end up in a body bag.

It occurred to him that he had an escape route. If he was unable to get the money, he might as well kill for something bigger. Hunt a whale so big that it not only took care of his immediate problem but netted him enough money to not worry about another job ever again.

He pulled out a loaded Smith & Wesson .357 Magnum. Flipping open the magazine, he took out the bullets, counting six as he placed them on the table. He pulled back the hammer and the trigger to test the revolver. The pulling of the trigger released the hammer and it struck the spot where the bullet would have been. It worked perfectly. He checked the barrel and reloaded the single-action revolver.

He pulled out a bag from his cupboard, threw in a magazine with spare bullets, and a large meat knife. He zipped the bag and walked out. The clock was ticking faster than he wanted it to.

~

Within five minutes, Tony and Adrian were hurtling down the highway at over 100 mph. Somewhere along the way, Tony saw a board: Washington DC, 160 miles. In the heavy traffic, it would take them four hours to get back.

'What the fuck is wrong with you, Adrian? Who did you see on the screen? Why don't you say something?'

Adrian was gripping the steering wheel tightly, really tightly. He was worried. When he saw that Tony was really furious at his not saying anything, he finally responded, 'It's not an Islamic terrorist group, Tony.'

'Then who is it?'

'That's what we have to find out.'

~

Josh drove past the gate and braked. It was dark. The streetlights were off. He picked up his bag from the passenger seat of his Ford pick-up and got off. He didn't lock the truck. It would have beeped. He walked slowly towards the house. There was a seven-feet-high wall all round the two-acre plot.

He threw a piece of metal wire over the periphery. No alarm went off.

The wall was the least of the challenges. He had climbed walls much higher than this one. In a couple of minutes, he was in and making his way towards the house. A few guards would be stationed at the entrance to the main building, he was sure. If he could get past them, the rest would be a cakewalk. The nearest cop picket was at least six minutes away. But for them to respond, someone would have to call them.

~

On the way, Adrian called FBI headquarters. Thankfully, Robert Brick was in office. Adrian told him everything he had seen. Robert was shocked too.

'Can you send us some back-up at the site, Robert? We will reach in twenty minutes.'

'Right away!'

When Adrian got into action, it was difficult to figure out who the boss was.

~

Josh hid behind a pillar and scanned the main entrance. Two guards, busy chatting. This was going to be easy. He screwed the muzzler on to the barrel of his .357. Standing a good 30 feet away, he took aim and waited for the right moment. It didn't come. He was running out of time. Not wanting to wait any longer, he muttered a prayer and pressed the trigger.

A puff of smoke. And the guard fell face down on the marble. He didn't even have time to scream in pain. That's what a bullet to the brain does. The other guard pulled out his gun and looked around frantically. He reached for his walkie-talkie and whispered into it.

The surviving guard tried to withdraw towards the pillar to his left. In the open, he was vulnerable.

And then he heard it. The clank of a revolver's hammer. He turned. Only to stare straight into the barrel of Josh's gun. Josh didn't waste another moment and fired. The only sound that could be heard was that of the guard's gun hitting the portico.

Josh walked in. It was a big house. The occupant would most probably be asleep. Killing was not his first option. He wanted to quietly take away what he had come for. Something that would make him rich beyond his wildest dreams. Something he had helped create.

He quietly padded into the living room. His shoes were stuffed in his backpack. It was familiar territory.

There was one bedroom on the ground floor. He opened the door and looked in just to make sure everyone was asleep. There was nobody there. It looked like a teenage girl's room. Posters of Justin Bieber covered the walls. He moved on to the first floor. The first room to his right was the study. He stood in the corridor, weighing his options. He heard a light snore from one of the other rooms. He thought for a moment and then walked into the study. Carefully, he shut the door behind him. There was a bookshelf to his right, and a study table and a window to his left.

He switched on the light and walked up to the table, stopping long enough to draw the curtain. Books were neatly arranged on the table. He looked at them carefully. He rummaged through the drawers but found nothing there. He was conscious of the time. If the second guard had managed to alert them the cops would be arriving any minute now.

'Where would you hide your deepest and most valuable secret?' he muttered. He was looking for a file containing documents or a CD or a hard disk. But who hid them like that these days? It had to be in a laptop but he couldn't find one. Had the FBI confiscated it? He panicked.

'What the hell are you doing here, Josh?' It was the moment he had been dreading all along. He turned. The door to the study was open and she was standing at the door with a baseball bat in hand.

'I came for a few papers,' Josh responded, innocently.

'In the dead of the night? Like a thief?'

'Some things cannot be done in Midland Café, in the light of day, sweetheart.'

That caught her by surprise. She thought she had done well

enough to hide her identity. It didn't cross her mind that someone could have seen her there.

'Perhaps you can care to tell me what you were doing at Midland Café the other day. Tailing me?' he ridiculed.

'None of your business, Josh,' she yelled.

'Well then, perhaps I should get back to my business. If you would care to go back to sleep now, I can finish my work in peace.'

'I called 911. They should be here any moment. Perhaps I will go to sleep after that.' And she waved the baseball bat at him.

That's when he saw it. He had found what he was looking for. But the mention of 911 sent him into a rage. In one swift movement, he pulled out his gun, pointed it at her and fired. A shrill scream pierced the silence of the neighbourhood as the bullet passed through her and embedded itself in the door behind her.

Adrian's car screeched to a halt the moment he heard the scream. Damn! Was he too late? He jumped out of the car and rushed in, Tony in hot pursuit. He pushed the main gate open and ran in. On the portico, he found two guards from the state police department lying on the floor. They appeared to be dead. He dashed in. All the lights were off except for the one in the room on the first floor. It took him some time to figure out where to go. He ran up the stairs and turned right. And immediately collided with Josh and took a tumble. Josh kept running.

'Freeze! FBI!' Adrian hollered.

Josh didn't stop. Adrian made a split-second decision and fired. He missed. The bullet shattered the glass door of a connecting room instead.

Tony was faster than Adrian. He sprinted and got closer to Josh who ran out the main door, jumped over the body of the first cop and was about to leap over the second cop when he got unlucky. Tony fired, Josh leapt and landed right in the pool of blood that the second cop was lying in, and slipped.

By the time Adrian reached Josh, Tony was there. Josh lay motionless. When he slipped, Tony's bullet had hit him in the neck.

Tony felt his pulse then looked up at Adrian and shook his head.

'Take charge of his bag, and do a body search. I will look inside,' Adrian said.

He turned and walked in. He switched on all the lights and walked up to the rooms on the first floor.

He opened the door to the first room. There was no one there. The moment he reached the second room, he involuntarily covered his mouth, feeling nauseous.

Nikki Tan was lying on the floor. She was unconscious but she was breathing. Miraculously, the bullet had missed her heart. The 911 response team arrived just then.

Adrian looked at her. 'Hold on, Nikki, hold on. Help is on its way,' he said as he rubbed her right hand. The moment he held it in his hand, he felt something gooey and let it go. It fell with a thud. Her body twitched in pain.

The EMTs took her away, leaving Adrian wondering what had just happened.

Only two people could tell him that. One was dead and the other had almost died in his arms. Nikki Tan looked so pretty even in that state. Even prettier than she had looked in her floral dress on the CCTV camera on Coney Island Avenue.

# 45

# Mumbai

The eTIOS issue was fast becoming a matter of national pride and importance. India's reputation as an IT giant was at stake. Pretty much all the world outsourced its operations to India. If the data breach was not dealt with quickly, it would lead to a loss of faith and consequent losses in business.

What made matters worse for eTIOS was that a security breach had been detected three months ago. It was plugged but not reported. That was a mistake. It was seen as some pranksters trying to hack into the system for fun. No one took it seriously. And then it happened again—on the day of the ATM heist. But by the time it was detected and plugged, the miscreants had done the damage.

Preoccupied with the eTIOS debacle and Malvika's death, Aditya let Varun handle everything related to Indiscape. After all, Varun could do no wrong. Townsville's MAUs climbed to 600,000 within ten days of the start of the Facebook promotion. There wasn't a country in the world where someone wasn't playing Townsville.

This was the context in which the head of programming came to Varun.

'Varun, we have a minor problem.'

'Yes?'

'There are close to 8000 gamers who are stuck at level six and are unable to move to the next level. The paid cheats are also not helping them. They have tried at least twenty times each to cross that level.'

'What could have caused this?'

'It's a bug in the system predictive algorithm. The game has gone into a loop. There is no way for them to get out and head to the next level. Until we intervene and change the program, they can't move on.'

'So what do you want to do?'

'We need to pull out four programmers for a week. They can make some changes and we can release an update so that the bug can be fixed.'

'Are you out of your mind? Four programmers for a week? Just when we are going full steam ahead on Townsville? It will set us back on game development.'

'But what about this bug?'

'Don't worry. We have 600,000 playing, of whom only a little over 1 per cent are impacted by the bug. What's the worst that will happen? They will stop playing, right? We'll live with it. Make some five to ten dollars out of those customers and let them drop off.'

'But, Varun . . . '

'Is there anything else?'

'No, Varun.'

'Thank you. Now if you will excuse me, I need to catch up on something.'

He walked back to his table, then turned around. 'Well, I can give you one resource. Here . . . ' He picked up a CV from his table and handed it over. 'Hire this guy. This CV came to me this morning, highly recommended. Get him to do the update you want. That's the best we can do.'

The director of programming looked at the CV. It seemed reasonable. 'Okay.'

Varun looked at his watch. It was hitting 8 p.m. He had promised Tanya that he would have dinner with her.

# 46

# Washington DC

'Adrian . . . Adrian!' Tony screamed.

The ambulance had just zoomed off with an injured Nikki Tan and the bodies of the two police officers. Josh's body would be released for an inquest only after the preliminary investigations. A forensic team from the FBI had also arrived on the scene. Tony was going through the contents of Josh's bag.

'Looks like he had come prepared for more,' Tony said, holding up the unused magazine that he had pulled out of the bag. He opened the backpack wide and looked in. 'What's this?' He pulled out a big meat knife and a piece of cloth. There was a key too. 'Our friend drove down here,' he declared.

'The car can't be far!' Adrian exclaimed.

'Wait? There is something else here. It feels cold. A sausage.'

'A sausage?' Adrian was surprised.

'Here we go . . .' Using a tweezer, Tony pulled out a four inch long sausage from the backpack. He held it up for Adrian to see and was about to drop it into an evidence bag when he shouted, 'What the fuck?'

Adrian rushed to his side. It was not a sausage. It was a human finger, chopped off from a body. He recollected the gooey feeling when he had rubbed Nikki Tan's right hand. He hadn't realized that it had only four fingers. He thought it was an injury caused in the attack.

'What kind of guy would chop off a victim's finger and carry it with him? A souvenir? How deranged can one be?'

As Tony dropped the finger into the evidence bag, Adrian couldn't help notice the sparkling gold ring that still adorned it.

# 47

# Washington DC

'I'd like to monitor the patient before I can comment.'

That was all the doctor would say when asked about Nikki Tan's condition. The bullet had gone straight through her, missing her heart by less than a centimetre. Enough to kill most people but Nikki was a strong woman. She had been through a lot in life. When Adrian had met her in the course of the investigation into Gillian's killing, he had been impressed with her strength and resolve.

After meeting the physician in charge, Adrian wanted to examine the room where Nikki was being attended to. He was reviewing the security arrangements around the ward when he saw her—Gloria Tan, Gillian and Nikki's daughter. Barely out of her teens, Gloria always looked delicately pretty but today she looked particularly vulnerable.

'She is going to be fine. I just met the doctor. Have faith,' Adrian whispered as he sat next to Gloria, taking care not to startle her.

'Are you going to find the attackers?' Gloria asked. It was clear she had been crying.

'He is already dead.'

'Are you sure he was the only one? What if there are others lurking about?'

'If there are, we will get them.' Adrian too had a lot of questions but they would have to wait.

His phone started to ring. It was Tony.

'Yeah?'

'Where are you?'

'At the hospital.'

'Can you get here in like . . . Well, soon?'

'Why are you so excited?'

'Come over and see for yourself!' Tony exclaimed.

Adrian had sent Tony and a team to retrace the intruder's steps. They had got a lead to his apartment's address through the GPS in his truck.

~

Adrian arrived at Josh's apartment thirty minutes later. The FBI chopper came in handy, though he struggled to find a landing spot in the neighbourhood.

'In here!' Tony yelled when Adrian opened the door to the apartment.

Adrian followed his voice and walked into the room where Tony was busy with some papers. The moment he entered the room, he froze. Arranged on the bed were wads of dollars. At least a hundred of them.

'Where the fuck did all this cash come from?'

'Our friend seems to have been involved in the ATM heist too.'

'What?'

Tony pointed towards a corner of the room where two large suitcases stood. 'The cash was found in these. Pretty elementary. He probably didn't expect his apartment to be searched.' He pointed to a pile of backpacks lying in another corner. Adrian counted twelve.

'All of them match the screenshots of the backpacks in the ATM video grabs. Can't be a coincidence, right?'

Adrian nodded in response.

Tony led Adrian to the far end of the room. On the table were several small packets.

'Marijuana. Small quantities. Not enough to book someone.'

'So he was a druggie too.'

'But here's something more interesting . . . ' He handed Adrian a notebook. 'I found this inside the vault that we forced open.' Adrian turned the first page and his eyes nearly popped. Written inside were some names and alphanumeric codes—codes he knew were the public keys for bitcoin wallets—and next to them were dates and values. Clearly this was some sort of a manual ledger meant for transferring bitcoins into and out of the wallet to the names written down.

'Why would someone transfer bitcoins across so many names? And under what circumstances?'

'Only if he is running some clandestine business where payment is made and received in bitcoins.' Adrian nodded.

Two laptops were also seized from the apartment, one of them a Mac. Both were sent for forensic examination.

The apartment owner was called. He gave them a picture of Josh's roommate, Stan.

'Run a facial scan,' said Adrian. 'Turn the apartment inside out. This guy holds the key to a lot more than the murderous assault on Nikki Tan.'

# 48

# Mumbai

'The bug is fixed, Varun!'

The programming head called in that morning. 'The guy you recommended did a wonderful job.'

'It's only been three days since he came on board.'

'Yes, but he rechecked the entire program and identified a simple change that was needed to make the fix. He tweaked it and now we are ready to roll. The update is being released today. Townsville is back on track now.'

'Good to hear that. You were unnecessarily getting worked up the other day.'

Varun was listening to the caller but his mind was elsewhere. He was thinking about Tanya. She had not left the confines of her house since the tragedy. Varun was concerned. Every day, after work, he went to meet Tanya, spent some time with her, and then headed back home. He hadn't had decent conversation with Aditya for over a week.

~

Times Now had been deliberating whether to carry the news of the finance minister's romantic liaison with the deceased CEO, and ultimately decided to bite the bullet. It carried a muted reference to the minister's possible affair with the CEO of NYIB but that was enough ammunition for the opposition parties. There was a ruckus in Parliament that day. The opposition was up in arms demanding the minister's resignation.

A few news channels backed by some eager political parties suggested that Malvika's death could have been a crime of passion, and not a suicide, and that the finance minister might be involved in it.

The finance minister fought off every challenge determinedly. When the prime minister, who was also the party president, called him and asked him to tender his resignation, the minister stoically refused. He had only one thing to say.

'Public opinion be damned! I know what I have done. And I have done nothing wrong. You want to sack me? By all means, do so. But I will not put in my papers. Resigning would mean tacit acceptance of the fact that I have done something inappropriate.'

The prime minister didn't have much choice. One of the perils of a coalition government. Over thirty-six members of Parliament owed their allegiance to the minister. A forced eviction could destabilize the central government.

~

Aditya's woes didn't show any signs of abating either. He had just finished an hour-long conference call with a client in the US when Sundeep walked in.

'Some more bad news, Aditya.'

'I'm getting used to bad news these days. I haven't heard good news on the eTIOS front in a long time.'

Sundeep extended a sheaf sheet of papers towards Aditya—a legal notice from NYIB.

'Matt has served us. He wants us to reimburse the 5 million dollars that they have lost because of the ATM heist. They are pinning it on us.'

Aditya didn't respond. He kept reading.

'They have also threatened to terminate our services if we don't reimburse them.'

After reading the document from end to end, Aditya spoke. 'From the looks of it, even if we reimburse them, they will terminate our contract.' He thought for a moment before continuing. 'We must respond to this. It is unacceptable. We have done no wrong.'

'Perhaps we should talk to them?'

'I don't think you should. They are looking for excuses to get rid of you.'

The sound came from the door. Both of them looked up. It was Swami.

'I tried to convince them not to do this. But they didn't listen.' He paused, waiting for a reaction from the two of them. When neither said anything, he announced, 'I have quit.'

Aditya shook his head. 'That's a big mistake. Why didn't you listen to me?'

'I couldn't take it any more. That asshole Matt makes me feel like a piece of shit. After so many years I deserve better, Aditya. I begged of him not to send a legal notice but he just refused to listen. What do you expect me to do?'

'It's okay, Swami. Don't worry. It will all work out fine,' Sundeep piped up.

'No. It's a big mistake,' Aditya reiterated. 'Now we won't know what they are thinking internally. We will be shooting in the dark.'

# 49

# Washington DC

Adrian had waited a long time for this day. Today he was finally going to interview Gloria Tan. Till now, he had patiently allowed her to tend to her mother.

Even though Nikki Tan's condition was still critical, Gloria had gotten used to the events around her and was in a settled state of mind when Adrian met her at the coffee shop a few miles from her home. For a girl who had lost one parent and was on the verge of losing another, she had tremendous poise.

'Do you have any idea what could have led to this?' Adrian started the conversation.

Gloria just shook her head.

'Any personal enmity? Family? Property? Wealth? Relationships?'

'Nothing that I'm aware of.'

'Was everything cordial between your parents?'

'It was in the initial years. But, of late, they were having quite a few fights.'

'Why?'

'Because of me.'

'You?'

Gloria nodded. 'Dad was worried about me. Mom felt he was overreacting.'

'Worried?'

'He was worried that I would embarrass him and compromise his position as a senator. I was like any other teenager. I'd go out with friends. I'd party, socialize, call people over. At times, we would skin up soft drugs after classes. It never went to a level for him to worry about but he always thought it could. Who doesn't do drugs these days? One of our Friday-night parties was busted by the cops once. Even then, they couldn't find anything illegal and after a few hours let us go. I had told mom about the raid.'

'Dad?'

'Dad didn't know about it. Never told him. Mom was always on my side. She knew that I was in control. She always told me that if I want to do such things, I should try them at home, not get adventurous outside. She was the one who introduced me to Cotton Trail.'

Adrian was shocked. He literally fell of his chair. 'She introduced you to the underground web for the drug trade?'

'Yes. I hope you aren't recording any part of this conversation Mr Scott. I'm telling you the truth because I want the men responsible for the attack to get the lethal injection. That's why I'm opening up to you. If any of this becomes public or implicates me or my mom, I will deny it.'

'You have my word,' said Adrian.

'Dad's behaviour stressed us out. Mom used to buy anti-depressants for me and at times for herself too off Cotton Trail. These were not over the counter medicines. She didn't want her drug purchases to be tracked by anyone and used against dad.'

'Who ordered from Cotton Trail?'

'Most times, she did. When she was travelling, she would provide for me and go. But if I ran out, I could order from Cotton Trail too.'

'She allowed you to do that?'

'Yes. Once in a while.'

'Doesn't Cotton Trail accept payment only in bitcoins?'

'It does. But I have a bitcoin wallet of my own. Mom kept a watch on it and transferred bitcoins into it.'

'Not entirely relevant, but did you use your bitcoin account responsibly?'

'By and large, yes. But occasionally when no one would notice, I would buy off it.'

'Buy what?'

'Mostly marijuana. Whenever we had a party at home. One day, dad found out. That day, dad and mom had a huge argument. She told him that I was doing these things with her explicit approval and that she was in control. She saved me that day. She really took good care of me even though I'm adopted.'

Adrian was hanging on to every word. The last bit raised his antennae but he kept quiet. He didn't want to interrupt the narrative.

'Dad chaired the committee of financial reforms. Actually, he was a bit of a liberal. In the committee, he was one of the few who supported bitcoins as legal tender. But seeing me use bitcoins to buy drugs set him off. He threatened to use his position to shut down Cotton Trail and ban bitcoins by making them illegal. Not that bitcoins enjoyed great credibility, but they had not been officially banned then. Both mom and I knew he couldn't have done it without the buy-in of others on the panel. And, in any case, it was not that we really cared.'

'You said you are an adopted child.'

'Yeah. From an orphanage in London.'

'Do you have any contact with your biological parents?'

'No. They died in the 1992 El AL Boeing cargo plane crash in Amsterdam. They were visiting relatives in Amsterdam when it happened. The plane crashed into their apartment complex. Thirty-nine people on ground were killed. My parents were among them.'

'I remember that crash. It was a cargo plane from the US, which had taken off after a stopover at Schipol.'

'Yeah,' she said, 'I was in London at that time with my guardians.'

'When did you find out about this?'

'A few months ago. Dad told me.'

Adrian was listening intently. Gloria's confession was muddying the plot.

'When he told you about you being adopted, did he tell you anything else about your biological parents?'

'I didn't care to ask. But yes. He did tell me. My parents were British.'

# 50

# Washington DC

As he narrated the story to Tony back in office, one question kept popping up in Adrian's mind, again and again. If Gloria was close to Nikki, so close that Nikki trusted her with Cotton Trail, why was it that Gillian was the one who told her about her being an adopted child? Why not Nikki?

'Is she a suspect?' asked Tony

'I'm not writing her off yet.'

'If she is, why would she tell you everything?'

'I'm not sure if she is telling us the complete story. Anyway, Tony, run a check on her arrest. If what she is saying is true, there should be a record.' He walked up to the table, shuffled a few papers, and asked, 'Has the forensic report come in?'

'Yes. A little while ago. I was going through it.'

'What does it say? Headlines, please.'

'Our friend Josh is a very complex creature. But for someone running an operation of this scale, his encryption is pretty elementary. His hard disk shows some interesting stuff. It has a list of many vendors who dealt in banned drugs on Cotton Trail. It could put the narcotic traders out of business in this great country.'

'How did it get there?' Adrian was all ears. This was like a labyrinth—so many blind alleys and passages concealed behind walls.

'Because our friend is an admin on Cotton Trail. He manages the entire back-end—vendors, payment collection from customers, technical problems with the website. He is the guy who does all that.'

'How do we know that?'

'Because of specific websites that he visited using the TOR network, from this laptop. One wouldn't normally visit those parts of Cotton Trail unless one is the admin. There is a trace on the hard disk. He even kept detailed notes about various bugs in the site. This also explains the bitcoin public keys that we found scribbled in his diaries. Those were of vendors who operate on Cotton Trail. Our friend used those keys to transfer their payments to them once goods were delivered to customers.'

'You are making it sound so easy. Wouldn't you have expected better levels of encryption from someone like him?'

'True,' Tony accepted. 'However, Adrian, our man here was probably not expecting to get caught which made him complacent. This is the first time his real and virtual worlds collided. Had he not been caught at Gillian's house, we would never have gone back to his apartment and seized all the equipment.'

Adrian nodded. 'Anything else that we know of?'

'Josh messed up some payments. Some of his mules disappeared with the money, and the guys behind the operation asked him to make good their loss. There are a couple of fairly aggressive mails on his laptop. How he landed up at Nikki Tan's residence is something we are still trying to figure out.'

'And you pieced all this together via email trails on his laptop?'

'Yes.'

'Where was he to deliver the money?'

'The Dominican Republic. We don't have a name but there is an address. The cash was to be delivered at a particular time.'

Adrian didn't respond. He was lost in deep thought.

'What do you make of it Adrian?'

'I don't know. Let's not make any assumptions. The problem with theorizing on the basis of incomplete facts is that we end up twisting the facts to suit the theory. We should be doing it the other way around.'

Tony couldn't have disagreed with this simple logic. 'You know Adrian, two questions have been on my mind from the time we reached the Tan residence. What was Nikki Tan doing at the cafe on the day of the heist? And why did Josh chop off her finger?'

'Unless there is a sect that believes in mutilating victims, it's completely incomprehensible . . .' He stopped. On the table in front of him were photographs of the crime scene, and the evidence collected from the site.

Adrian looked at the images carefully, again. There were images of the bloody meat knife. The chopped finger with the ring on it. He suddenly stopped scanning them and turned towards Tony. 'Show me the forensic report.'

The report described the ring. It was made of pure white gold, 22 carats, no patterns, no texture, handcrafted. An image of the cleansed ring was attached. Its undulating texture suggested that it was made with antiquated equipment, probably outside the United States.

The inner side of the ring, not visible entirely to the naked eye, had what seemed to be a code—a long, alphanumeric code. Adrian thought for a few seconds and got up to dial a number from his desk phone.

'Hi, Dan Malloy.' A nasal voice came on the line. Dan was the chief of the CRRU, the Cryptanalysis and Racketeering Records Unit, the FBI's code cracking wing.

'Dan, Adrian. Right time?'

'No time is right for you, you son of a bitch. What are you up to?'

'Neck-deep in work.'

'I met Brick the Prick a couple of days ago. He was ready to piss on you!'

'That would have been an unfairly violent reaction to anything that I might have possibly done to offend him.'

'Ha ha! Young man, he knows that you are his only officer capable of getting to the bottom of the Gillian Tan murder. So while he is seething at the delay, he doesn't have much of a choice.'

'Speaking of Gillian, I'm sending you an alphanumeric code

found on Nikki Tan's ring. I need your help to decipher it. I think I know what it is but I'd rather wait for your confirmation.'

'Let me give it a shot. I'll call you the moment I have any answers.' He hung up.

It didn't take Dan long to call back. Adrian switched on the speaker phone so that Tony could listen in.

'Looks fairly simple to me, Adrian. It is the private key to a bitcoin wallet.'

'Hmm, thought as much. Though I was a bit surprised that there were fewer than usual number of characters.'

'Bitcoin users are obsessed with keeping their private keys secret. Looks like Nikki Tan went a step ahead and got it engraved on a ring!'

Adrian responded, 'But why would she do that? Wouldn't it make it easy for anyone to get their hands on the key?'

'Well no. In this case, I suspect that she has not gotten the entire code engraved. Only twenty-four characters were engraved on the ring, whereas the bitcoin private keys have anywhere between twenty-seven and thirty-four characters.'

'So we don't know exactly how many characters are missing?' Adrian queried.

'Only Nikki would know that. So even if someone stole the ring, they wouldn't be able to do anything with it. With our decryption equipment and knowledge of check digits built into the code, we will be able to decipher the entire code in a week or so. The program will take that long to run. A layman wouldn't be able to figure out the missing characters in a lifetime.'

'Thanks, Dan. I will wait for a final communiqué from you.' He hung up and turned towards Tony, who was quietly listening 'It's the ring, Tony. Nikki was attacked for the ring. Her finger was chopped off for the ring.'

Tony agreed. 'Obviously she has enough funds parked in her bitcoin wallet for someone to kill her for it.'

'And the one who attempted to kill her is the admin on Cotton Trail. Do you think we have enough for Cotton Trail to be probed and . . .' he added after a thoughtful pause, '. . . and possibly shut down for ever?'

'Of course we do,' responded Tony, 'but getting to Cotton Trail is almost impossible. We don't know who runs it or where it runs from, If you think there is a way to get past that, it's definitely worth a try.'

# 51

# Mumbai

Tanya was furious after the Times Now report. She went public with her allegations. She gave media interviews accusing the finance minster of having a hand in her mother's death. She had always felt that he was using her mother. And that's exactly what she said in her interviews.

A few days later, an extremely agitated finance minister arrived in Mumbai. From the airport, he went straight to his hotel. This was a personal visit and he managed to evade the press.

A little after midnight, he left the hotel in a private car and drove to Malabar Hill with two accompanying cars. The cars stopped in front of a multi-storeyed apartment complex. The minister got off and walked in.

Tanya opened the door. She betrayed no expression, no emotion, even though she wasn't expecting him there.

'Yes? What can I do for you, sir?' she asked, keeping her anger in check.

'May I come in?'

Tanya stepped aside and allowed him to enter.

Varun was in the living room. The minister was surprised to see him there but didn't comment. He remembered him as the guy who was by Tanya's side on the day Malvika had died.

'What brings you here . . . sir?' Tanya asked again.

Varun got up to leave, but Tanya pushed him down by the shoulder. 'I want you to be here,' she said firmly.

'Tanya, I wanted to tell you something,' said the minister.

'I'm waiting with bated breath.' Tanya was extremely sarcastic. Nobody had ever spoken to the minister in that fashion.

'You have been reading a lot about your mother and me in the press. Not just reading, but you have also been speaking quite a bit about it. Even implying that I'm responsible for her death.'

'I'm sure the law will take its course. And if my mom was murdered, someone will pay for it.'

'That someone is not me, Tanya. I don't care what the world thinks about me but I wanted to tell you that I did not kill your mother.' He nearly choked as he said this. A confident orator, who could stand in front of the entire Parliament and hold his ground, was tearing up in front of Tanya. 'Your mother and I were extremely close. We were more than friends. We went back a long way, Tanya. I knew almost everything about her, and she was my secret vault. I would never confess it outside the room but I loved her. And believe me, she felt the same way. If things had gone well for a few more months, we might have gotten married.'

Tanya knew that the minister was a widower. His wife had succumbed to cancer a few years ago. She was taken aback by his emotional reaction.

'I didn't want you to be influenced by the media and start believing that I killed her. I am as sad as you are. That's why I came in person.'

'Thank you for being so considerate,' Tanya said arrogantly. 'But I'm going to need a stronger reason to believe you.'

'Look,' the minister started off, 'I didn't have to come and explain myself to you. The fact that I'm doing it should be reason enough for you to believe me. In any case, my conscience is clear.'

He walked towards the door. As he left, he asked, 'Is there anything Malvika left behind, which is marked to me? If you find any such thing, do let me know.'

Tanya didn't even respond. He walked out.

'Lying bastard,' Tanya exclaimed the moment the door shut

behind him. 'He thinks I'll believe every word he says. Rubbish!'

'Give him the benefit of doubt, Tanya. He didn't have to come here to explain.'

'Bullshit, Varun, BULLSHIT!' Tanya yelled at the top of her voice. 'There is clearly something of his that mom had. He came here to see if we've found it. He came here for selfish reasons. Not out of concern for me.'

'What could it be?'

'So many days, when I'd be away, he'd come and spend time with mom. Both of them would drink together. It is possible that, on one of those drunken nights, he left something here . . . something he thinks can implicate him. Or perhaps he gave something to mom for safekeeping.'

'Oh okay!' Varun exclaimed. 'You've never spoken about this before.'

'I have. In fact, I also told you that I once came back and saw two unfinished whisky glasses and food on the table. One look at mom and you could tell what she'd been up to.'

'Hmm . . .' Varun thought for a second and added, 'but you know, I don't think the minister drinks. Remember the night of your mother's death, we asked him if we could get him a drink and your mom asked for a soft drink for him. He categorically told us that he doesn't drink.'

Tanya shook her head. 'He could have been fasting, or probably lying about being a teetotaller! These guys are totally different in public and in private, when they let their hair down.'

Varun nodded vigorously.

'But if, for a minute, I assume that you are right, then who was mom's companion while I was away?'

# 52

# Mumbai

'Thank you!' A beaming Sundeep disconnected the phone and rushed to Aditya's room.

'The report of the Cyber Intrusions Wing of the Department of Cyber Laws has come in, Aditya. They have given us a clean chit.'

Aditya's eyes gleamed with excitement. 'Really?'

'They have said that this intrusion could have taken place in any organization. According to the report eTIOS has met all the requirements for system security and this hack was not because of any negligence on our part.'

It was a huge relief for Aditya. He had been fighting the agencies, which had accused his team of lapses, like a mad man. 'With this acquittal, it's time to grow our business again. Once Swami serves out his notice period with NYIB and joins us, we will have a strong team. You, Swami, Varun—what more can I wish for? Perhaps it's time for me to retire!'

'Come on, Aditya. You are not genetically wired to sit at home.'

For the first time in a long time, they were smiling and joking.

'What's the status of Townsville?' Aditya asked.

'No clue.' Sundeep replied, suddenly curt. 'You should be asking Varun.' He turned and left the room.

Aditya was surprised at Sundeep's abrupt response but didn't say anything. Sundeep had been upset not only at Varun's induction into the team but also by Varun's success. Under Varun, Indiscape was going from strength to strength. Townsville had touched 2 million users, all on Facebook. Newsfeeds were stuffed with people playing Townsville, inviting friends to join in. People inviting friends got free coins, which could be exchanged for game cheats and short cuts. It was fast becoming a way of life.

# 53

# Washington DC/Mumbai

Ed Walsch, chief of the FBI's Cyber Command Unit, was in his office when Adrian came calling.

'Something dramatic must have happened, Agent Scott, for you to seek me out,' Ed started the conversation. He didn't quite like Adrian but that was more because Adrian was a popular field agent who got to wield rifles, shoot at the bad guys, do all the sexy stuff, whereas all the brain work that Ed did never got the attention it deserved.

'Cotton Trail.'

Adrian said the word and looked at Ed, completely ignoring his caustic comment.

'What about it?' Ed asked.

'I want to know everything that the FBI knows about it.'

'Why do you want to know? I'm not authorized to share information with anyone. Even a fellow officer.'

'We believe the Gillian Tan assassination has a Cotton Trail link.'

'Most of it is classified. Way above your pay grade, Agent Scott.'

'Whose authority would you require to open it up to me? Would POTUS do?'

'Well, that's a big name to drop!'

'Gillian was his confidant. He was working for the President on a classified committee on alternate currency. Specifically bitcoins.'

'No one mentioned that to us. And we are supposed to be the Cyber Command!'

'Probably because it's way above *your* pay grade, Ed.' He took his revenge. 'Now don't be a prick. The President is following up with the chief on this assassination almost every week. The last thing he would want to be told is that the murderers got away because one Ed Walsch in Cyber Command didn't share information.'

'I must admit that's pretty convincing,' said Ed, smiling. He got up and walked out of the room.

Adrian knew he was going to make a call, to check the veracity of his claim. He was back in a couple of minutes. 'Meet me in the evening. At 6 p.m. And now, if you will excuse me, I have work to attend to.'

# 54

# Washington DC

Adrian met Ed at a roadside cafe in the Capitol Hill precinct. Ed was carrying a large briefcase full of papers.

'Thanks for coming, Ed. Appreciate it.'

'Look, Adrian, this could get you killed so watch your back!'

'We could have met at the headquarters. Why here?'

'I didn't want this to be seen as an official meeting. I know I'm being watched. There are moles inside the FBI who don't want anything to be done to Cotton Trail. Commercial interests, I guess. They will go to any lengths to protect the drug mafia.'

'Thanks, Ed.'

'Here are the papers. They have all the details of our pursuit of Cotton Trail, and what we have found so far.' He strained his neck, looked around, and raised his hand. A waiter came to take their orders and came back with two cups of coffee.

'Who runs Cotton Trail?'

'We will soon get to that. As of now, we do not know for sure.'

'What do we know that could give us a lead into Gillian Tan's murder?'

'Last month, the FBI along with the CIA, got into a server in France called . . . '

'Hacked into,' Adrian clarified.

'. . . yes, hacked into a server in France called Freedom Hosting. It was the provider of turnkey services for hidden sites—special websites with addresses ending in .onion. You know what TOR is, right? TOR hidden sites are used to evade . . . '

'I know what TOR is!'

'Cool. We hacked into it because we had information that 90 per cent of the child pornography sites are hosted by Freedom Hosting.'

'Hmm?' *Come to the point. Come to the point!* Adrian was screaming inside.

'Freedom Hosting was the server that rented out space to Cotton Trail.'

'What? You know who hosts Cotton Trail?'

'Yes.' Ed nodded.

'Why don't you take them down?'

'For two reasons. Of late we have the traffic to the site come down dramatically,' Ed explained.

Adrian realized that this may have been because the admin had been taken out, leading to payment-related issues and consequently customers and vendors were staying away for the time being.

'And,' Ed continued, 'there are hundreds of Freedom Hosting equivalent servers in the world, spread all over from Iceland to Romania to Latvia. If we take Cotton Trail down on Freedom Hosting, they will simply host their site on any of the other servers and be up and running almost immediately. If we have to close it down for good, we have to get the brains behind Cotton Trail. But we made one big breakthrough—we now have the source code of Cotton Trail.'

# 55

# Mumbai

It was a big day for Indiscape.

The press had congregated in huge numbers at a five-star hotel in suburban Mumbai where the senior management of Indiscape was expected to make an announcement. The moment they caught sight of Aditya and Varun, the photographers went mad. Varun was the newest celebrity in town. He was on his way to becoming a youth icon. Aditya was happy to let him have his moment in the sun.

'Ladies and gentlemen, it's a landmark day for Indiscape today,' announced Varun, once they were inside the hall and everyone had settled down. 'Today we are venturing into something new. Something that has never been done before.'

Everyone waited, eager with anticipation.

'Today, for the first time in the world, a gaming app that has become extremely successful in the world of social media is being launched as a mobile app. Indiscape is proud to present the world's first gaming app that can be played on a computer, a tablet, and a phone seamlessly. All you have to do to ensure this seamless integration is log in using your Facebook ID. We are launching the Android version today.'

Thunderous applause.

'And guess what?' Varun roared over the applause. 'For the next week, this app is entirely free!'

The applause, which had abated, rose to another crescendo. 'So go out and get your Indiscape Townsville mobile app. This is one addiction you won't regret!'

The announcement was followed by a Q&A session. Aditya and Varun addressed all the queries related to the game and its development. Sundeep was seated with them on the dais. When someone from the media asked Aditya about eTIOS's track record and how the hacking incident would affect security of the mobile app, Varun stood up and confidently countered, 'We have tried to make this game as foolproof as possible. No one can hack into it. We take full accountability for anything that takes place in our organization. While investigations have cleared eTIOS, we still take our learnings from the events and move on, rather than brood over what happened.' The press seemed satisfied.

Varun spotted Tanya in the crowd, standing in the corner, a laptop bag hanging from her right shoulder, and waved. He knew she'd come in late. Hair open, no make up, she looked beautiful.

After the event, on the way home, Varun and Tanya stopped by the beach. The waves rushing up against the sand formed the perfect backdrop for Tanya to let her hair down and vent her pent-up frustrations. When the talk steered towards her mom, she broke down and started to cry. Varun hugged her. They stood there like that for a long time.

# 56

# Washington DC

Adrian finally got lucky. The facial scan of the man in the tweed coat showed up in a database. Umar Farouk, a second-generation American Muslim, ran a small trading outfit in New York. One of the increasing breed of white American Muslims, he had taken over the family business after his father passed away three years ago.

The video grab was not proof enough to convict him but reason enough to subpoena him for interrogation.

Unfortunately, the interrogation did not lead to anything conclusive. Umar admitted to being at the coffee shop in Coney Island. He had recognized Nikki Tan as the wife of the late senator and had walked up to her to offer his condolences. Dropping her to the car was a normal courteous gesture. That was it. When confronted with the video that showed the ATM robbers acknowledging him and him stiffening up, he claimed that he was intimidated by the three guys and the stiffening up was due to fear. Adrian couldn't argue with that logic.

Adrian was frustrated. Everything was leading to a dead end. He decided to seek help from his mentor and knocked at his door again.

'Adrian?' Dan smiled when he opened the door for Adrian to come in. 'I expected you . . . but not at this hour. Come on in!'

Adrian followed him into the house. Dan was his mentor, an eccentric genius. He had been slated to take over as second in command of the FBI, till a crazy turn of events had put him out of political favour. That had devastated Dan, turning him into a bit of a recluse. The story in the FBI was that if Dan couldn't figure out something, nobody could. Dan's eccentricity had cost him the second most influential job at the Bureau but his intellect was intact. That's why he was still the head at the CRRU.

'Dan, how do I unravel Cotton Trail? It could give us the key to many a mystery.'

'That day, the moment I saw the ring, I knew. I knew exactly what you were looking at. I also know what the FBI is doing to fix Cotton Trail. Unfortunately they have no clue how to go about it.'

'Why?'

Adrian knew that Dan was right more often than not. He wished he had knocked on his door sooner.

'Because they are chasing the wrong leads!' He sank into the plush leather sofa in his living room and continued speaking. 'When you stop chasing the wrong things, you give the right things a chance.'

Dan continued, 'The FBI is only looking at what Cotton Trail does currently, how to break into it, how to get to its vendors and customers, how to prevent payments and transactions . . . They are waiting for Cotton Trail to make a mistake. If I were responsible for the operation, I'd handle things differently.'

'And how would that be?'

'I'd start from the beginning. I'd go back to where it all began. Cotton Trail started a year ago. Or, at least, that's when it started getting noticed, if my memory serves me right. Even assuming it was word of mouth and not advertising that fanned its popularity, someone would have had to market Cotton Trail. That should be your starting point.'

Adrian was confused. 'Where does one even begin to look?'

'Look, Adrian, the guy who founded Cotton Trail would have looked for customers from the real world, people like you and me, who would not visit the anonymous TOR web in the normal course. The founders would want us to know about Cotton Trail so that we could start buying off it. The first thing we need to know is how the founders promoted Cotton Trail to the public at large.'

'Yes!' Adrian exclaimed. 'And that information will lead us to the founders!'

'If not the founders, the interested parties for sure. That will be something to work on. It's not going to be easy. You will have to go through loads of data, information on blogs, online forums, problem-solving websites, video forums, and so on.'

'How long would you take for this, Dan?'

'Me?' He smiled.

'Yes, Dan. I don't think I can do this without you.'

Dan chuckled. 'I can't say. It could take a few hours, a day, a week, or even a year. Perhaps never, if I don't get lucky, or if the founders have hidden their trail well enough. Let me begin by trying for a week. If I make some progress, I'll let you know.'

Adrian knew there was no point in arguing with Dan. He never kept buffers for negotiation. And, in any case, he was doing Adrian a favour.

As he left, Dan looked at him and said, 'Adrian, it shouldn't be that tough. We just have to go far back enough in time—to the point when no criminal thinks that far ahead. That's where you will catch him with his guard down.'

# 57

# Mumbai

'Tanya! We broke into the top ten!' Varun blurted out in excitement when Tanya came on the line.

'Top ten?'

'Yes, top ten! Within a week of its launch, the Townsville mobile app is now number nine on the Android store. Our free download offer ends tomorrow.'

'How did you pull this off, Varun?'

'I'd like to believe it's a good game!'

'Yeah, yeah! As if there are no other good games doing the rounds and people downloaded only yours. You are a smart cookie. The Android store hasn't figured you out yet.' Tanya sounded sceptical. 'I know you, Varun. You want to succeed at any cost. So I'm sure you fixed this.'

Varun laughed. 'I really wanted this to break into the top ten before the free offer ended. As a result, from tomorrow, when we price our app at 1.99 dollars, there will be enough visibility and word of mouth for people to buy it on impulse.' He chuckled and added, 'The Apple and Android stores are smart but our download bots are so well designed that no one has figured out that they are not real customers but computer codes programmed to download the app from the store. So, 40,000 downloads a day gets me a spot in the top three free apps. The bots we designed download roughly 25,000 times a day, and we get about 10,000 downloads a day from genuine customers. That makes it 35,000 downloads a day. And this explains my No.9 position on the "most downloaded" list, sweetheart.' He laughed. 'Now we will get greater publicity and figure on all the "most downloaded" lists. That gives us a better chance at revenue generation once we turn into a paid app.'

'Do you think this is ethical, Varun?'

Varun whirled around. Sundeep was standing behind him. 'Not only are you cheating the buyers, you are cheating yourself too. Aren't you?'

Varun hung up on Tanya promising to call back. He turned towards Sundeep and, with an irritated look on his face, said, 'Listening into someone else's conversation is not good manners at all, sir.'

'Varun, we have always run this business in a strictly above-the-board manner, without resorting to means of suspect integrity. Your dad always says that reputation has no insurance.'

'I am with you, sir, but this is the first time we have built an app of this magnitude. If we are not able to push it up the rating scale, how will people see it? Imagine the word of mouth it will get by breaking into the top ten in the first week! The app store will promote it on its home page. More people will see it, so more people will buy it.'

'But buying your own apps?' Sundeep rolled his eyes. 'Isn't that stupid?' Though he was angry he kept his cool because he was talking to Aditya's son.

'Yes. But since we are keeping this mobile app ad-free, the only way to generate revenues is to get people to buy it.'

'This amounts to . . .'

Before Sundeep could finish, Varun cut in, 'If I were to promote the app through ads, I would need a 100,000-dollar marketing budget. Instead, I will spend 75,000 dollars on building bots to buy the app. It's nothing but a different form of marketing spend.'

'I need to tell Aditya. He may not subscribe to this.'

Sundeep turned and walked away.

'Asshole!' muttered Varun the moment Sundeep was out of earshot. 'Wonder how dad puts up with him!' He grumbled, as he called Tanya again. She had moved on to a completely different topic and sounded quite excited.

'Varun!' she exclaimed. 'Did you watch the TV?'

'No, sweetheart, I didn't. I'm in office, remember?'

'The finance minister has resigned.'

# 58

# Mumbai

A furious Aditya barged into the conference room while Varun was in a meeting with the game development team. On seeing a team of fifteen in the room, he sobered down. He looked at Varun and said, 'Can you see me once you are through?'

'Yes, dad. Anything urgent? We can stop this meeting. We were just discussing some service issues.'

'Service?'

'Yes. We received feedback that the Townsville mobile app is processing-intensive and is slowing down other aspects of phones.'

'How many such complaints have we got?'

'Three. Not many, but we thought it better to address it before it goes out of hand. It's a Grade 3 complaint. Low impact. We are refunding the amount paid by these customers and asking them to delete the app. Once we release a fix for the bug, we will let them download it free of cost.'

'Sounds good to me.'

Aditya left. Within fifteen minutes, Varun knocked on Aditya's door.

'Varun, Sundeep spoke to me this morning. How could you even think of manipulating the "most downloaded" list?'

'Dad, it's just a marketing gimmick. We are using bots to download a few copies of our program so that the sales figures appear high. Once Townsville stays in the "most downloaded" list for some days, we will remove the bots. It helps because . . .'

'I know how it helps, Varun!' Aditya was furious. 'You need to realize that I have run this business with some rules and values. I have been happy with the limited success I have had. The only solace is that no one can dare to point a finger at me and say that I use inappropriate means to grow my business. But now, it will all come to naught if my son does not follow the same rules. Do you get that?'

Varun didn't know what hit him. For the first time, Aditya was ripping him apart. He looked out of the room. Sundeep was pacing up and down the corridor.

'I let you handle this business because I felt that you would run it with dignity and integrity. I will have none of this bot business to prop up my app sales. I have asked Sundeep to oversee the entire compliance for all our businesses. I will ask him to focus more on gaming now.'

'I don't have any problems with Sundeep uncle looking into it.'

'And son,' said Aditya, having cooled down somewhat, 'success is not always measured in terms of dollars earned or turnover. It is measured in terms of the difference you have made to the people around you.'

'Yes, dad'.

Varun turned to walk out of the room.

'Get the bots deactivated now,' Aditya reiterated.

Sundeep was still outside. Varun glared at him but didn't say anything as he walked back to his office.

# 59

# Washington DC

At 6 p.m., Adrian parked his car on the road outside Dan's house and walked in.

'Heard of magic mushrooms?' Dan asked, the moment he saw Adrian.

'Yes, but that's one thing I've never had.'

'Adrian, you must. If you are in this trade, there must not be a single drug you don't know about. Magic mushrooms or psychedelic mushrooms, also called shrooms, cause serious differences in mood perceptions and behaviour.'

'Tripping. Yes, I know about it. When one is in a state of disarray under the influence of drugs.'

'Then you must have heard of Shroomery?'

'Yes. What about it?'

Shroomery was a site dedicated to illegal mushrooms and visited largely by people interested in the recreational psychotropic drug. Given that magic mushrooms could easily be foraged or grown, several people visited Shroomery for advice on how to cultivate it.

'Eight months ago, a user who goes by the name "Altoids" posted on Shroomery.org to promote Cotton Trail.'

Adrian showed no emotion. He had no idea what was coming his way.

Dan rummaged through the pile of papers on his table and pulled out one. He took out his reading glasses, wore them way down his nose, and started to read.

'*I came across this website called Cotton Trail. It's a TOR hidden service that claims to allow you to buy and sell anything online anonymously. I'm thinking of buying off it but wanted to see if anyone here had heard of it and could recommend it. I found it through Cottontrail420.wordpress.com, which, if you have a TOR browser, directs you to the real site at http://tydgccykixpbu6uz.onion. Let me know what you think . . .*'

Dan handed over the paper to Adrian. While Adrian was reading the comment, he logged on to Shroomery on his computer. 'There you go,' he said, as he turned the computer screen towards Adrian. 'We think this Altoids fellow is your guy.'

'What makes you suspect him?' Although he sounded sceptical, there was a glimmer of hope in Adrian's eyes.

'A few reasons. Most important, Altoids is a recently created ID, roughly a year old. Since then, in the entire year, it has made only one post on Shroomery. That could mean that the ID was created with the sole intent of promoting Cotton Trail. This post is from around the time Cotton Trail came into the public domain. So Altoids is probably closely linked to Cotton Trail, if not the promoter himself.'

'Do we have any traces on the ID? Where did he log in from?' Adrian asked.

Dan shook his head. 'Altoids used TOR to make the post, rendering it untraceable.'

'Damn!'

'The question, Adrian, is why a regular guy would use TOR to make an innocuous comment?'

'Not exactly. He could be a Libertarian, someone who fiercely protects his identity online. There are people like that, Dan,' Adrian played devil's advocate.

'True, there are but how will you explain a similar post appearing on bitcointalk.org just two days later? Again by Altoids.'

'He did that?'

'Yes. Bitcointalk.org hosts every detail of all developments in the bitcoin world. Why would he post on bitcointalk.org about Cotton

Trail if he weren't promoting it? He ended both the posts with "let me know what you think…" Too much of a coincidence. Similar post, similar request. I don't know if you can see it but this Altoids was on a mission to generate interest in Cotton Trail.'

Adrian was simmering with excitement. Even though he had thrown the libertarian concept at Dan to derail his logic, he knew, that such people were very rare. If Altoids had posted on Shroomery and bitcointalk.org using TOR, he had to have something sinister in mind. It was definitely not normal. Now they had something to work on.

'We need to get this guy,' was all he could say.

# 60

# Mumbai

Things started to move when the Central Bureau of Investigation took over the Malvika suicide case. The CBI called many possible witnesses to depose and sought extensive data from NYIB and other sources. From NYIB, in particular, they sought information on Malvika's email trails, her telephone records, and so on. The meeting with Tanya was also a part of this inquest.

Kabir Khan, the deputy director of the CBI and officer in charge of the case, arrived with people from the Crime Branch of the Mumbai Police and a sub-divisional magistrate.

'We are sorry to have asked for this meeting at such short notice, Ms Tanya.' Kabir was apologetic. 'As you can imagine, the pressure on the CBI has been intense.'

Tanya nodded silently.

'Have you read the post-mortem report? It does not indicate any possibility of a murder.'

'It doesn't but I don't believe it.'

'So you suspect that she could have been killed?'

'Mom was very strong-willed. There is no way she could have committed suicide. She fought her whole life, so committing suicide would have been cowardly.'

'It could have been an accident.'

'It was not an accident!' She screamed. Tanya was beginning to get upset. 'You are only interested in giving the minister a clean chit. You don't care two hoots about the truth.'

'That's an unfair accusation.'

'How else can you explain the fact no one asked me about my mother's relationship with the minister? Neither the CBI nor the Mumbai Crime Branch is interested in treading down that path. They know there is a landmine there.'

'Though there has been intense media speculation, our investigations haven't revealed a shred of evidence linking them,' said the bureaucrat. 'Can you provide us any evidence in support of your mother's alleged relationship with the finance minister?'

'That's for you to investigate and establish. The problem is that you've made up your mind and just want to check the "have investigated" box.'

The three men looked at each other. Kabir was beginning to get annoyed by her impudence. 'How was your relationship with your mother?'

'Like any other normal mom and daughter we had our ups and downs.'

'There were signs of a rift between the two of you. Was there a problem that we should be aware of?'

'Which mom–daughter pair does not have problems? There are fights but always in mutual interest.'

'Was your mother comfortable with your relationships?'

'I'm not in a relationship right now.'

'What about Mr Varun Rao?'

'He is a very good friend. Is this inquest about me or my mom?'

'About your mother, Ms Sehgal, but we need to be sure about what we are doing.'

'Wonderful, but let me tell you that mom liked Varun. So even if we had something going, it would have been fine with her. Will that be all? Or do you gentlemen have any further questions?' Tanya asked curtly.

None of them responded.

'Thank you.' She got up.

Kabir got up too. Now, he was fuming. 'Do you want us to do our job or do you want us to be your puppets, young lady? Just watch out. While I have a huge amount of patience, I do not tolerate crap,' he barked as he opened the door and stormed out.

# 61

# Washington DC

Dan found one more mention of Altoids and called Adrian.

'A few months after Altoids's first appearance in October, he posted a wanted ad on bitcointalk.org for "an IT professional in the bitcoin community". He asked interested parties to email frosty@ frosty.com.'

'Frosty?' Adrian asked.

'Yes, Frosty. I checked it. It's a valid email ID,' Dan confirmed.

'Why would you . . . ' Adrian was about to say something when he was interrupted by his assistant and Tony who barged into his room.

'Hold on for a sec,' he said and looked up. 'Can't you guys see that I am on a call?'

'I'm sorry, sir, but there is an urgent call on line two!'

'Who is it?'

'The White House.'

'What?'

'Sir, Mike Hendricks, the President's chief of staff is on the line.'

'Put me on right away! Dan, I will call you back. The White House is on the other line.'

~

'Evening, Adrian. Is this a secure line?'

'Yes, sir, it is.'

'Good. I'm calling on behalf of the President.'

'Sir?'

'The day Gillian Tan was killed, he had sought a meeting with the President who had agreed, given their close association. The meeting was scheduled for right after the meeting of the Committee on South Asian Policy, which Gillian was to chair.'

'Thanks for telling me, sir.'

'That's not why I've called, Adrian. Gillian wanted to meet the President because he wanted to share with him something that had come up in his personal life, something he felt that the President must know.'

'Do we know what it was, sir?'

'No, we don't. The President and the Senator went back a long way. The President knows the family very well and is a bit anxious to find out what it could be.'

Adrian thought for a minute. 'We haven't come across anything out of the ordinary yet, sir.'

Hendricks responded softly, 'The President is keen that, during the course of your investigation, should you do come across any information that might put the Tan family reputation at risk, you should get it cleared by the President himself. He trusts your discretion, Agent Scott.'

'I won't let the President down.'

'Thank you, Agent Scott.'

'Mr Hendricks, I have a request.'

'Go on.'

'Gillian Tan chaired the classified committee on alternative currency. It is a committee of financial sector reforms, and bitcoins are among its most important agenda items. I would like to see the minutes of the meetings, sir. I'm told that Gillian Tan, the libertarian, was a huge supporter of bitcoins, till he had a change of heart because of some personal incidents, and turned completely against them.

'The minutes are classified so I can't make any promises but I'll try my best.' And Mike Hendricks disconnected the line.

Adrian was confused. He looked at Tony. The message was

strange. What confused him even more was the fact that the President had chosen to convey it to him so late in the day. Why had he waited for so long?' He described the conversation to Tony.

The phone rang again. Mike Hendricks again.

'A day before he was killed, Gillian did chair a meeting of financial sector reforms. Contrary to what you indicated, he made a strong pitch to make bitcoins legal tender. Call me if you need anything else.'

Adrian was quiet for a long time. 'Tony,' he finally said, 'didn't Gloria say that Gillian had threatened to ban bitcoins and Cotton Trail?'

Tony was not in the room. Adrian looked around, walked out of the room, and asked his secretary. That's when he saw Tony rushing back towards him.

'Where the hell did you disappear, Tony?' he yelled.

'This looks strange, Adrian.' Tony said, without bothering to respond to Adrian's question. 'We have thoroughly checked all police records for the last three years. Gloria's name does not figure in them, neither as a convict, nor as a rounded up suspect. In fact there is no trace of the busted party that you mentioned. It seems to have been wiped off the police records.'

'Her father was an influential senator, Tony,' Adrian reasoned. 'He could have got the records erased.'

'But didn't I hear you say that Gloria told you that Gillian didn't know about the incident?' Tony's question left Adrian searching for answers.

# 62

# Washington DC

Adrian relayed the conversation to Dan.

'A call from the President's office has to mean something.'

'We don't even know if the message has the President's endorsement. To me, this is a pink elephant,' announced Dan, confidently.

'Pink elephant?'

'Yes. Remember Richard Nixon and Watergate? The most famous nine words ever spoken, words that rocked a nation!'

'Dan, please! I'm a bit slow. Can you please be specific?'

'At the peak of the Watergate scandal, in 1973, President Nixon went on air and said, "There can be no Whitewash in the White House." These nine words turned the American nation against their President. Till then, people hadn't linked the White House with a cover-up until Nixon himself made the connection. His own denial created the story. A pink elephant, Adrian, is a negative in a conversation that gives you hints on what is being covered up.'

'Does that mean that Mike has inadvertently told us what to look for?'

'He is scared that we will unearth something that could spell trouble for him and probably the President. Something you have done recently has got to him.'

'And that is mired in the personal lives of the Tans.'

Adrian began to make all kinds of connections in his head.

Dan disappeared into the bar, and returned with a bottle of

Glenmorangie and three glasses. He told Tony, 'If you want ice, you will have to get it from the basement.' He poured out three large drinks.

'Coming back to Altoids . . . and the ad he posted on bitcointalk. org. The ad was quite revealing. It said: *I am creating an economic simulation to give people first-hand experience of what it would be like to live in a world without the systematic use of force. Need an IT professional who is well versed in the TOR, and willing to adapt to the world of bitcoins.*'

'What does that mean?'

'That he wants to create a world of bitcoins. A world without borders. Where capital can flow freely without government control. Everyone anonymous yet free.'

'Isn't that what Satoshi Nakamoto wanted? The creator of bitcoin. The ultimate Libertarian. He sounds so much like how Satoshi would have sounded. Is Altoids the founder of bitcoins?'

'We can't say that conclusively but Altoids definitely is the promoter of Cotton Trail.'

'You seem to be extremely confident about that?'

'Hold on. I haven't told you the most important thing yet. Whoever he is, he did slip up once.' Dan announced, with a grin.

'While we do not know who Frosty@frosty.com is, the FBI has the source code of Cotton Trail. Ed Walsch told you that, didn't he?'

Adrian nodded.

'Given the illegal nature of Cotton Trail, it is fair to expect that the person managing it would not log in from the same spot repeatedly. Restricting mobility would mean vulnerability They would be on the run most of the time.'

'True.'

'However, when we analysed the source code of Cotton Trail, it showed that the admin section can only be accessed through a unique IP address. That would mean someone was logging in either from the same computer or the same wi-fi router. Clearly a contradiction, unless . . .'

Adrian was listening quietly.

'. . . unless Frosty or Altoids, or whosoever it is, uses a Virtual Private Network or VPN to log in to Cotton Trail.'

'How do you say that . . . in English, Dan?'

'I thought you would know!'

'For a minute, let's pretend that I don't.'

'Okay, okay! If they use a VPN, they can log in to Cotton Trail from anywhere. A VPN can be accessed through a code known only to those who use it. A VPN will trick Cotton Trail into reading the IP address as a unique address hardcoded into the Cotton Trail source code. Hence they get the desired mobility as well as security. It's common for banks to use it. When customers log into the Internet banking facility of a bank, they log in through a VPN, using their passwords.'

'Okay!' Adrian nodded. He hadn't understood it completely but he knew that he would pick up as the discussion progressed.

'Two months ago, the email account Frosty@frosty.com was accessed from an Internet cafe in Washington DC.' He paused. 'Two minutes before this email was accessed, the VPN network was accessed from the same Internet cafe. From the same computer. The VPN provider, under fear of a subpoena and a threat to cancel his licence, gave me the details this morning.'

'Are you saying that Frosty and Altoids are the same?'

'Yeah! Altoids, for sure, is one of the admins. Unless, of course, Altoids went to the same Internet cafe at the same time as Frosty, and sat at the same computer around the same time.'

When he saw the worried look on Adrian's face, Dan added, 'Our friend is not particularly careful. He is leaving trails wherever he goes. So I'm sure we will get something on him soon. He is not as smart as he thinks he is.'

Adrian thanked Dan and got up to leave. Dan gave him the papers he had printed out. 'Remember, these cannot be used as evidence, because we haven't obtained these formally from Google and the

VPN service providers. You will have to go through the process if you crack this case.'

'Thanks, Dan,' Adrian said, accepting the papers. He was about to hand them on to Tony, when he noticed a map showing the location of the Internet cafe. 'Is this where the last login was registered?' he asked.

'Yes, it is,' said Dan.

'It's just not possible.'

Tony looked at him wondering what went wrong. Dan was also curious.

'This is less than half a mile from the Tan residence.'

# 63

# Mumbai

Swami was in office. He still had a month of his notice period to serve. He'd asked Matt if he wanted him to go on gardening leave and not come to office but Matt had graciously told him to continue as head of retail banking till the last day of the notice period. He did not want Swami to go out in a fit of rage. That would have been detrimental to the morale of the team.

A buzz from his computer alerted Swami. Someone had pinged him.

'Hi, sir!'

Mukund had pinged him on Sametime, NYIB's internal chat interface. He was in charge of foreign exchange remittances.

'Yes, Mukund?'

'Sir, I've sent you an approval request for Vaishnavi Metal Strips. You need to sign off.'

'What approval is it?'

'Sir, they are remitting 750,000 dollars overseas to settle an import bill.'

'Can you scan and send me the bills please?'

'Already done, sir. Should be in your inbox by now.'

'Let me see.'

'Okay, sir, we are nearing our cut off time. So if you could look at it and let me know, it will be great.'

Mukund was in the trade finance department. Three quarters of a million dollars overseas remittance for a retail bank customer was a huge sum of money.

Swami scrutinized the bill. Vaishnavi Metal Strips had imported furnaces and ovens for diffusion, oxidation, or annealing of semiconductor wafers. Something didn't add up. Why would Vaishnavi, which was into steel trading, import material normally used by semiconductor companies?

He pinged back. 'Hi, Mukund, I have a few questions about the bill.'

'Yes, sir, please tell me.'

'Why does Vaishnavi need to import this?'

'Not too sure, sir.'

'Has anyone inspected and physically verified the imports?'

'No, sir.'

'Aren't you supposed to do so before you release large foreign exchange?'

'We do it in the normal course of business but in the case of Vaishnavi, Malvika had asked us to release funds without verification.'

'Do you have it on record?'

'Yes, sir, approval by mail.'

'Whatever Malvika did . . . well, she did what she did. I need to see the consignment before I approve. Meet me in ten minutes.'

Swami had never done anything like that. He was just acting on instinct.

And his instinct proved right. The consignment turned out to be a heap of rags neatly packed with layers of insulation and other material, designed to give it much-needed authenticity and, more important, to ward off any attempt at opening the boxes. The goods mentioned in the import bill were nowhere to be seen. It was a clear case of fraud. The importers were remitting money overseas for goods that were never imported in the first place.

'Tell Vaishnavi that we will not remit the amount. Also inform them that we will report them for a fraudulent attempt to launder money.'

'Sir, they were very close to Malvika.'

'Who told you that?'

'In the last year, they have remitted funds at least four or five times, and Malvika had signed off on each of those transactions.'

'Are you kidding me?'

'I can send you those approvals. I remember very well because I also noticed that the imports were not consistent with their core line of business.'

'Send me the details. Irrespective, put this remittance on hold. We are not releasing the forex.'

Swami had barely returned to his office when he got a call on his landline. He looked out of his cabin towards his secretary's workstation. She had left for the day. Left with no option, he took the call.

'Swami *garu*?'

'Yes.'

'Saar, I am Naidu from Vaishnavi Metal Strips.'

'Tell me, Mr Naidu,' said Swami, leaning back in his chair. He was impressed with how quickly the call had come.

'Saar had come to our office today.'

'Yes, I was there to inspect the consignment.'

'You should have told us, saar. We would have taken care of you.'

'Aren't you ashamed, Mr Naidu? You are trying to cheat the bank and the country. You are laundering money overseas.'

'Saar, can I meet you?' Naidu had summarily ignored Swami's comment.

'I will ask my branch manager to arrange a meeting with you. By the way, we are lodging a police complaint.'

'Saar, please meet me for five minutes before you do anything. I'm sure we will satisfy you.'

'Enough, Mr Naidu! We are not dishonest bankers whom you can manipulate at will.'

'No, no, saar! That is not what I meant. I'm at your reception. If you give me five minutes, I will explain.'

Swami looked at his watch. He did want to know the transaction history. Perhaps he could manage five minutes. He instructed the receptionist to seat Mr Naidu in the conference room. In another five minutes, he walked in.

'Yes, Mr Naidu?'

Naidu stood up. 'I am very sorry that you had to take the trouble for me.'

'It's fine, Mr Naidu. It's our job. Tell me what you wanted to meet me for.'

'Saar, this money has to go today, or latest by tomorrow morning.'

'So, you expect us to remit money against a fraudulent invoice? Your imports are not even worth 10,000 dollars and you want to remit close to a million dollars against a fake invoice?' Swami was furious.

'Saar, you don't understand. If money not go, I will be in big trouble.'

'That's your problem.'

'No, saar. It is your bank's problem too.'

'My bank's problem?'

'Yes, saar. I am telling you in strict confidence. This is the sixth instalment of an amount Vaishnavi needs to give to the central government, for allowing a group company to continue mining in Chhattisgarh. This remittance was advised by the finance minister. He said he would speak to the CEO of your bank to remit funds overseas. That is why I am doing this. This is the sixth and last instalment. Total amount 5 million dollars, including this one. You can check old records, saar. All this is being sent to an overseas company controlled by the finance minister. Benami, saar.'

'What?' Swami was shocked.

'Yes, saar. Your CEO know about it. She only give approval. This is last instalment. Please let it go. No one know. If it stops, I will be in trouble and I expose your bank.'

Swami didn't know what to say. He went back to his room and

called Mukund, asking for all the forex transactions that Malvika had approved. Naidu was right. Swami had known that Malvika was not the most straightforward of people. Now he wondered what Malvika's cut had been in the entire deal.

He walked back to the conference room. Naidu was talking on the phone.

'Give us time till tomorrow,' he requested Naidu. 'And no, we are not reporting this to anyone yet.'

Naidu left, promising to return the next day.

That night, Swami met Aditya and Sundeep.

'Don't get into this at all, Swami. Just approve it after documenting the fact that the customer has been routing these transactions through NYIB in the past and that Malvika had approved five of them.' Aditya advised.

'I agree.' Sundeep endorsed the suggestion.

One thing was clear to them. Malvika's dalliance with the finance minister was much more than personal.

# 64

# Washington DC

Adrian drove to the George Washington Critical Care Hospital where Nikki Tan was still under observation. She had not come out of the coma.

Adrian sat at her bedside and looked at Nikki. She looked so calm, as if she'd wake up any minute and tell him everything.

A few questions about her were bothering him though. He had never seen a mother who would help her daughter acquire drugs to keep her away from other problems.

But the larger problem was the ATM heist. What was she doing at the venue with someone who was mixed up with the perps? Tony had visited the Internet cafe down the street from the Tans' residence. The cafe had shut down, replaced by a Dunkin' Donuts. They had tried to access old security systems and CCTV camera footage but everything had been destroyed when Dunkin' Donuts took over.

A knock on the door disturbed his deep thoughts.

'Gloria! How are you?' He didn't realize that Gloria had walked in and was now standing at the door.

'Oh, hello, Agent Scott!'

'I was passing by. Thought I'd check on your mom,' he explained, getting up to give her a warm hug.

The two of them walked out of the room. He had a thousand questions on his mind. Unable to decide whether the time and place were appropriate, he decided to go with his gut. 'Gloria, there was

an Internet cafe down the road from your house, right?' He showed
her the map.

She looked at it and said, 'This is where Dunkin' Donuts stands
today, isn't it?'

'Yes. Was it a popular place?'

'Not sure about that. But Mom used to go there.'

'To the Internet cafe?'

'Yeah. But very rarely. Maybe once or twice. To talk to her
friends. But only when she wanted privacy. Being a senator's wife
can mean putting up with fair bit of intrusion, Agent Scott.'

'Who were these people?'

'Some were people who helped her adopt me. Dad didn't like
her talking to them. He felt that being in touch with them would
constantly remind her of my being adopted. Some people at the
adoption home in London. The staff at the hospital where I was born.
A couple of relatives of my biological parents. A few friends too.'

'Have you ever met any of them?'

'Some of them, yes. When I was visiting last time.'

'Which was when?'

'September. End-September. We were there for over a month.
We went all over Europe. Just me and mom. It was so much fun . . .'
She had tears in her eyes, as she recollected moments from her last
vacation with her mother.

Adrian's interest was piqued. 'Would you have their contact
information?'

'I might. Let me check.' She dug into her bag and pulled out her
iPad. She browsed and gave him a few details.

'Thank you!'

An excited Adrian turned around and left. Gloria and her mom
had gone to London in end-September for a month. The last login
from the Internet cafe by Altoids was in October. It couldn't have
been them. Once in his car, after a lot of thought, he called Tony.

'You game for a trip to London this weekend?'

'Weekend? Today is Friday.'

'Yes. Leave tonight and be back by Sunday.'

'What for?'

'For a quick meeting with Nikki Tan's friends.'

Tony kept aside the newspaper he had been reading. He had an irritated look on his face. Two stories in the newspaper had caught his attention and he was completely engrossed in them when Adrian had called.

One was about an upmarket hooker in New York who claimed to have bedded over 200 famous people—athletes, celebrities, politicians—in the last few years. She had begun publishing her escapades on her blog, two every week. Tony made a mental note to read the blog posts. Confessions of a hooker—the title of the blog was too enticing for him to ignore.

The second was about a student at University of Rhode Island whose pants caught fire when the battery of his Dell laptop exploded. He'd slept off while working on his sociology project with the laptop on, well, his lap. Only to be woken up by his pants on fire!

# 65

# Mumbai

Revenues from Indiscape's Townsville had started to slow down. Varun was tracking them closely. He had all the answers even before the questions were asked.

He walked up to Aditya and said, 'Dad, we are going to release a new update to our gaming program, both on Facebook and on the mobile platform.'

'Why is that?'

'Our games were designed to go viral on Facebook. Every time a player went up a level, acquired a new apartment, or built a new hotel, it was posted on Facebook and became a part of his friends' newsfeeds. That drove our popularity but it had its flip side too. Many users complained to Facebook that their newsfeed was getting clogged by posts from some apps, including ours. Facebook changed its algorithm, so that game-related posts now get lowest priority in the newsfeed. So friends of many of our gamers may not even see the posts from our games.'

'And we have committed 25 million dollars to Facebook this year. And more in the coming years,' Aditya responded.

'Yes. Most of which will come from the revenue we earn from the game itself. Until now we had underpriced the game, cheats, level changes, game coins . . . We are now bringing them to a reasonable level. Hopefully with this new update, our gross revenues will go up. And, in any case, our mobile app has now become a paid application. Revenue from that will start kicking in too.'

'Great. Well done, Son!' Aditya was a proud father. 'Do pump in some information to my desk on the revenue numbers, at least on a weekly basis.'

'Sure, Dad. Aren't you going home?'

'No, no! I have to respond to this query from the Department of Revenue Intelligence. It'll take some time. Sundeep is working on it. Need to send it out by tonight.'

'Cool. I'll have the team upload the updates and leave.' He looked at his watch.

Aditya could make out that he was not happy about something. 'Out with it. What's bothering you?'

'Nothing, Dad. Its only six thirty. The gaming server downtime is scheduled at nine thirty. That's when we will upload the update. I have to wait till then, only . . . '

'Is Tanya waiting?'

'Come on, Dad,' Varun said, sheepishly, 'it's not that!'

'Leave it with me. I'll log in from here and authorize the upload.'

Varun's eyes lit up. 'I'll ask the team to hand over the program to Sundeep uncle. He'll help you with it. It shouldn't take more than twenty minutes. Our scheduled downtime is 9.30 p.m. to 11 p.m. IST.'

'This will take care of both the game on Facebook and the mobile app, right?'

'Yes, Dad, both.'

And Varun left for his date with Tanya.

Not wanting to eat out, Tanya had cooked a basic meal for him at home. Varun told her everything that happened that day and also how he had delegated the update upload to Aditya. Tanya laughed. 'He's such a nice guy. You shouldn't take advantage of his goodness!'

'Yes indeed. I wish I hadn't stayed away from him for so long.' He smiled at Tanya and looked at his watch. It was nearing 11 p.m. 'If you are in the mood for a drive, why don't we head back to office to check if everything is done?'

'You go on. What will I do there? How long will you take?'

'Thirty minutes, at best.'

'Okay, then let me get my laptop. I'll finish my work while I wait for you.'

Aditya was still in the office when Tanya and Varun reached. 'I thought you guys had a date. I didn't know a date meant time in office!'

'No, Uncle. Varun was feeling bad that he left you alone. So we came back.'

'Ha ha!' Aditya laughed and started packing his bag to leave for the day.

# 66

# Mumbai

The CBI interrogated the entire top management of NYIB, including Matt. Nothing objectionable had been discovered in Malvika's email or phone records. The finance minister too had stuck to his stance that he hadn't done anything wrong. He dared the opposition to prove his guilt.

Swami was extremely forthright in his depostion. When asked what he knew about Malvika the banker, he told them what he'd discovered about the money laundering. The finance minister's involvement, Naidu's confession . . . he told them everything. Malvika was a pawn that the minister used, he said categorically. Not that it proved in any way that the minister was involved in her death but it definitely gave the CBI a possible motive.

While all other depositions lasted about thirty minutes, Swami's went on for over two hours. He backed up every statement with documentary evidence. Of all the people that the CBI interrogated, Swami's statement was the most revealing and the most shocking.

~

That evening, Kalpana was alone at home, watching TV, when a telephone call disturbed the peace.

'Mrs Kalpana Swaminathan?' asked the voice on the line.

'Speaking,' she answered softly.

'There has been an accident.'

# 67

# USA

Eighteen more laptop explosions were reported in the next week. Fortunately all the laptops were in sleep mode when they blew up, so there were no serious injuries to the laptop owners.

The Rhode Island University incident was clearly not an isolated one. India recorded seven laptop disintegrations; Ukraine, South Africa and Argentina recorded eight each; and there were over twenty each in the US, Austria and France. All of them were Dell laptops. When the problem was reported to Dell's headquarters by the local country management, they blamed faulty power supply and battery. All the laptops were replaced.

What started off as a trickle, within two weeks, had snowballed to over 1000 complaints. Until then, Dell had ignored the issue, assuming that the customers were overreacting. They could not comprehend the gravity of the situation because the complaints were distributed all over the world so when a country head looked at these numbers, they were small. In the monthly customer service review, when consolidated numbers from across the world were presented to the executive committee, panic set in. The service matrix was not looking good at all. Worse, the complaints were across all laptop models.

Computers heating up, even when not in use, was fast becoming the single largest problem. What started out as a problem with Dell computers soon snowballed into a problem for all laptop manufacturers.

Something was drastically wrong.

# 68

# Mumbai

Kalpana was devastated. Everyone at NYIB was aghast. First, Malvika had committed suicide, and now Swami had died in a hit-and-run. That's what the cops were treating it as and had registered a case against an unknown person.

The post-mortem report cleared any doubts. It was a clear case of death due to trauma caused by the accident. Onlookers had seen the truck lose control and ram into the car waiting at a traffic signal, with Swami inside.

Kalpana found it impossible to come to terms with Swami's untimely death. God had been extremely cruel to the family. She worried about Swami's mother, who had gone into a daze the moment she received the news.

It was not difficult for the cops to piece together the events leading up to Swami's death. After long and sustained discussions with witnesses, Swami's colleagues and his family, the cops came out with their version of what transpired that fateful evening.

That day, Swami had called Kalpana and told her that some important work had come up in the bank, and that he needed to meet Matt before coming home. He wanted to brief Matt about his deposition to the CBI. This was around 1 p.m. He had then tried to reach Matt. But Matt was not available.

The CBI inquiry had drained Swami of all his energy. He was too tired, mentally, to last out the day in office. He decided to pack up and leave. That's when Aditya called, to check on how the deposition had gone. Swami told him briefly and said that he would meet him at night and give him the details. Aditya was in Delhi for a business summit but was taking an evening flight back, so a late night meeting with Swami was possible.

Sadly none of that could happen. In the intervening few hours, a speeding truck collided with Swami's car, killing him on the spot.

The driver of the dumper had fled the scene, fearing public outrage but walked into the Santa Cruz police station later that evening, and surrendered.

An accident case, a dead victim, the accused in custody—there was nothing much to be done. As far as the cops were concerned, this was an open-and-shut case.

Aditya spent the night trying his best to console Kalpana and Swami's mother. Sundeep and Natasha were there as well.

'I don't believe Swami's death was an accident.' Aditya dropped a bombshell on Sundeep when they stepped out to get some fresh air. 'Could his candidness at the deposition have led to his death?'

'The CBI refuses to disclose the details of the deposition but say that he didn't say anything of consequence or significance to this case,' said Sundeep

Aditya declared, 'He briefly told me what he told them, and that was definitely not "nothing". I will do everything possible to get to the bottom of this.'

# 69

# Washington DC

'No trace of Gloria's kin.'

When Tony said this, it surprised Dan. 'Didn't you say that Gloria and her mom visited them last September?'

'I did. That's what Gloria mentioned. I checked the emigration data, and they did visit London in September last year. Our field officers in London and Amsterdam launched a search operation. They could trace the kin of most of those killed in the El Al disaster, but not Gloria's.'

'Wait!' Adrian exclaimed and walked to the table. He picked up his cellphone and dialled a number.

'Pan American Insurance. How may I help you?'

Adrian spoke for a few minutes and hung up. He looked at Dan. 'Let's wait.'

Within five minutes, Adrian got a call. After he disconnected the line, he looked puzzled. 'This is not normal. Weird, in fact.' And went on to tell them the entire story.

'Should we speak to Mike? Perhaps he can tell us what this is about.'

Dan walked up to the computer. He had this know-it-all look on his face. 'Let's wait till tomorrow morning. We should be sure about what we want to tell Mike.' He logged in and accessed a classified database.

Seeing him get busy, Adrian decided to leave and come back the next morning. He bid goodbye to Dan and got into his car.

He had hardly driven for a mile when his phone rang. He looked at the phone and then at Tony. 'Why is he calling now?'

'Adrian!' Dan sounded very excited. 'Come back. Come back right now!'

'Okay, turning around. Five minutes and we'll be there.' Adrian took a U-turn at such speed that Tony went crashing into the passenger window.

'Hey!'

'Hang on!' Adrian screamed back, as he steadied the car. A couple of minutes later, the car screeched to a halt in front of Dan's residence, and the two of them jumped out and rushed in. The door was open.

Dan was stooped over his computer. He was staring at something. Intently. It was a map. Hearing them walk in, he looked up.

'Altoids. One more log in. Last night. I just got the details.'

'Where?'

'It's a post asking for help to recover lost digits from a bitcoin code.'

He handed over a piece of paper to Adrian. It was a printout from bitcointalk.org:

*I have a problem. I had written down a few characters of my bitcoin private key on a piece of paper. These fucking termites. They tore through the paper, which was kept in a safe. All I have now is pulp. Is there a way to reconstruct the key from the remaining characters that I have stored elsewhere? Any help would be appreciated.*

# 70

# Mumbai

After sending a legal notice along with a claim for 5 million dollars in damages, Matt Metzger promptly sent a letter to Aditya, terminating the services of eTIOS. In the normal course, he would have waited till Swami's notice period ended. But with Swami dead, there was no need for niceties.

A detailed exit plan was also sent to Aditya along with the termination notice. Aditya was devastated. NYIB had sent a legal notice earlier but Aditya had hoped to bring them around. Now, that didn't seem likely. NYIB was the first account that eTIOS had secured when Aditya had quit the bank to set up his own business. Riding on the back of the NYIB relationship, Aditya had built the eTIOS business. He took the rejection personally.

He emailed a few old friends who worked with NYIB in New York. However, given the mood and the issues related to privacy and data integrity, he knew that not much would come of it.

# 71

# Washington DC

'Three days! I get out of the country for three days on a nice holiday that looks like work and you track me down here too!' Mike Hendricks complained the moment he came on the line. He was in Davos for a precursor to the World Economic forum.

After exchanging a quick round of courtesies, Adrian came to the point. He narrated the story of Tony's London visit. 'When our field operatives could not trace Gloria's kin, we began to wonder if there was a different story there. Last night, I called my contacts at Pan American Insurance, and I was shocked . . . ' He paused. No response from the other side.

Then, 'I'm listening. Go on, Adrian.'

'Pan American Insurance paid out half a million dollars each to the families of twenty-nine people who died on the ground in the El Al disaster of 1988. In the case of Gloria's biological parents, they paid out *1.5 million dollars each* to the kin.'

'Could be a deal with Pan-American Insurance.' Mike was unruffled.

'We would have thought so too, had I not found out something else last night. Something that takes the cake, Mike,' Dan butted in. 'Last night, I accessed the federal database.'

'Do you have access to it?'

'Yes, I do. I got into the Combined DNA Index System. Got a hit on Gloria Tan's DNA.'

The Combined DNA Index System, known as CODIS, is a software platform that blends forensic science and computer technology. It contains over 10 million DNA profiles from the fifty states of America: of individuals—offenders, arrestees, detainees— as well as DNA of forensic interest, unidentified human remains, missing persons and relatives of missing persons. CODIS allows investigators to search for and match DNA profiles, a feature which comes in handy in crime resolution.

'Why would that interest you?' Mike Hendricks asked.

'The fact that the insurance payout was three times the regular payout raised eyebrows. Secondly, as per Gloria's own admission, she was rounded up during a suspected after-school rave party. Police records do not indicate any such detention. That got me curious. I wanted to see if Gillian was protecting her.'

'That would be quite normal for him to do. Right?' Mike responded. 'He was a doting father.'

'Well, yes. Would have been normal for him to do that, had he known. But Gloria also mentioned to us that Gillian was not aware of the incident.'

'Okay?'

Adrian could sense irritation in Mike's tone.

'And guess what. We found Gloria's DNA fingerprint in the National DNA registry. The NDIS.'

'How did it get there, Dan?'

'It's mandatory these days to collect the DNA samples from all arrestees or detainees irrespective of whether the person is convicted or not. Gloria's DNA samples would have been collected during the round up before someone bailed her out and erased the police records pertaining to the incident. The person who erased the police records, missed the fact that the DNA samples had already been collected. That explains why the DNA profile exists in the database, even though there are no police records.'

'You need to give me the headlines, Dan. I need to rush. Don't have much time.'

'Terribly sorry, Mike. Let me try and wrap it up. We ran Gloria's DNA strains for a match. To see if it matched with any other profile on the database.'

Silence.

'I got the report this morning, Mike.'

'It matched,' Mike responded.

It was not a question. It was a statement. Dan could make that out.

'Yes, Mike. One match. A high stringency match. You know about it, don't you?'

Adrian was shocked by Dan's latest revelation. Dan had not mentioned it to him.

'Yes, Dan,' Mike replied, 'Gloria is Nikki's daughter. Nikki's and mine.'

'The truth is stranger than fiction!' Tony was stunned as well.

Mike explained, 'We met in London, when she was in her early twenties, and fell in love. That's when Gloria was born. But, over time, we realized our aspirations, our goals were different and we drifted apart. Life does this to you. When she married Gillian after a brief courtship, she kept the story under wraps. She was sure that Gillian would not accept her child. Especially given that, by then, I'd become his political adversary. But she eventually succumbed to her motherly instinct and told Gillian. He was livid but eventually accepted the child. The El Al disaster story was spun to give credibility to a three-year-old walking into the lives of Gillian and Nikki Tan. It was convenient. We presented Gloria to the world as the daughter of a couple killed in the disaster. We bought the family's silence by paying them through Pan-American insurance. No one bothered to figure out anything till you guys got involved. I expect extreme levels of discretion from you.'

'But then what about Nikki's and Gloria's trips to London?'

'Nikki and I no longer meet but Gloria is my daughter too. Nikki gets Gloria to London for me to meet her and spend some time with her as a mentor.'

'Does Gloria know that you are her biological father?'

'Yes.'

'Then why did she lie to us?'

'She has been told what to say when asked about her parents. So it is not surprising that she told you what she did.'

'That explains it, I guess.' But Adrian was not entirely convinced. 'One question crops up repeatedly though. Why did Nikki mastermind the ATM heist, knowing very well that she would be under our watch?'

'Do you think she is capable of masterminding such a task? A global heist? I'm not too sure about that, Agent Scott. We can ask her that once she wakes up from the coma. Till then, I guess, we have to exercise caution.'

Adrian decided to let that be, and moved on to the next issue.

'There is a strong possibility that Gillian Tan's murder and Cotton Trail have something in common.' Adrian went on to detail all the findings till date.

'What do you need from me?' asked Mike.

'Permission to travel to India. Open back channel communications with the Indian foreign ministry to allow us to investigate. In particular, we will need the assistance of the Indian cyber cell.'

'Why India?'

'Because the latest login into the Altoids account is from Mumbai,' Adrian explained.

Mike said just one word. 'Granted.'

After disconnecting the call, Adrian looked at Dan. 'How did Mike Hendricks' DNA make it on to that database. Does he have a criminal background?' He also wanted to ask Dan why he hadn't mentioned this to him. But didn't. There was no point arguing with Dan.

'I don't know,' Dan responded.

'What do you mean?'

'Politicians at this level would have been detained some time or the other in their lives. And the way the law enforcers are zealous about capturing DNA samples for detainees I was sure that Mike Hendricks' DNA would be in the database.'

'I don't understand.'

'The day Mike Hendricks called you to convey the President's message to you, I knew something was amiss. Remember, the Pink Elephant. Something was not right about Gloria's background. The insurance pay-out was the clincher. I threw in the bait. Mike Hendricks knew his DNA was in the database. He knew it would match with Gloria's because he is her father. What he didn't know was that the DNA of people at his level is not accessible to anyone below the secretary of defence. He is relatively new to politics. He took our bait and told us the truth.'

'You lied to him?'

'A white lie to catch a pink elephant is acceptable. Isn't it, Adrian?' Dan smiled. 'Elementary my dear, Scott. Elementary.'

# 72

# Mumbai

Tanya's plea to release her mother's belongings, which were lying with the cops, came up for hearing in front of the holiday bench of the Mumbai court. When the CBI representative did not object, the prosecutor did not contest the appeal. The court ordered the release of all seized belongings of Malvika. Tanya went with Varun and promptly brought them home.

She opened the packet and pulled out a blue cotton saree. It was bloodstained and gave off a horrid, unbearable stench. She fondly hugged it and buried her face in it.

There was a packet of jewellery too. It contained a pair of earrings, a necklace, a mangalsutra. No bangles, no rings. A Corum watch.

'Malvika sure had style,' Varun thought.

Tanya put everything away inside a cupboard. She walked to the kitchen to make a cup of tea. The maids had left. They normally left on Friday afternoon and returned on Sunday evening. Tanya preferred it that way as it gave her some privacy, particularly if she wanted to be with Varun.

Varun followed her into the kitchen. He stood there, hugging her for a few minutes. Tanya turned to pull out the jar of tea leaves. The water in the kettle was boiling. Varun took the jar from her hand to keep it back once she was done. As he kept it inside the cabinet, he looked around for something to munch on. He picked up a tin of peanuts and spotted a jar of green-coloured, wasabi-flavoured nuts right behind it. He knew Malvika had liked wasabi. Tanya had told him that. He kept the peanuts back on the shelf and picked up the wasabi nuts. As he was opening the jar, Tanya turned with a cup of tea in her hand.

'Wait, wait, wait! Where did you pick that from?'

'From here.' He pointed to the cabinet.

'Check the expiry date. Mom used to keep fresh stock on the other side.' She walked to the other end of the kitchen and pulled out a new jar.

Varun smiled, kept the old jar back and took the new one.

'I will trash it,' Tanya said as they sat down at the table, drinking tea. For a long time, she sat like that. Varun got up to keep the tea cups in the sink. He picked up some more wasabi nuts and turned around.

Tanya was crying. Despite her best efforts to be quiet, he could hear her sobbing. Her shoulders were shaking in sync with her crying. He walked up behind her and hugged her gently, kissing the side of her neck.

Tanya turned around and hugged him tight. 'Promise me you will never leave me, Varun! Promise me.'

He smiled affectionately and hugged her back. She stepped out of his embrace and kissed him on his lips. Varun wanted to kiss her but wasn't sure if it was the right time. Tanya solved his predicament. She pulled him towards her and kissed him, then pulled him into the bedroom. They made love passionately. Tanya wanted to forget all that she had been through and the best way to take her mind off it was to immerse herself in Varun. Exhausted, they collapsed in each other's arms and let sleep take over.

It was almost 6 p.m. when Varun was woken up by the incessant ringing of his phone.

'Yeah, Dad?'

'Where are you, Varun? Call me when you are free. Need to talk to you.'

'Okay, Dad, give me half an hour.'

He hung up and looked at Tanya. She looked like a goddess,

more so when she was naked in bed. He got out of bed and looked around for his clothes. Twenty minutes and a shower later, he kissed Tanya on her forehead and left.

He took the stairs instead of waiting for the elevator. At the third floor, he saw a man walking into an apartment. Varun stopped for a moment. Their eyes met briefly before the man hurried inside. Varun shook his head, and walked on towards his car.

# 73

# Mumbai

Any investigation by a foreign law enforcement agency in India had to be cleared by the Ministry of External Affairs. In this case, when Mike Hendricks' office got in touch with the ministry, they were referred to the CBI.

The CBI was quite happy to have the FBI investigate the ATM heist and the possible Cotton Trail linkages in India. They conferred with the director-general of Mumbai Police and assigned Assistant Commissioner of Police Dibanker Shome of the cyber crime cell to work with them.

Adrian had worried that the Indian government would throw a spanner in the works. While seeing him off before his flight to Mumbai, the CBI director had whispered, 'Mr Scott, the Indian government does not take kindly to surprises. So make sure that there are none. And if there are any significant findings, please keep me in the loop. While it is easy to give permission to FBI, it is easier to deport errant officers. And please, no media interaction. Not a word!' Adrian nodded. He decided to take it as it came.

When Tony and Adrian arrived at the airport a team of officers from Mumbai Police was there to receive them. They were escorted to the Trident Hotel in the Bandra-Kurla Complex, which would be their home for the next few days.

The biggest challenge for Adrian was that the cops in India hadn't even heard of bitcoins or, for that matter, Cotton Trail. It took Adrian a fair bit of time to lay it out for them. At the end of it, one thing was clear: ACP Shome couldn't offer him anything more than logistic support. Tony and Adrian would have to do the actual investigative work.

The IP address from where Altoids had logged in, asking for support to figure out the missing alphanumerics in the private key, had been easy to identify. It was a node on the VTS network, one of the largest telecom service providers in India. It surprised Adrian, and even Dan for that matter, that Altoids had been careless enough to leave a trail. He never expected to be caught.

'Is it a phone? A tablet perhaps?' Adrian asked the legal head at VTS, when he met him the next morning.

'No, it is a leased line. Communication lines that feed corporates.'

'I know what a leased line is,' said Adrian. The legal head looked pointedly at ACP Shome who was struggling with these terms. 'Which company does this leased line connect to?' Adrian asked. Once he had the name and address of the company on record, he could then track the specific individual.

'I'll have to check and get back to you.'

Adrian raised his right eyebrow. 'You don't know?'

'I . . . actually, you see . . .' stammered the legal head.

Adrian cut in, 'As in you will have to find out. Or will you have to check if you can disclose the names?'

'Legally, I cannot give out the information, unless there is a request from the concerned judicial authorities or the cops.'

Adrian looked at ACP Shome. 'You can instruct him to give us the information, can't you?'

'No.' ACP Shome was apologetic. 'Need a court order. Even the director-general's order will do.'

'How long will it take to get it?'

'A week,' said ACP Shome. And then he surprised Adrian further, 'If we are lucky.'

Adrian could see that VTS's legal head had a few papers in a folder on his table and that it seemed to contain a lot more than just IP address-related documentation. From where he was sitting,

Adrian tried to read the contents of the page on top. He couldn't. They couldn't wait for a week.

He got up from his chair, and looked at ACP Shome. 'If we have your permission, can I have a word with him alone?' And he pointed towards the legal head.

'Sure,' and ACP Shome started to get up from his seat.

'No, please stay seated. We don't want to trouble you. Sir, if you don't mind, can I have a word with you outside?'

The legal head got up and walked out with Adrian.

'Sir, I did not want to say this in front of the ACP but this is a very important case for the FBI. Anyone who helps us get to the bottom of this will be rewarded . . .' He paused, and added, '. . . in whatever way you deem fit.'

'I admire your arrogance, Mr Scott.' The legal head had an angry look on his face. 'You Americans think you can get anything you want. Yes, there are a few people who will be swayed by your green paper, but not me. I'd rather you left before I report this obstinacy.'

'Sir, it's understandable that you are upset but do you realize the good you will be doing? If the US gets to the bottom of Cotton Trail and the people behind it, we will be able to prevent thousands of teenagers from getting addicted to narcotics. Smuggling, pornography, paedophilia—all these evils can be stopped if you help us. All we need are the details of the IP address I gave you.' Adrian made a moral appeal.

'I'm sorry, Mr Scott. I'd love to help but our company will provide the details once we are asked to disclose it . . .' He turned, and added, '. . . through proper channels and not a moment before.'

The three of them thanked the legal head and left. In the police jeep in the car park, Adrian asked, 'Where to now?'

Tony smiled. He pulled out his cellphone and brought up a picture of a paper with an address on it.

'Here,' he proclaimed, and looked at ACP Shome, who was trying to conceal a smile. 'You will get me sacked for sure!'

The jeep pulled out of the parking lot and moved towards the address in the image.

Adrian's phone beeped. It was a message. From Dan: *Get your hands on the latest press release from my unit in FBI. We have a lot of work to do.*

# 74

## Cupertino/Mumbai

The press conference at Cupertino, California, was unprecedented. Apple Inc. announced a major overhaul of its operating system. It caught everyone—users, programmers, app developers, competitors—by surprise. A major upgrade of the operating system was not due for at least three months.

The same day, the FBI issued a press release signed off by Dan Malloy.

> *At the request of Dell, the world's largest laptop computer manufacturer, the FBI will be investigating the blowing up of over two dozen Dell computers in the west coast of the US and an unidentified number of laptops all over the US and the world in general.*
>
> *Normally such acts are under the purview of local law enforcement agencies. However, given the suspected cyber terrorism roots and the fact that a much more serious scenario could ensue if such unprecedented acts increase in frequency, the FBI has been asked to investigate.*
>
> *Dan Malloy, Chief of Cryptanalysis and Racketeering Records Unit at the FBI, will lead the investigation.*

When Adrian saw this on his mobile, he was surprised. He couldn't comprehend what it was about and called Dan. 'What's the story, Dan?'

'You saw the release?'

'Yes, but what's it about? Couldn't figure out much.'

'It's not what is in the release that is important. It's what is not there that raises eyebrows.'

'And that is?'

'I spoke with Tim Cook.'

'The Apple CEO?'

'Yes. The new version of the operating system released by Apple was created to tackle the overheating problem.'

'What's the connection?'

'There is a malware in the system. No one knows where it came from. There exists no antidote for it. It has infected over 100,000 computers in the US alone. What's worse is that it is suspected to have infected over 1 million smartphones. All kinds, iOS and Android.'

'And what does the malware do?'

'It scans the computers and phones for bitcoin wallets. The moment it identifies a bitcoin wallet on the hard disk, the program steals the private key and transfers all the bitcoins to a clandestine wallet, precoded in the malware. We have no clue how many customers have lost their bitcoins like this.'

'Shit! That's dangerous.'

'Apple is so worried that it came out with a new iOS version, which categorically asks customers to reload all necessary apps. They have taken care to back up and reinstate core data. Any data not in core form and all executable files are deleted. This extensive reformatting is going to inconvenience users for sure.'

Adrian didn't say anything. He was trying to take in the gravity of the situation.

'That's not all, Adrian. The software also leaves an executable file on the system boot disk, which forces the computer to join a network based in Ukraine, whenever it is on the Internet.'

'A botnet!'

'Yup, a botnet. Once the system joins the hub in Ukraine, it automatically downloads the bitcoin mining software. This software then resides on the computer. Whenever the computer is in sleep mode, the software takes over and the processing capabilities of the computer are added to the network and used up to remotely mine bitcoins. To get new bitcoins as and when they are issued. It is a Graphics Processing Unit intensive act and heats up the unit. This causes the computers to blow up. It is one of the smartest designed, self-destructing malware I've seen. It regenerates every five minutes and, when it does, it destroys the older version, thus destroying any evidence of its earlier presence on the machine.'

'Doesn't sound good at all, Dan.'

'Nope. The only saving grace is that such malware never spreads on its own. Obviously people are clicking on something, which activates its transfer. Hopefully we will find something soon.'

'Let me know in case you need our help.'

After disconnecting the phone, Adrian looked at ACP Shome. 'Let's not do this in a hurry. I think there's more to it. Let's meet our suspect only when we are ready. He isn't going anywhere.'

Adrian was distressed. His mind was on the malware.

# 75

# Mumbai

Aditya woke up at 6.15 a.m., picked up his Blackberry from his bedside table and walked to the bathroom, scrolling through the mails. The two minutes of tooth brushing time was also Blackberry scanning time.

He went through a few office mails. Nothing urgent. A couple of direct mailers. There was a 50 per cent discount at Shoppers Stop. When was the last time he'd shopped there? A mail from Apple, giving him the daily sales figures of his apps. Another mail. From Apple? He stopped brushing. The subject line just had one word: 'Congratulations!'

He clicked the mail open. His face broke into a wide grin the moment he read it. Hurriedly, he spit out the remnants of the toothpaste, rinsed his mouth and rushed out. 'Varun!' He called out excitedly. 'Varuuuuun!'

He briskly walked across to Varun's room. Not there. He dialled Varun's number.

'Morning, Dad.'

'Where are you, Varun?'

'Out for a jog. You know I go for a jog every day.'

'Oh yes! But I needed to tell you this now. Couldn't wait.'

'Dad, you sound really happy. What happened?'

'You did it, Son! Townsville is the number one app on the Apple store's "most downloaded" list!'

'Wow, really?' Varun too had a wide grin on his face.

'Yes. I just saw the mail from Apple. It's a huge achievement, Varun. Never before has any app from India made it to that position.'

'It's all because of you, Dad. You built a fabulous company. You deserve every bit of credit for this.'

'You know, Varun, this could not have happened at a better time for us. After all the issues with eTIOS and NYIB pulling out, we desperately needed some good PR. This will do it for us! We'll definitely get some good stories in the media.'

In his excitement, Aditya forgot that Varun was out for a jog. Varun indulged him for a bit and then hung up. He turned to his right and smiled. 'We are number one on the Apple store. How cool is that?'

'Come on!' Tanya rolled her eyes. 'What's the big deal?' She shrugged her shoulders. 'You probably used bots to download your program.'

'Shut up, you idiot,' Varun retorted. 'I stopped using bots the moment we became a paid app.'

'Huh?' She pretended to be unimpressed and ran off towards the junction of Worli Seaface with the Bandra–Worli sea link.

'Wait! Wait!' Varun called out loudly as he took off behind her. 'This is a wonderful piece of news. You don't know the worth of a game, you layman!' He caught up with her, held her by her shoulder, imploring her to stop.

She laughed. Her pretty face lit up. 'You rock, Varun, you rock. I was kidding.' And the smile became even broader.

'Wait, rock reminds me of something.'

Varun fumbled in his pocket and pulled out a tiny box. The maroon box had a wavy 'T' embossed on it. He went down on his knee, one hand on his heart and the other holding the ring he had taken out of the box.

'Marry me!'

Tanya looked at the Tanishq solitaire in his hand. She couldn't take her eyes of the glittering diamond ring.

'Tanya?'

'Were you saying something, Varun?' Tanya asked, mischievously.

'Will you marry me?'

'Idiot!' Tanya said. 'Of course I heard it the first time. I was testing your patience.' Her hands went up to her cheeks and she shut her eyes with her fingertips.

'My knees are hurting.'

'Of course I will, Varun.' She pulled him up and hugged him. 'I will, Varun, I will. You are the only one I have.'

'Give me your hand,' said Varun. Tanya extended her left hand towards him. He held her ring finger and was about to slip the ring on when he saw an old ring. 'Take it off.'

Tanya tried to pull it off but it didn't budge.

'Let me try,' Varun volunteered.

'No it's fine. It's an old ring. It's gotten stuck. Slip yours on this finger.' And she extended the finger adjacent to the ring finger towards him.

Varun quietly slipped it on the other finger.

Tanya looked at the solitaire, kissed it excitedly and hugged Varun again.

'I love you, baby,' he said.

'Me too, Varun. Be with me for ever.'

'Can I make one call? It's important.' Tanya nodded.

'Dad!' Varun screamed into the phone. 'Tanya said yes, Dad. She said YES! This is the best day of my life. Bye, Dad.' And he hung up.

He turned around. Tanya hugged him again. 'I wish I had someone I could call and share this with.'

Varun hugged her even more tightly. 'I'm there now.'

After a few moments, he released her and said, 'Come, let's go. I have to pack for my trip to Ukraine tomorrow.'

'Oh yes.' Tanya knew that Varun was going to Ukraine to take a look at a small gaming company, which an investment banker had recommended they could buy.

'When will you be back?'

'Three days. But today calls for a celebration, Tanya. Dinner? Tonight? What say?'

Tanya was not in a mood for dinner. 'Let's go for a movie?' Varun agreed.

That night, when they returned from the movie, Varun came up to drop her to her place.

The moment Tanya unlocked the door, she let out a gasp. 'Oh my God! What the fuck?' Her hands instinctively went up and covered her mouth. Varun sidestepped her and walked in. The whole house was a mess. The furniture was in disarray, papers were strewn everywhere . . . Somebody had come in when they were away and ransacked the house.

Varun was shocked. He walked from room to room, looking at the chaos.

'Looks like your mom had something after all and someone wants it desperately.'

'But what? Who?'

'I can only think of one person whose behaviour was out of the ordinary.'

When a perplexed Tanya looked at Varun, he clarified. 'The finance minister. Remember what he asked you that day? If your mom had left something for him . . .'

'Motherfucker.' That was all Tanya could say, as she looked around in dismay.

The local cops were promptly called in. Aditya too landed up.

Much to their surprise, the CCTV camera in the building was not working when the break-in had occurred. Strangely, the building had suffered a power outage for a few minutes that evening. The fuse had been tampered with. Since power outages are unheard of in south Mumbai, most buildings do not have any power back-up.

The watchman and other support staff in the building were quizzed. No one knew anything.

When Varun and Tanya tried to lodge a complaint with the police, the cops refused to register a case. They fought and argued, but to no avail. They left the police station, threatening to pull strings.

On the way back, Varun asked Tanya if she wanted to stay with him and Aditya for a few days. She politely refused. There were too many memories associated with her mother. 'I can't leave, Varun. I just can't leave this place and move.'

# 76

# Mumbai

Tony had just woken up. He was lying on his bed, naked from the waist down. A towel lay on the floor beside the bed. His iPad was next to him, on top of the quilt. He unlocked it and the screen came up in a flash. *Confessions of the Hooker*... proclaimed a huge banner running across the top of the site. He was now looking at the blog of the infamous hooker in United States who claimed to have bedded over 200 celebrities.

The blog post that she had released the previous day was about a British cricketer whom she had met on one of his trips to New York. The *Huffington Post* that Tony had read on his flight to India had carried excerpts from the blog; the article was attempting to guess the identity of the blogger. No one knew who she was. Tony prayed for her safety. When important people are tickled in their pants, it can get extremely uncomfortable

*Huffington Post* had rated the blog as one of the most erotic of all times, though it was mediocre in terms of language and literary excellence. 'What else do you expect from a hooker?' said the article.

Tony concurred. Her blog posts were really erotic and could turn on even a dead man. Irrespective of what the *Huffington Post* said, the blog had become quite popular in the United States.

The events of last night flashed before his eyes.

He was already horny. He hadn't had a woman in over two weeks. It was getting to him. He was scared of trying anything adventurous in India. Stories of how people in India extorted money from foreigners in the name of sex had scared him. And how long can one live on porn? He decided to give *Confessions* a try. 'An erotic book is always better in bed than a stranger. If not better, at least safer.'

The first post he read was an escapade with an ageing Hollywood star. A star she called Grizzly, because of the humungous amount of body hair he had. She went on to reveal how, at the age of 63, and at her insistence, the ageing star decided to wax and have all the hair removed from his body. She went on to describe in explicit details her sexual escapades with him, and how removal of the hair around his manhood made him a lot more appealing to her than his earlier avatar.

The way she described their rendezvous turned Tony on. Something stirred down there. Once he was done playing with himself, he kept the iPad aside, rolled over and went off to sleep.

# 77

# Mumbai

Tanya wanted to complain to the CBI about the break-in and make it a part of the deposition she had given a few days ago. Kabir Khan was waiting for her. She had called him before making the trek to the CBI office.

When she had settled in the chair in front of Khan's table, he began to speak. 'I know you would be concerned about the unannounced raid on your house last night.'

'Raid?' Tanya was surprised. This angle hadn't occurred to her.

'Yes, madam. The CBI raided your residence last night. Yours truly is the culprit.'

'How can you do that? It's illegal! I will drag you to court.'

'Be my guest,' thundered an arrogant Kabir. 'We had the requisite court permissions. Two *panchas* were with us.' He shrugged.

'What did you take from my house?'

'The list of the items we seized and the panchas' declaration have been handed over to the court. You can take the list from the court in due course.'

'This is ridiculous. I will complain.'

'To whom?'

'To the home minister.'

Kabir took out his pen, tore out a piece of paper from a pad in front of him, and wrote down a number. 'There you go.' He gave the paper to Tanya. 'The home minister's number. I'll tell his personal assistant to put you through when you call.' And he laughed. 'That will be all, Ms Sehgal. Thanks for coming by.'

He had exacted his revenge for Tanya's misbehaviour when he had gone to her house to interrogate her.

# 78

# Mumbai

'Are you sure you want to do this?' asked Tony, the moment he saw Adrian and ACP Shome waiting in the lobby. He was late by five minutes. Adrian was wearing jeans and a white shirt.

'Yes, of course. Why else would we be here waiting for you?'

'Don't you think you will tip him off? Make him a bit more careful?' ACP Shome asked. 'It might be better to monitor him for some time.'

'No, Mr Shome. The thing about cyber crime is that the tyre marks are already there, and they cannot be covered. Irrespective of how hard you try. In fact, the harder you try, the more tracks you end up making. So by alerting him, we might prevent any further traces from coming up. What we have already will be enough to nail him.' Adrian countered as he got into the car. 'And, Tony,' he continued, 'the more I see of this case, the more I am convinced that there is a link between the ATM heist, Cotton Trail and Gillian Tan's assassination. It's just that we don't know what it is.'

The Toyota Innova made its way through the busy streets of Mumbai. ACP Shome had a job to do. To trail the two FBI agents and make sure things didn't go out of hand. And also to make sure that if any victories were to be had, the Mumbai police got information about them well in advance to claim credit. The night before, he had given his daily report to his boss, the head of Mumbai police, about the visit to the VTS office. And how Adrian had coaxed the legal head of VTS out of the room while a seemingly disinterested

Tony had clicked away happily at the documents lying on the table. ACP Shome had been told to look the other way, as long as matters didn't blow up. Their actions had CBI approval, he was told.

In no time, they were at the address mentioned in those documents.

~

Aditya was engrossed in work. After the recent debacle, eTIOS wanted to hire the services of a systems security firm to audit them on a regular basis, recommend upgrades and plug loopholes. Given how he was a stickler for quality, he only wanted the best in class. They had shortlisted four international firms and three of them had been called that day to make their pitches. He had just returned to his office after one such meeting when his intercom buzzed.

'They are here, Aditya.' It was his secretary.

'Hmm. Show them in. And can you also organize some coffee for us? Black for me.'

'Yes, Aditya.'

~

'Good morning. Thanks for meeting us at such a short notice, Mr Rao.'

'I've got used to this gentlemen, especially after the problem you had in New York.' Aditya smiled.

'These are Special Agents Adrian Scott and Tony Claire of the FBI.' ACP Shome made the introductions.

'Thank you, ACP Shome. Hope all is fine and safe under your watch.'

Shome smiled.

'The FBI is extremely grateful to you, Mr Rao, for being so candid and open about the happenings at eTIOS. Our purpose of meeting you today is to understand from you if your internal investigations have hinted at the involvement of any insiders in the data infringement that led to the ATM heist in New York.' Adrian was not there to inquire about the heist, but it did provide a good opening.

Aditya looked at ACP Shome. He was a bit confused. He had been subjected to such questions from the day of the incident. His intercom buzzed again.

'Yes?'

'Aditya, the next team is here. Should I ask them to wait?'

'No, ask Sundeep to meet them and start the presentation. I'll join them.' And hung up. He looked at the three visitors and volunteered. 'We are meeting a few international firms to audit our system security on a quarterly basis. Just to make sure that we are fully covered and not exposed.'

'That's nice. Who all are you meeting?' Adrian was just being courteous.

'We just started this morning. So far only FireVault has presented its case. We have three more meetings during the course of the day and tomorrow.'

'Really gracious of you, Mr Rao, to have met us on this busy day.'

'No, no, not at all. In fact I'm sorry that I kept you waiting. We digressed during the presentation and started talking about an incident in Pondicherry a couple of days ago. That took up a lot of our time.'

'Incident?' Shome was curious.

'Oh, you would probably know,' he said, looking at Shome. 'The incident where a French woman was molested by an American inside Auroville in Pondicherry. The molester was thrashed by some people who had gathered, on hearing the woman cry for help. He is admitted in a local hospital.'

'Is that so?' Shome tried to think but couldn't recollect anything.

Aditya continued, 'The interesting bit is that the American's passport was found to be fake. The police are now trying to identify him. Security and infringement is an issue everywhere, you see. Not only in our systems.' He smiled.

Tony was taking copious notes.

'In any case, let's get back to the matter at hand.' Aditya spoke about the entire episode and the aftermath and how they had dealt with it. About how it had impacted their credibility and how they had worked towards restoring customer confidence. He brooded over the fact that they had lost the NYIB account. For almost fifteen minutes everyone just listened to what Aditya had to say.

Tony suddenly got up and walked to his bag, kept in a corner of the room. He dug out something and walked back to the table. As he got closer, he extended his hand towards Aditya. He was holding a box.

'Mint?'

'No, thanks.'

'Sugarfree Altoids.' The stress on the word 'Altoids' was evident and intentional.

'No, thanks,' Aditya repeated firmly. 'I'm not a mint person.'

'What about you, Adrian? ACP Shome?' Tony turned to the two of them and offered mints. Adrian picked one while Shome too declined.

'Wonderful. All this is now for me,' Tony said cheerfully himself and kept the box in front of him. Adrian was keenly observing Aditya's response. There was no change in his demeanour.

The discussion continued. The brief Altoids interjection didn't impact anything. After about twenty-five minutes, Adrian got up to leave.

'Thanks, Mr Rao. Appreciate your time.'

'Not at all. If you have any other queries, please feel free to call me or mail me.'

'Will it be okay if I email you at the Frosty.com ID?' Adrian sprung a surprise.

'Frosty.com?' Aditya seemed genuinely surprised. 'I don't have any ID by that name. My ID is on the card I gave you. Please use that ID. I'll make sure someone from my team responds immediately.' As he said this, Sundeep walked in. 'Hey, Sundeep, good you are here. Meet Agents Adrian Scott and Tony Claire from the FBI.'

'FBI? I came to check if you'll take long. If not, we'll wait for you and not begin the presentation.'

'We are almost done, Sundeep. These gentlemen are here to get an update on the lead up to the ATM heist.'

'Oh, okay. You should have called me, Aditya.' Sundeep was visibly disappointed that it was just by chance that he had stumbled upon the meeting.

～

After they left, Sundeep repeated, 'Aditya, you should have called me. I would have given them the correct picture.'

'It's okay. I handled it. I'd have called you in case I was getting stuck somewhere.' He put his arm around a sulking Sundeep. 'In any case, you have too much to do as it is.'

～

After exiting the eTIOS office, Tony and Adrian got into the police jeep with Shome.

'Strange. He didn't show any reaction when we confronted him with references to Altoids and Frosty,' began Adrian. 'If he did mastermind the heist, he should have been shocked when we mentioned those words.'

'But we have clinching evidence against him, don't we?'

'Not sure if you can call it clinching, Tony. In fact, under the circumstances it may not even be enough.' Adrian was concerned. 'The pictures that you clicked showed that the IP address corresponded to the wi-fi in Aditya's room. Perhaps his laptop. But what does that prove? He could be Altoids but we still don't have evidence of Altoids's involvement in the ATM heist. We just suspect him of being the brain behind Cotton Trail.'

'So we have nothing else to go by. We are at a dead end. One and a half day in India, and we are in a blind alley,' Tony lamented.

When they reached the hotel, Adrian turned to ACP Shome, 'Give me half an hour. I'll freshen up and be down soon.' He headed towards the elevator. Tony followed him. ACP Shome stayed in the lobby.

'Once we get to the bottom of this, we should go somewhere and chill. And bed some dumb French woman, like the one Aditya mentioned,' said Tony, as soon as they entered the elevator.

'Ha ha!' Adrian laughed. 'You and your libido, Tony. How are you managing?'

'Making do with the confessions of the hooker.'

The elevator had just came to a halt on Adrian's floor when Dan called.

# 79

# Mumbai

'We've hit a dead-end, Dan. What should we do now?'

'We should try a different approach. Wait for a couple of days and send a response to the latest post where Altoids asks for help on the missing alphanumerics of the bitcoin private key. Tell Altoids that you can decipher it. Only an idiot will give you the remaining characters and ask you to decipher the missing ones. So he will have to engage to find out how to get it done. Let's see if it draws him out. That will give us an opportunity to get to him.'

'I doubt if he will take the bait so easily, Dan. He is too smart.'

'He will try everything to get the key.'

'Let's see. What's happening on the laptop blow-up and malware issue, Dan.'

'Some interesting stuff there. We have acquired the mirror image of the Ukrainian server that was pumping malware into desktops, laptops and cellphones across the world.'

'Jeez, how did you manage that?'

'The FBI invoked the Mutual Legal Assistance Treaty that Ukraine has signed with the US. Under that, Ukraine is bound to share this information.'

'But, Dan, if someone intended to infuse malware, wouldn't that someone use a server in a location that does not have any such treaty with the US?'

'Coincidence, Adrian. We signed the MLAT with Ukraine only a week ago. This is the first instance where the treaty has been invoked.

When the criminals were planning this, Ukraine would have been a safe haven for them.'

'That's a good omen, Dan.' Adrian was excited. 'What does the server mirror image tell us?'

'Too early to say but we're trying to find out more. Hopefully we will have something by tomorrow evening. The team is on it.'

He hung up and was about to get into the shower when he got a call on the hotel landline.

'Adrian!' It was Tony. 'I'm sending a link to your phone. Take a look.'

Adrian walked to the table, picked up his phone and came back to the landline. He touched the screen and Tony's message opened up. There was a link to the *Times of India* website.

'Damn!' he exclaimed the moment he saw the link. 'What is he doing here?'

'Exactly! What's Stan doing in Pondicherry under a false name and identity, while the FBI is looking for him the world over?'

# 80

# Sangamner/Mumbai

Ram Sarvate had just returned from his farm in Sangamner, 150 km from Mumbai. He was sitting on the ledge outside the house, taking in the happenings of the evening, when his wife came out. Seeing him, she went back inside and returned a minute later with a glass of water. Ram took it and almost immediately dropped it to the floor. His wife, who was going back into the house, stopped and turned. His face had tanned. 'Probably the heat,' she thought. But his eyes told her another story. They had shrunk like those of a dead, dried-up fish.

Then she saw his hand.

'Oh my God!' she exclaimed, dashing back to his side. 'What happened?' His hand was swollen. The forearm was bleeding badly. The elbow joint was out of place. His right ear was bleeding, from a cut. He had draped a sheet around him. When she removed the sheet, she saw his vest was drenched in blood.

'What happened? Oh my God! What will I do now?' She was hysterical.

'Quiet! Quiet!' Ram tried to calm her down but she was having none of it. She forced him to see the village doctor, who packed them off almost immediately to the government hospital in neighbouring Nasik.

When Ram returned home the next evening, he had seventeen stitches for the cut next to his ear, and his right arm, which had a broken elbow and two forearm fractures, was in a cast.

All this was a result of his running feud with the local politician who wanted to usurp his land.

A week later, when his physical condition improved, he gathered the necessary courage to head to the police station and lodge a complaint against Govind bhai, the local henchman who had attacked him. Three of his neighbours, who has seen the ghastly attack, went along with him and signed off as witnesses.

Govind was a well-known goon of the area and the cops knew where he lived. When they went to his house to arrest him, they discovered that he was in Mumbai where he had been arrested a week ago. On what grounds, nobody knew. Later that day, the inspector at the local police station called the Mumbai police to verify Govind's whereabouts.

When he kept the phone down, he was in a state of shock. He sent word for Ram to come and meet him. The moment Ram entered the police station, he walked up to him, lifted his hand and brought it down hard in one swift move on Ram's cheek.

'Liar!' he screamed.

Ram looked at him, tears in his eyes, wondering what he'd done to upset the inspector.

'How could Govind have attacked you when he was involved in an accident in Mumbai on the same day? He is in jail for killing someone in a road accident, and that too in Mumbai. The time of the accident is exactly the same as the time he is supposed to have attacked you. The time that you have stated in your FIR. You son of a bitch!' He slapped Ram again.

'Aaaah!' screamed Ram.

The incident was first reported in the Sangamner local press but was soon picked up by the national media. If media speculation was anything to go by, Swami was supposedly murdered by Govind after he had deposed against the finance minister.

Televised debates that night focused on the minister's involvement in the murders of Malvika and Swami. The minister himself maintained a stoic silence and refused to talk to the media.

'Swami uncle had found out something where your mom helped the minister move some money out of the country. She was probably being arm-twisted by him,' said Varun

'Yes, you told me that the day he told your father.'

'Do you think he mentioned that to the CBI? And the minister found out about it somehow?'

'Former finance minister. He has resigned,' said Tanya, angrily.

'All right, all right, former minister.'

'I hope he rots in hell.'

'I tell you what . . . ' and Varun walked up to her desk and picked up her laptop. 'Let's write to the CBI telling them exactly what Swami uncle told me and dad. In case the CBI knows about this, great. In case they don't, it might help them. We will also release a copy of this mail to the media, so that everyone knows about it.'

He opened Tanya's laptop, and settled on a lounge chair to type up a note for the CBI. He wrote out everything he knew. Tanya walked up to him. 'Don't you think this will sully mom's reputation too?'

'Not any more than it already has been. Everyone and his uncle are saying whatever comes to their minds. By sending this to the CBI, we can set the record straight.'

Tanya didn't respond. She was thinking. 'Are you sure, Varun?'

'Yes. Unless you think otherwise?'

'No, I'm fine with whatever you say.' She headed to the shower but didn't seem too confident or convinced.

Varun finished the note and tried to log into his email. The laptop was not connected to the Internet.

'Tanya!' He called out. She was in the shower. 'What's the wi-fi password?'

'There is a pen drive in the top drawer of my dressing table. Use that and transfer the file to the other laptop. That one will connect automatically to the wi-fi.'

Varun transferred the file and sent it to Kabir Khan, promising to send a signed declaration the next day. He mentioned that the declaration was also being released to the press at the same time.

After he sent the mail, he waited for Tanya to come out. She was taking a long time. 'Probably washing her hair,' he said to himself.

Might as well play some games on the laptop, he thought, and settled back on the lounge chair.

~

Dan called Adrian that evening.

'Adrian, the server analysis for the Ukrainian server has come in.'

'What does it tell us?'

As Dan started explaining, Adrian's eyes widened in disbelief.

'Tell me you're kidding, Dan!' That's all he could say after sixteen minutes of listening.

Dan paused. 'Now that this has come up, I see no point in you guys staying back there. I recommend that you come back immediately. There are more serious issues to be addressed.'

'You're right. Tony and I will be out on the first flight home.' He hung up.

Shome dropped them off to the airport that night. He said, 'I can't figure out why you are leaving in such a hurry!'

'Something important has come up. We will try to come back soon, Mr Shome,' said Adrian.

'Okay. Hope you get to the bottom of this case. If you need anything from India, do let me know.'

'Thanks, Shome. You have been a wonderful companion all along.' Adrian shook hands with ACP Shome and walked towards the check-in counter. Tony started to follow but whirled about to wave to Shome and bumped into a young man. He apologized immediately. It was his fault that he didn't watch his step.

'Not a problem, sir,' Varun said and moved on. He was on his way to Ukraine.

'Close the deal one way or the other. Don't let it hang. Do what it takes,' Aditya had told him as he dropped him off at the airport a few minutes ago.

# 81

# Mumbai

Tanya was not the only one feeling lonesome with Varun away, trying to crack the deal in Ukraine.

Aditya too was feeling the pinch. Even though he had lived alone for the better part of his life, he had quickly gotten used to Varun's presence in the house. Coming back to an empty house was not easy for him any more. As a matter of routine, he spoke to Varun every night for updates on the negotiations with the Ukrainian gaming company.

After speaking to Varun that night, he tried to get some sleep but couldn't. He kept tossing and turning in bed. Finally after an hour without an iota of sleep, he got up and logged on to his computer.

There were a few routine mails. He responded to them. A thank you mail from Adrian Scott. He ignored it. The line of questioning by the FBI had angered him, though he hadn't shown it. The next was a mail from the World Gaming Council. He was about to mark it as spam but decided to read it.

*Dear Mr Rao,*

*The World Gaming Council is happy to invite you to the inaugural conference to be held in Washington DC, from 28–30 October. We are happy to inform you that Indiscape Corporation has been nominated for awards in two categories:*

1. *Fastest growing gaming company in the world*

2. *Best gaming company in emerging markets*

*It would be wonderful if you could accept the award in person (should Indiscape win in either category) on behalf of the company. The ceremony will be held at the end of the conference. The attached brochure has more details.*

*Accommodation has been arranged at the Ritz Carlton, the venue of the event, and you will be covered for business class travel from India to Washington DC.*

*We request you to confirm your attendance.*

*Warmest regards,*

*Smith Barney*

*Curator — World Gaming Council*

Aditya suddenly perked up. This was the first time someone had recognized the contribution of Indiscape to the gaming world. And that too an international forum. Excited, he called Varun instantly and read out the entire message to him.

'First the number one spot on the Apple Store and now this recognition! You deserve it, Son. I will write to them that you will be there to receive the award.'

'Dad, they have invited you. You need to go.'

'No, Varun, it's yours. You have worked relentlessly on this for the last few months.'

'When did you say it was, Dad?'

'From 28th to the 30th of this month.'

'Dad! It's Tanya's birthday on the 28th. She will kill me if I am away.'

'Take her with you.'

'I don't think she'll go. I've suggested to her a few times to take a break. But she is too traumatized to do anything. I suggest you start packing your bags.'

Aditya replied to Smith Barney, confirming that either he or his son Varun would make it to the conference. This was another PR opportunity for Indiscape.

# 82

# Washington DC

*Confessions of the Hooker* had America hooked. The revelations were coming three time a week now. It had become a national pastime. Tabloids, TV news, magazines—all were talking about it.

Aditya landed in Washington DC, early on a sunny Friday morning. He was a bit tired. The two stopovers had taken their toll. Someone from the Ritz was waiting for him with a placard that had his name on it. He signalled to the person and followed him to the parking lot. On the way to the parking lot, he called Varun to tell him he had reached and asked him to wish Tanya a happy birthday.

The driver led him to a waiting SUV. In no time, they were speeding down the highway. Forty minutes later, they were at the Ritz. As he was checking in, Aditya picked up a tabloid placed on a stand in the reception. On the front page was a story of how the hooker had bedded an NBA star player in the minutes leading to the NBA finals. This is America, he thought as he checked in and was escorted to his room by the hotel staff.

He showered, changed, and settled down with a mug of coffee from the self-service kettle. He was about to log in to his laptop when there was a knock at the door.

Two white men, wearing smart black suits stood outside.

'Mr Rao?' asked one.

'Yes. What can I do for you?'

'Can you come with us? We need to do a dry run at the venue.'

Aditya was surprised. 'Dry run?' He had never heard of events like these doing a dry run. But they were the hosts. He didn't want to offend them. 'Give me five minutes. Let me change into something more appropriate.'

Within five minutes, Aditya was in the lobby. The two men directed him to a waiting car and they got in. Inside the car were two other similarly dressed men, one driving and the other in the passenger seat. The ones in front didn't even bother to acknowledge his presence as the car sped through the streets of DC. It was still early morning. Peak-hour traffic had not yet clogged the streets. In twenty minutes, twenty long and silent minutes, the car entered the basement of a huge building via a side entrance. Aditya couldn't make out where they were.

'Is this the venue?'

No one answered.

'I asked a question!' Aditya said forcefully. No one bothered to answer him or return his glance. 'Is this the way you treat your guests?' He raised his voice just a bit, betraying anger as well as panic. The car came to a halt in a parking lot in the basement, and three of the men got out.

The fourth, to Aditya's right, looked at him and instructed sternly. 'Please get out of the car, Mr Rao.'

That's when it struck Aditya that they may not be representatives of the World Gaming Council. 'Who are you?' he asked, racked with anxiety.

'You will find out soon. Please follow us.' And the last person got out of the car.

Aditya looked around. The basement was empty. He had no option but to get out and follow them. He pulled out his phone to call Sundeep or Varun. No signal. Obviously the building had jammers installed.

Aditya started to sweat.

# 83

# Mumbai

When Aditya had called him from the airport immediately on landing, Varun was still in office. It was late and he was about to leave to pick up Tanya for her birthday dinner. He had promised to take her to Celini, a popular Italian restaurant in the Grand Hyatt in suburban Mumbai. He had already reserved a table for two.

'Are you ready, Tanya?' He called her to check.

'Long ago. Waiting for you. I'm hungry.'

'I will be late by about half an hour, baby. Something has come up. Will finish it and leave. If I don't do it now, it will not get done till Monday.'

'Tell you what. You work. I'll come and pick you.'

Twenty minutes later, she was in Varun's office. He hugged her as she entered his room. 'Come, come, sit . . . I'm just about finishing.' And then he realized his faux pas. 'You are looking soooo . . . ' He couldn't think of the right word. After a moment's pause, he added, '. . . yummy!'

'You had to think that hard?'

'Had to think of the right word, Tanya! Wrong words won't do, especially on this special day.' He smiled, exposing his dimples.

'So you want to go for dinner or you want this yummy babe for dinner?' she asked sensuously. She sat on the sofa and spread her legs seductively, running her fingers up her thighs.

'Come on, Tanya! This is an office,' Varun chided her in jest.

He went close to her, bent down and kissed her on her lips. 'You are looking *wow* today.' Tanya smiled. He kissed her on the lips again. Tanya was in a crazy mood. Though there were a few people in office at that late hour there was no one in sight. She held his head and pulled him towards her as she sucked on his lips. She didn't let him go in a hurry. She ran her free hand up his thighs. She could feel it. He was turned on too. She tried to undo the clasp of his belt.

'Wowowwow! Someone is in an awesome mood today,' joked Varun, as he pulled himself back. 'There are CCTV cameras here, baby.'

'Let's go to the washroom. Come quick!' Tanya got up.

'People around, baby. Can't you see?'

Tanya looked around. She could see some heads, above the workstation dividers.

'Take me somewhere where there are no cameras.' She thought for a second and added, 'Your father's room. Come let's go. It's got a wooden door. I saw it last time.' She took his hand and pulled him towards Aditya's room. There was no one on that floor. They hurried in. She kicked the door shut and locked it. Varun just looked around to make sure they were alone. When he turned back to Tanya, she had already taken off her top and was undoing the zipper of her skirt. Then she was all over him, her mouth, her lips, her hands. In no time, she had pushed him on to the lounge sofa and her hands were fumbling with his belt. The trousers came off, the shirt was ripped off and she was on top of him, riding him. Thankfully, there was no one on the floor. Varun was certain Tanya's moans and groans could be heard all over the floor despite the wooden door.

When they were done, Varun got up. Tanya walked into Aditya's private washroom. While Tanya was inside, Varun got a call from one of his tech guys.

'Hold on, hold on, dude. We can fix this. In fact, you should be calling the gaming director for this.'

Tanya walked out of the washroom, smiling and looking pretty. Varun blew a kiss at her but continued talking.

A few moments later when she tugged at his shirtsleeve, Varun put the phone on mute, and said, 'I'll be back in ten minutes. Then we can leave.' Tanya nodded. Varun walked out and headed down to his cabin.

He returned in a little less than an hour. An irritated Tanya was sitting at Aditya's desk, surfing the net. 'I'm going to become a bored housewife for sure,' she grumbled to herself.

Just then he returned and announced, 'I'm ready to go.'

'Great. After tiring me like you did a while ago, if you don't feed me, I'll collapse any moment,' she said, holding him by his arm as he led her out of the room.

# 84

# Washington DC

Aditya was led into a room with one large window. In the middle of the room stood a rectangular table and three chairs—one on one side of the table and two on the other. He was made to sit on one chair and everyone exited the room.

For the next thirty minutes, he was alone, wondering what could have gone wrong. Why was he going through this? He tried to connect the dots to figure out who these people could be and why they were doing this.

The door opened with a bang and four men walked in. 'Good morning, Mr Rao. You have no idea how excited I am to see you here,' said the man in front. He had a huge smile on his face. Dressed in a grey suit and red tie, he looked a lot more intimidating than the day Aditya had met him in Mumbai.

'Agent Scott? What's going on? Why have I been brought here like a prisoner?'

'Well, well, Mr Rao!' Adrian walked towards him. 'I'm surprised you don't know why you are here.' He placed a hand on Aditya's shoulder and pushed him back in the chair. Gently. 'Please make yourself comfortable. We have a long day ahead.'

'What? I have no idea what you're talking about. Where am I, Agent Scott?'

'Hmm, Mr Rao, let me set some ground rules here. Today, I ask the questions and you give the answers. The day we came to your office, you were very nice to me. It is my turn to reciprocate.'

The sweat was now beginning to make it difficult for Aditya to keep his eyes open. This was the first time he had been in a situation like this. The world had only seen one side of him, that of a law-abiding citizen. Adrian pushed a box of tissues towards him.

'Thank you,' said Aditya and pulled out a couple to wipe his face.

'You seem nervous, Mr Rao.' Adrian was beginning to enjoy this. 'However, given that this is the first question you asked me, I will answer. You are at the FBI office in Washington DC.'

'FBI? Why?' Aditya demanded.

'Didn't you hear me, Mr Rao? I ask the questions today. You will get your answer as we go along. But if we have your permission, Mr Rao, can we begin our . . .' and he paused, '. . . uh, our discussion?'

Aditya didn't even respond. He looked the other way. 'I want a lawyer.'

'Request denied.' Adrian was quick to respond.

'You can't deny me legal aid. It's against the laws in your country.'

'I know the laws of this country better than you, Mr Rao. If it comes to it, we will deal with it.' This response scared Aditya. So did the look on Adrian's face. The agents who came in with Adrian stood by the door. Adrian walked around the table and sat down on one of the chairs on the other side.

'What do you know about bitcoins?'

'Just as much as one could know from newspapers, magazines and web articles.'

'Is that all?

'Unless you know something else that I don't.'

'Do you own bitcoins?'

'No, I don't. But the last time I checked, owning bitcoins is not a crime. Or is it?'

'No, not at all.' Adrian was smirking. 'It's certainly not a crime.' He reiterated, 'So if I hear you correctly, you do not have any bitcoin holdings.'

'No.'

'Ever considered buying or dealing in bitcoins? Interesting, this business, eh?'

'Never. For our gaming company Indiscape, we did consider accepting bitcoins as a means of payment from customers who play our games. But then, due to the enormous state of flux and the volatility of bitcoins, we did not implement that idea. That's the closest we have ever come to bitcoins.'

'Have you heard of Altoids?'

'The mint?'

'I am not particularly in the mood for a joke, Mr Rao.'

'The only Altoids I have heard of is the mint, Agent Scott. What is so funny about that?' Aditya was getting restless.

'Cotton Trail? Does that ring a bell?' Adrian carried on.

The door to the room opened and a fourth agent walked in. He looked at Adrian Scott and spoke. 'Agent Scott, Dan Malloy wants to speak with you.'

'Can you please inform him, politely, that I will be there in thirty minutes?'

# 85

# Mumbai

The staff at Celini had cordoned off a private space for the two of them. Tanya looked ravishing in a short red skirt and a matching top that she had bought from Zara a few days ago. Varun was in smart office casuals. Checked shirt, corduroy jeans, Friday dressing.

Salads, pizza, red wine and tiramisu—this was staple diet for anyone who visited Celini. Tanya loved the pizzas there. In fact, she was the one who had picked the restaurant. The Italian wines they served there would make anyone a fan.

When the clock struck midnight, a clutch of musicians walked up to them and played 'Happy Birthday' on violins. A cake was brought in, and the staff stood around singing along with the music. Tanya was overwhelmed, and teary-eyed. Varun hugged her and wished her. 'One thing I must do when I marry you is figure out a way to stop this constant flow of water!' He joked as he kissed her.

They were there for the next three hours. Tanya was drunk by the time they left. She had no clue about what was going on. Varun held her close as he led her out to the car. Carefully, he seated her in the front seat of the Mercedes, fastened the seat belt and got into the driver's seat. He drove straight to Tanya's apartment complex and walked her up to her apartment. The moment he opened the door, Tanya pulled him towards her and kissed him. Varun kissed her back. She pulled him into the house. Varun kicked the door shut. Hurriedly, she unbuttoned his shirt. It surprised Varun that she was doing all that when she couldn't even hold herself steady or walk straight! But all that didn't matter. He led her to the bedroom and dropped her on the bed. She didn't even wait for him to join her, as she undressed herself. Varun went to the restroom; he was a bit drunk too, and wanted to wash some of it away before he got into bed.

By the time he got back, Tanya was fast asleep. He looked at her and smiled. She did look pretty. He walked out of the room, into the kitchen. He groped around in the cabinet, looking for something to eat. When he heard Tanya moaning in her sleep, he returned to her side. He slipped into bed silently and held her close.

His arms came around and hugged her from behind. His elbows rested on her waist and his palms cupped her breasts. She moaned as she brought up her hands and pulled him closer, begging him to hug her tighter. He moved closer. Her fingers tightened around his even as he gripped her breasts firmly. He could feel her nipples stiffen. She moved her hand a bit.

'Ouch!'

He exclaimed and pulled his hands away. He brought his left hand up and looked at what had caused the momentary pain. There was a deep scratch on his index finger. Blood was oozing out. Wondering what had scratched him, he reached for Tanya's hand. She had no clue what was going on. He turned her hand around and realized what had scratched him. It was the ring on her finger. He reached out for it. He knew Tanya was having some trouble removing it. He twisted it and off it came, almost effortlessly. He pulled it off but then, remembering how emotional she was about it, carefully slipped it back on to her finger.

Varun lay there for a while, eyes wide open. Sleep had deserted him. Thoughts of how the last few months had reshaped his life flashed in front of him. After a while, he suddenly got up as if he had remembered something. He wore his clothes and tiptoed out of the house and walked down the stairs. He didn't want to wake Tanya up. He went down to the parking where his car was parked. From the boot, he pulled out a huge teddy bear. He had initially planned to give it to her on the morning of her birthday. He opened a small niche in the boot and took out a small back object which looked like a battery charger, covered in plastic. He locked the car and was back in the apartment in no time. Tanya was still fast asleep. Drunk. He walked up to her. Without waking her up, he carefully placed the bear next to her and brought her arms around it. She would wake up in the morning cuddling it. He placed the other object in her hand and walked to the kitchen. He was thirsty. He drank a glass of cold water and was wiping his hands when he heard a noise. He hurried back to the bedroom, tissue still in hand and saw that Tanya had turned over; the teddy was in her arms, but other object had fallen down. He walked around the bed, to the other side, tissue still in hand, picked it up and dumped it inside her cupboard. He undressed and slipped into bed with her. The blood had stopped oozing from the scratch on his finger.

The next morning, Tanya woke him. She had nuzzled up to him and was kissing him delicately on his lips, trying to wake him up. 'I love you, Varun,' she said as she sucked Varun's bottom lip into her mouth. Varun smiled.

He wanted to tell her about how her ring had cut his finger but didn't say anything. It was her birthday and he didn't want an uncomfortable conversation.

# 86

# Washington DC

'So where were we, Mr Rao?' asked Adrian, having dealt with the interruption. An evil smile played on his face. 'Ah, bitcoins. We were discussing you and bitcoins.' He paused for a second, evil smile intact. 'Does Cotton Trail ring a bell, Mr Rao?'

'No. I don't know what you are talking about,' Aditya responded.

'Okay, for a minute, let's assume you are speaking the truth.'

'I *am* speaking the truth,' thundered an irritated Aditya.

'Fine, fine. We'll take your word for it. Indiscape is your company, right?'

'Yes, it is.'

'And you own 100 per cent of it.'

'Actually 88.3 per cent. The balance is owned by some friends, investors and a few employees.'

'Wonderful. This makes it easy.' He looked up at Aditya and smiled. 'Townsville?'

'What about it?'

'Very successful game, right? Climbing the charts all over, huh?'

'Yes. It's our game. That's what brought me to the US. We won the award for the best gaming company in emerging markets.'

'For the record, there is no such award.'

'What?' Aditya hollered. What was Adrian talking about? 'I have an invite. They even sent me the ticket.'

'The World Gaming Council meet is on but this award was added at our behest . . .' and, smiling at Aditya, he added, '. . . on paper.'

'What do you mean?'

'It won't be announced at the meet. We had no other way of ensuring that you would come to the US. In India, you would have escaped, given that Indian technology laws are so frivolous and vague.'

'You must be kidding!'

'Does it look like I am?'

Aditya was really worked up by now. This was not a regular interrogation. They had planned it all. He had been tricked into coming to the US so he could be arrested here. But arrested for what?

'But why? What have I done?'

'We will figure that out Mr Rao. Townsville is the most popular game on social media, on smartphones, and in a standalone state. The world knows it. But there is something the world does not know. Something that only you know, Mr Rao.'

Aditya looked at him blankly.

'Why did you do this, Mr Rao? Why? You put out a software update on your game?' Adrian left the question hanging.

'We did release a software update recently. It's a routine process. What about it?'

'Was it only a software update? Or something else?'

'I can't understand what you are getting at, Mr Scott. A software update is a software update. What else can it be?'

'It can be malware too, can't it?'

'What?' Aditya screamed. 'Are you out of your mind?'

'Well perhaps you might have a mind good enough to explain why the update contained a self-replicating virus, which spread to every single computer, smartphone and tablet that your customers played your game on.'

'My company is one of the most honest you can find in the entire Indian subcontinent!'

'Guess that's why the guys behind the ATM heist chose your company to hack into. Or did you help them . . .? Anyway, we will come to that later. Your virus scanned millions of computers for bitcoins. When it found any, it identified the private key of the bitcoin wallet and transferred all the bitcoins to an unknown wallet. And that unknown wallet can only be yours, Mr Aditya Rao.'

'Rubbish!' Aditya hollered. 'I'd rather die than do anything like that.' People had called him names in the past, had been offended by many of his actions, but there was one thing which no one had ever dared to call him—a cheat.

'Not only did your virus scan computers for bitcoin wallets, but it also made the computers and smartphones join a Ukraine-based network. Once connected to the network, the malware downloaded bitcoin mining software and ran that on the computer. Bitcoin mining is a computationally heavy process so what better than to combine the computing powers of a million smartphones and hundreds of thousands of laptops across the globe and get them to mine bitcoins for you. Brilliant, I must confess. How did you have the confidence that you won't get caught?'

Aditya's hands went up to his face. 'No! No! You've made a mistake.'

'This is what has happened, Mr Rao. Under your instructions. Using your password. From your network.'

'Impossible!'

Adrian handed Aditya a piece of paper with an IP address on it. 'Your game is hosted on the Ukrainian server and a few other mirror servers around the world. The software update, which included the malware, was uploaded from this IP address on to the Ukrainian server. The upload was authorized using your ID from this IP address.'

Aditya was shocked. His face turned red with anger and embarrassment.

'Don't pretend, Mr Rao. Let me put this on the record. I'm not talking to you here because of this malware. We checked it out. Your legal agreement—the terms and conditions that every gamer has to accept before he can play your game—covers you. It even says that any gains on account of this will be entirely yours.'

'I don't think we specifically put that in the T&C. Ours is a standard T&C that most gaming corporations the world over use.'

'True. All you gaming companies fuck with five condoms. Right? Cover yourself for every breach. The legal terminology will let you escape there. But what's more important, Mr Rao, is what you will tell us now. What is your role in Cotton Trail?'

'I haven't even heard of it, Agent Scott. When will you believe me?'

'Are you one of the promoters of Cotton Trail?'

Aditya didn't respond. He looked the other way.

'Who is "Altoids"?'

'How would I know?' Aditya raised his voice.

'You know damn well, Mr Rao.'

'No, I don't. How many times do you want me to tell you?'

'Frosty?'

'What Frosty?'

'Who is Frosty, Mr Rao?'

'I have no clue.' Aditya was on the verge of breaking down.

'Have you killed anyone, Mr Rao?' Adrian thundered.

'Never!'

'Are you sure?'

'Never more sure.'

'Gillian Tan?'

'Who is Gillian Tan?'

'You murdered Senator Tan a few months ago!' Adrian yelled at him, then whispered into his ears, 'Did you enjoy the sound of the blast that killed him? Don't you remember, Mr Rao?'

'Enough!' Aditya screamed as he got up from his chair.

'Sit down or I will have to restrain you!'

The threat worked and Aditya sat back. 'Agent Scott, I don't know how to get you to believe me. The names you are dropping don't mean anything to me. You are barking up the wrong tree.'

'How is it then that the malware got uploaded from your ID?

'I don't check the technical details of every software that is uploaded.'

'Okay, accepted. But how is it then that Altoids logged in from your laptop, from your wi-fi network and posted updates and messages regarding Cotton Trail and bitcoins?'

'My wi-fi? My ID?'

'Yes. I showed you the IP address, Mr Rao. Altoids logged into a VPN network from that IP address and posted details about bitcoins. The same Altoids has been all over the net promoting Cotton Trail. Can you explain this? If you are not the promoter of Cotton Trail, what's your motivation in spreading awareness about Cotton Trail, Mr Rao.' Adrian paused. A grin came up on his face. 'Or should I say . . . Mr Altoids?'

'Someone else could have misused it.'

'In the normal course we would believe this, Mr Rao. But given that the malware was also uploaded from your ID, your defence doesn't seem to be so airtight. Especially when the only person using that exclusive wi-fi network in your office is you.'

'My conscience is clear.'

'So is the evidence,' said Adrian.

Suddenly, the door swung open and Dan walked in.

'What the hell is the problem with you, Adrian? I've been trying to reach you for a while.' He looked at Aditya and smiled. 'Give us a minute, Mr Rao.' And he pulled Adrian out of the room.

The moment they were out, Dan said, 'He is not the one we are looking for.'

'Dan, you are much smarter than that. Have you fallen for his innocent looks?'

'No. Altoids just signed in and sent us a message. He is willing to engage. To figure out how to get to the missing characters in the bitcoin private key.'

'What?'

'Yes. The message was sent a few hours ago in response to our post. And this fellow has been in your custody since before then. How can he be in your custody and send messages at the same time?'

'Dan you pulled us out of India because you felt that if we interrogated this guy in India, particularly after the gaming malware became known, we would hit a dead end. Now, after all this, you are asking us to let him go?'

'It is what it is, Adrian.' He shrugged. 'Someone is clearly playing this guy.'

'Now what do we do with him?'

'Let him go,' Dan recommended.

'No. He knows quite a bit through the interrogation. If he is the one being played, let's use him to help us.'

# 87

# Washington DC

Aditya was in his room at the Ritz. For the last twenty-four hours he had been holed up in his room. He had stepped out only once to attend the World Gaming Council event. In fact, Indiscape was even awarded the prize for being the 'best gaming company in emerging markets'. Adrian had felt guilty for having put Aditya through the trauma and had impressed upon the organizers to go ahead with the award. Given that the instruction came from the highest level in the FBI, the organizers obliged. Aware of this, Aditya didn't even bother going up to the dais.

Adrian had apologized profusely to Aditya but Aditya was a worried man. Someone was taking advantage of his organization, his reputation. Someone was playing him. It had turned out to be far more serious than what he had imagined. The assassination of a sitting senator, bitcoins, Cotton Trail, malware—these were not issues to be taken lightly.

So when Adrian requested him to stay back for a few more days, to help the FBI in their investigation, he readily agreed. In return, he wanted them to help fix issues that seemed to have crept into his company. The FBI agreed and instructed him not to share their observations with anyone in the company as that might hamper their investigation. This was the reason why Aditya was in his room that day, watching TV. Fox News, the ultimate gossip channel in the garb of mainstream news, was playing on loop. By afternoon, the main news programmes had disappeared and the channel shifted to the latest expose by the Hooker which had the nation in its grip.

An entire thirty-minute slot was dedicated to the Hooker hullabaloo. He was not sure if it was a regular affair or got thirty minutes that day because there were multiple disclosures. Fox didn't name the three individuals who the hooker claimed to have bedded, because they were influential people and the news could not be verified.

The news programme had intrigued Aditya. He walked up to his laptop, keyed in the URL of her blog, brought it up on his screen, and started reading. He started with the latest one. The post was quite scandalous and Aditya found he was very turned on by it. As he read further his eyes grew wide. Was she lying? Or was she writing the truth?

He walked up to the phone and placed a call.

'Good . . .'

'Good afternoon, Agent Scott. It's Aditya Rao.' He didn't even wait for Adrian to complete the greeting.

'Mr Rao, I was about to come and see you today.'

'Please do. It would be great to have a drink together in the evening.'

'Yeah, I'll drop in.'

'I was reading the latest in the *Confessions of the Hooker* series.'

'It isn't healthy to read trash at this age, Mr Rao,' said Adrian, chuckling.

'Agent Scott, if it is good enough to do it at his age, it is definitely good enough to read at mine. Have you read the latest confession? Please read it right away, then call me.' He hung up.

Within five minutes, Adrian called back. 'Holy motherfucker! Where did this come from?'

'Is our drink on, Agent Scott?'

'Yes, of course. Twenty minutes.'

# 88

# Mumbai

After spending the birthday weekend with Tanya, Varun was back at work on Monday morning.

As usual, he logged in to his laptop and pulled up the weekly sales MIS. It gave him the number of Townsville downloads every day, from the time Indiscape had put it up on the app store.

At first glance, the MIS didn't look too good. Weekly sales had dropped... in excess of 30 per cent over the previous week! He broke it down. From Monday to Friday, sales were steady. On Saturday, sales went up. They normally did on a weekend. But Sunday shocked him. Sales were down by 80 per cent as compared to Saturday. In the normal course, Sunday sales of gaming apps either tracked Saturday sales or, in certain cases, were higher. An 80 per cent drop meant something was surely wrong.

He logged in to the app store to check. The details were there. The price was there. The reviews were there . . .

The download button was missing.

Anyone who visited the app store and searched for Townsville would find it, but would not be able to download it.

'WHAT THE FUCK!?' he shouted. He could be heard throughout the corridors of Indiscape. He called his secretary. 'Get the Townsville gaming director in my room right away,' he hollered into the phone.

Within five minutes, the director responsible for Townsville was in his room, laptop and lunch bag in hand. 'Sorry, sir. I was in the parking lot, when your secretary called. I came straight to meet you.'

'We have a problem with the Townsville app. The download button is missing on the online store.'

'I'll check it out, sir. Give me ten minutes.'

In two minutes, Varun got a call on his office line.

'Sir, it's not a problem with the Apple store alone. We are facing issues on Facebook too. We are checking it out.'

'On Facebook too?'

'Yes, sir. It does not load. Whenever someone clicks on the Townsville link on Facebook, it returns a blank screen.'

'Damn. So no one has downloaded or played Townsville for sixteen hours now. This in a disaster. All the effort we have put in to popularize the game will come to naught. Everything will collapse if users cannot and do not play the game. Do you get it? Hurry up and fix the problem!' He was yelling.

'Yes, sir. You don't worry, sir. I will put the team on the job.'

A few minutes later, Varun was sitting in his chair, elbows on the table, palms covering his face, when the phone rang again.

'Sir, I checked with the folks at Apple. They say it's an error and they will look into it.'

'Did they give a timeline?'

'Twenty-four hours for resolution.'

'That's too long. What about Facebook?'

'Their link with the Ukrainian server has collapsed. We are providing them with alternative server details. They will connect to those to restore service.'

'Why the fuck didn't we have multiple servers connecting to Facebook mainframes in the first place? Isn't that the normal business continuity protocol?'

'That's the way it was programmed. Strangely now when we check, the connectivity to Facebook is only through three servers located in Latvia, Ukraine and California. It was supposed to be twelve as per the initial program. We are looking into how this happened.'

'Put your star performer on the job. The guy who debugged your program in three hours. He is still working for us, right?'

'Yes, sir. He is.'

'And how long will Facebook take to restore connectivity?'

'Four to five hours is what they've committed. But judging by past experience it can stretch to beyond twelve hours.'

'We will be fucked! Our screw-ups give customers a chance to sample the competition. In business, when you're ahead, hold your customers tight. Don't lose sight of them for even a moment. The only way to hold on to them is by giving them so much that they just don't have the time to look at the competition. Because if one customer switches, and begins to like the competitor's product, chances are that all our other customers may like it too.'

Varun got up and walked to the third floor to Sundeep's room. In Aditya's absence, he had to keep Sundeep informed. 'Let's fix it and move ahead,' was all that Sundeep said. Their relationship, dismal as it had been, had broken down completely after the bots fiasco.

As he was walking down the corridor to the staircase, he looked up. There were over 200 people working on that floor, some on gaming, some on eTIOS, and others on a new project Aditya had begun. He looked around. Many of them were alien to him. This was not a floor he normally came to. As he looked around, he saw one familiar face. And then he turned and walked back to his office.

Back in his room, Varun called Aditya but couldn't get through. He tried calling him on the hotel landline but there was no answer. Varun left a voice message, asking him to call back.

# 89

# Mumbai

Moments later Varun received a call from Ukraine. It lasted for a few minutes and was interspersed with furious gesticulation. By the end of it, Varun's face was red with anger. He had to do something. Quickly.

After thinking for a few minutes, he called Aditya's cellphone again. Aditya didn't pick up, so he called again letting the phone ring. He was losing patience when he heard Aditya's voice. 'Hi, Varun.'

'Dad! Hi.'

'What's up, Son? I was sleeping.'

'I figured that, Dad. But there seems to be a problem.'

'What happened? Is everything okay between you and Tanya?'

'Yes, Dad. No issues on that front.'

'Then?'

'Is there a problem in the US?'

'No. Why?' asked Aditya, calmly.

'Because you extended your trip.'

'I just extended it by a few days. Felt like meeting a few of my old friends. Remember I worked here many many years ago.'

'I can understand, Dad. But we've had some problems here.'

'What problems?'

'Did Sundeep uncle call you?'

'Oh, that problem. Yes he called me. It will set itself right. You guys are overreacting.'

'No, Dad. We are not overreacting.'

'Relax, Varun.'

'It's the FBI, Dad.'

'What?'

'Yes, Dad. It's the FBI. Townsville has been pulled out from the servers and Facebook on instructions from the FBI.'

'How can you be so sure?' Aditya was very curious, because the FBI had assured him complete secrecy. They had also promised that once Aditya's team cleansed the game, they would not have any issue with it being reloaded on to those servers.

'The company that we have made an offer to buy, in Ukraine, is a minor stakeholder in the company that owns the server space.'

'Oh?'

'I checked with them.'

'And what did they tell you?'

'The FBI apparently asked them to shut down the access to our app on their servers. So people logging in to our game will not be able to play. The official line as dictated by the FBI is that it's a technical snag. Because they can't just pull down anyone's access to a server outside their jurisdiction. I suspect Facebook too has been given the same story and they are parroting the FBI's line.'

'Damn! That's not a good sign.' Aditya swore into the phone.

Varun thought his tone was strange. 'Dad, did you know this was going to happen?'

The question caught Aditya off guard. 'What kind of a question is that?'

'Sorry, perhaps I'm confused. In any case, when are you coming?'

'This weekend.' That was the end of the discussion.

Tanya came to visit him in office that evening. When he told her the issue he was facing, she was concerned too. She called off their dinner plans and decided to head back home.

# 90

# Washington DC

Aditya didn't feel good about lying to Varun. He didn't have a choice, though, since his calls were being monitored by the FBI. He wanted the entire episode to end. It was causing him more damage than anything else had in his whole life.

There was a knock at the door. 'Agent Scott!' he exclaimed, surprised to find Adrian standing there so soon after he had left earlier that evening. Is everything okay?

'I need to ask you some questions.'

'About what?' Aditya said as he moved aside and let Adrian in. Adrian walked to the sofa next to the window and settled down. He picked up an apple from a fruit bowl on the table in front of him and bit into it. 'I haven't had dinner.' He volunteered an explanation.

'Do you want to go down to the coffee shop and grab a bite?'

'If you don't mind, can you order a chicken club sandwich for me? I'll have it here.'

Aditya nodded and walked up to the telephone. 'What's wrong? Obviously something is bothering you. And you are figuring out how to ask me without offending me again.'

'Are you in any way involved in the murder of the CEO of NYIB?'

'Malvika? Oh no! For God's sake!'

'Why then?'

'Why what?'

'Why then do we have a request from the Mumbai Crime

Branch, routed through the CBI, to make sure that you return to India on time?'

'Is that normal? Is the FBI bound to comply? Just asking out of academic interest, for I don't intend to do anything stupid.'

'Well, no. But the request has also been forwarded to the US government through your home ministry. You seem to be in a terrible mess, my friend. All I could gather from them is that it's about that CEO of the bank involved in the ATM heist.'

'So', Aditya looked at him, 'what now?'

'Nothing. Tomorrow you will head back. Tony will accompany you. I'll join you in a day. Something seems to be cooking there. I have some work in California.'

'California?'

'Yes. Following up a case lead there.'

'Anything to do with *Confessions of the Hooker*?'

Adrian shrugged non-committally, as he walked out of the room. 'See you in Mumbai,' he said just before the door shut.

# 91

# Mumbai

Aditya landed in Mumbai in the wee hours of Friday. The CBI team picked him up from the airport and whisked him away. No one even knew that he had returned to the country.

A day later, early in the morning, a team of CBI officers swooped down on Sundeep Srivastava's residence and packed him off in an unmarked van. His wife protested, threatened to call influential people, but before she could do anything of the sort, Sundeep was gone.

Varun was at Tanya's that night. He'd just woken up and was having a morning cup of tea when a team of officers knocked at the door. In no time, Tanya and Varun were speeding towards the CBI office in Bandra-Kurla Complex. All their questions went unanswered, all their protests unheard. The officials said that all would be revealed once they reached their destination.

ACP Shome from Mumbai Police's cyber crime cell and Tony were in the room when Tanya, Varun and Sundeep were brought in.

'I know you want answers. Give us five minutes, and we'll explain everything,' ACP Shome announced to the group when he sensed the simmering tension. 'The CBI regional director will be here.'

The five minutes stretched to ten. An hour passed. Nothing happened. The three of them sat huddled in a corner, occasionally talking to each other but largely brooding, wondering where things were headed.

Finally, at 2.30 p.m., a good four hours after they had arrived, the door swung open and three people walked in

'Aditya?' Sundeep exclaimed, while the other two looked on. 'When did you get back?'

'Hi, Sundeep. I got back yesterday,' Aditya said. His eyes were trained on Varun, who was surprised to hear his response. He didn't offer any explanation about why he didn't get in touch with anyone. Varun kept staring at him, wondering what was going on.

The person next to Aditya began, 'My name is Adrian Scott and I am with the FBI.'

'Kabir Khan, CBI.' The regional director introduced himself.

'Okay, let's begin.' Kabir started off brusquely. 'Folks, we have a few questions to ask you. We can either do this the easy way or make it difficult. If we do it easy, we can finish our work quickly and head home in time for dinner.'

No one spoke.

'Okay, first question. Was Malvika Sehgal, the CEO of NYIB, murdered or did she commit suicide?'

'I told you and your CBI, she was murdered,' Tanya said angrily. 'The minister was using my mom. She aspired to become the RBI governor. He promised her the post and then went back on his word. I think she threatened to expose his misdeeds to the entire world, so he killed her. Even if he didn't physically kill her, he was definitely responsible for driving her overboard.'

'Had you ever seen your mother with the minister?' asked Kabir.

Tanya thought for a minute. The CBI had asked her this question earlier too. She shook her head. 'No.' She looked at Varun. This was exactly what he had told her too.

'Isn't your accusation based on hearsay? How can you insinuate, without evidence, that a person of this stature would be involved in such a crime?'

'Doesn't matter what I think. The minister himself confessed that he liked my mom and that he cared for her.'

'Is that what made you accuse the finance minister of being romantically involved with Malvika?'

'He confessed to it! He visited us after mom's death and said that he was extremely fond of her.' Tanya vociferously defended her earlier hypothesis. 'He said that had things gone on well for another six months, the two of them would have got married.'

'Come to think of it, it could also be because he wanted to justify to you why he couldn't have killed your mom, Tanya!' Varun butted in. Tanya glared at him.

'If I'm wrong then how do you explain those long conversations with the finance minister, sometimes stretching late into the night? On days when I was travelling, I'd find that someone had visited her at home and stayed over. One can tell what's going on in one's house.'

'Yes, you can,' Kabir agreed, 'but you assumed that it was the minister. We have checked Malvika's mobile history. Not a single call to the minister was made at any inappropriate time of the day. How do you account for that? And the minister has denied that his relationship with Malvika was anything but professional.'

'He is a liar. Are you on his payroll? Why are you defending him?' Tanya pounced on him. Kabir didn't like the way Tanya was talking to him. 'My mother is dead. And he killed her! Why don't you question him?' Tanya was getting hysterical. 'Or at least let us confront him.'

'I don't think there is any need to ask the finance minister about it, Tanya,' Aditya spoke for the first time. 'Because . . .' and he paused, searching for the right word, '. . . because,' he repeated. 'Because it was me. It was I who visited her when you weren't at home. The half-empty whisky glasses that you saw were mine.'

# 92

# Mumbai

Tanya was shocked.

She pointed at Aditya, her mouth wide open. 'You?'

'Yes.' Aditya nodded.

'Were the two of you in a relationship?'

Aditya nodded again. 'And I'm not ashamed of it.'

'No! No! That's not what I meant. You are, in any case, a far superior man than the finance minister.'

'Who are we to comment on that? Anyway, we stopped seeing each other a month ago. It was a mutual decision but it was harder on her. And as far as the finance minister is concerned, I guess I should have mentioned this to the CBI earlier. *She* was using the minister, not the other way around. He was always under the impression that he and Malvika were in a relationship. As far as she was concerned, the only reason she entertained him was because he was her ticket to a position on the RBI board, possibly leading to the position of governor. He was her pawn.'

'Why did you stop seeing each other?' Kabir asked.

'Seeing the two of them get close . . .' and he pointed towards Varun and Tanya, '. . . I told her that we needed to put an end to our relationship.'

Tanya looked at Varun. He was taken aback by this turn of events. He had no idea how to react.

'Just imagine if we'd gone ahead with our relationship . . . What would the two of you have done? What would you call yourself?

Stepbrother and stepsister? Siblings in an incestuous relationship? What? There was no option. We had to call it off. I was clear. She supported the decision. But I guess it was too much stress for her . . . Perhaps she cracked.'

'Why didn't you tell us earlier?' Varun asked.

'What could I have told you?'

Varun had no answer.

'This is a good enough precedent for us to assume that she committed suicide on her birthday.' ACP Shome tried to take things to their logical conclusion. 'A failed relationship.'

'No, it isn't.' Aditya was very vocal. 'She couldn't have committed suicide that day.'

'And why is that?' Kabir asked. His tone indicated that he was holding his cards close to his chest.

'Because, that night, she planned to ask Tanya if she was serious about Varun. We had planned to go out with Tanya and Varun after the party. Just the four of us. Fifteen minutes before she died, she reminded me. If she intended to commit suicide, why would she remind me that we had plans after the party?'

Sundeep, who had been very quiet all this while, finally spoke out. 'How come you never mentioned any of this to us, Aditya? We thought there were no secrets between us. First it was Varun who came as a surprise and now this.' His tone was rather accusatory.

'Neither you nor Swami liked Malvika. My relationship with her could have affected our equations. So I chose to be silent about it. And Malvika was extremely uncomfortable about me speaking about it. Wouldn't you respect your partner's point of view?'

'Enough of this family drama, folks! Let's move on with our next question. Assuming there was foul play involved, how was she murdered?' Kabir kept up the inquisition. 'And why?'

When no one responded, Kabir elaborated, 'The last few people who spent time with Malvika were the minister, Aditya, Tanya, Varun, Sundeep and Swami, who is dead. All of you present here were among the last few to see her alive.'

Everyone nodded.

'The post-mortem didn't indicate any struggle or any other telltale signs of murder. So it was very easy to assume that Malvika had jumped off the building,' Kabir Khan continued.

'Which is what we did.' Shome made his presence felt.

'But was it?' Kabir looked at everyone in the room and asked. Everyone looked back at him. Then he looked at Aditya alone.

'As I said earlier, it couldn't have been a suicide,' reiterated Aditya. 'But why and how she was killed, I have no clue. I do not know!'

'What I do not know, I do not think I know,' said Adrian, smiling at Kabir. Kabir smiled back. He had a look of arrogant authority on his face.

'Five hundred years before Christ lived a Greek philosopher. A philosopher who changed the way the Western world thought. Who altered their mindset. He felt that wrongdoing was a consequence of ignorance and those who committed wrong knew no better. Do you know who I'm talking about?' Kabir asked the group.

'Socrates?' Sundeep responded. He had read about it in school, but wasn't sure whether it was Socrates or Aristotle.

'Bingo!' Adrian said, excited. 'Socrates. 479 BC. Very impressive, Mr Srivastava, I must admit. Then you must know how he died.'

'He was killed by the state. Sentenced to death. The charge against him: corrupting the youth of Athens and impiety—not believing in the gods of the state.'

'Yes. He was a hero to many but a villain to a few knowledgeable souls. He was given many chances to flee, to escape death. But he stayed put and paid for it with his life,' Kabir added stoically. 'But my question was how he died, not why he died. You see, Mr Srivastava. How? Why? There's a difference.'

'What's the connection, Officer?' Tanya asked.

'Wait, my nightingale. We have only just begun. We have a long way to go. Let me first complete my story, then I will sing an "Ode to a Nightingale".' Kabir's voice was full of ridicule. Tanya was extremely peeved. But there was little she could do about it so she looked the other way.

'Ah. "Ode to a Nightingale". John Keats. Wonderful! I didn't know that the CBI had a poetic touch to it. I'm very impressed,' said Adrian. He rattled off the opening verse:

My heart aches, and a drowsy numbness pains
My sense, as though of hemlock I had drunk,
Or emptied some dull opiate to the drains
One minute past, and Lethe-wards had sunk:

'Hold on, Mr Scott, hold on! How dare you steal my thunder?' Kabir chided Adrian in jest. He walked up to his briefcase, which was on the table, and opened it. He pulled out a plastic pouch and held it up. Inside were egg-shaped seeds. They were flat-sided, two-sectioned, greenish-brown, about quarter of a centimetre long, and thick-ridged with protuberances. Holding the pouch high above his head, he shook it vigorously. 'This is a bonus round. Anyone knows what this is?'

There was silence in the room.

'No one?'

Silence again.

Kabir looked at Adrian and said, in a mocking manner, 'Either they are too smart or complete idiots. What do you think?'

'I think they are too smart.'

'Well, for the moment, let's pretend they are not smart.'

'Mr Srivastava, what were you saying about Socrates? Do you know how he died?'

'Not sure. He was executed. That's all I know.'

'Ah . . . yeah, he was indeed.' He turned to his right. 'And Nightingale, would you know how he died?'

'Don't call me nightingale,' Tanya snapped.

Kabir's eyebrows went up. 'Aaah! 'My apologies, Ms Sehgal. I'm very sorry. Now you tell me, do you know how he died?'

'No, I do not.'

'Well, am I mad? How can I expect you to remember how Socrates died 2500 years ago?'

'History has it well captured, Mr Khan,' Adrian interrupted again. Much to Kabir's displeasure. Whether it was a choreographed act or genuine disappointment and anger, one couldn't make out. Irrespective, Adrian went on. He pulled out a tablet from his bag, touched a few buttons, looked at the screen, and started reading. 'Well, this is how Pluto describes Socrates on his death bed in *Phaedo*:

*The man . . . laid his hands on him and after a while examined his feet and legs, then pinched his foot hard and asked if he felt it. He said 'No'; then after that, his thighs; and passing upwards in this way he showed us that he was growing cold and rigid. And then again he touched him and said that when it reached his heart, he would be gone. The chill had now reached the region about the groin, and uncovering his face, which had been covered, he said—and these were his last words—'Crito, we owe a rooster to Asclepius. Pay it and do not neglect it.' 'That,' said Crito, 'shall be done; but see if you have anything else to say.' To this question he made no reply, but after a little while he moved; the attendant uncovered him; his eyes were fixed. And Crito when he saw it, closed his mouth and eyes. Socrates was dead.*

And Adrian made a face as if one of his own had passed away. He looked up from his tablet. 'Well, 2500 years pass and the means of killing remain the same.'

Varun, who had been silent all along, finally spoke. 'I am sorry, sir. You are wasting our time here. None of us can understand anything you are saying.'

Kabir screamed, 'What did you say? Wasting your time? Fuck you, young man! We have wasted our time following up on this ridiculous drama and you can't indulge us for five minutes. We have indulged all of you for so fucking long!'

Adrian walked up to him and patted his back.

Kabir shrugged him off and paced around the room like a man possessed. He was in top form now. He sniffed hard, looked up and down intermittently, and finally took a deep breath and settled down. He still had the packet in his hand. He raised it up again, pointed to it, and sniffed hard again. And then, he said, in a very matter-of-fact manner, 'This is what killed Malvika.'

# 93

# Mumbai

'What is that?' Aditya asked.

Everyone had the same question but couldn't muster the courage to ask.

'Hemlock seeds.'

'Hemlock seeds?' Aditya exclaimed.

'A herbaceous biennial bushy plant. Largely found in Europe, Africa and parts of Asia. Seeds of the hemlock plant are extremely poisonous. A small dose is enough to kill a person.'

'Hemlock seeds are also called conium, from the scientific name *Conium maculatum.* It derives its name from the Greek word *konas,* which means "vertigo", one of the symptoms of ingestion of hemlock seeds,' explained Adrian. 'Remember what Keats said in his poem... "My heart aches, and a drowsy numbness pains, My sense, as though of hemlock I had drunk" . . .?'

Kabir nodded. 'Socrates was killed using hemlock seeds. He voluntarily drank the poison he was administered. Malvika, however, drank the poison, or rather ate the poison unknowingly.' He paused. He wanted to observe the reactions in the room.

'The most important chemical in hemlock seeds is coniine. Coniine causes death by blocking the neuromuscular junction. This results in an ascending muscular paralysis, which begins in the feet and rises up, eventually killing the person when it reaches the heart. Remember Pluto's description of Socrates death. That's what happened to Malvika. But before it could reach her heart, she fell because of the instability caused by the paralysis of her lower limbs. The low parapet of the terrace didn't help. You see, 2500 years have passed since the day poor Socrates was killed, but things haven't changed even today!'

# 94

# Mumbai

'We'll talk about Socrates later,' said Kabir, and looked at Adrian. 'You want to take it from here?'

Adrian turned and looked at everyone in the room. 'Satoshi Nakamoto? Anyone?'

'The bitcoin founder?' asked Varun,

'It is widely suspected to be a pseudonym. No one knows who he is. And, strangely, the name is a combination of four Japanese technology companies: sa from Samsung, toshi from Toshiba, naka from Nakamichi, and moto from Motorola. Obviously, someone who goes by this name has a fascination for Japanese products or technology.'

'What has Satoshi Nakamoto got to do with Malvika?' Aditya asked.

'Well, nothing,' said Adrian. 'Over the last few weeks, a blogger going by the name "Hooker" has been creating fair bit of excitement through her *Confessions of a Hooker* blog. The post has the rich and famous worried that their names might be on the list. No one knows who the Hooker is, so no one knows if they are next. This weekend, the Hooker released a mega post, which linked her to three celebrities: an NBA player, a Hollywood star and a politician. One senator Gillian Tan.'

Aditya smiled with pride. After all he was the one who had pointed it out to Adrian.

'Do you guys know him?' Adrian asked.

'Yeah, I heard about the assassination,' Tanya volunteered.

'Me too. I read about it in the papers,' Sundeep meekly responded.

'Gillian Tan was very close to the President of the US. Anything that affected his stature could directly or indirectly affect the position of the President. When he was assassinated, we searched his residence for clues that could lead us to his killers. But we did not find anything. This time around, after the Hooker's confession, the President got worried and asked us to reinvestigate. We got moving quickly.'

Everyone in the room looked blank. They didn't know what was going on.

'We scanned Gillian's house. His regular laptop, which we seized the first time around, didn't contain anything sensational. But when we did a second search of his house, we found a niche in his study table. A niche wide enough to hold a MacBook Air. Tucked away under three layers of encryption in the MacBook was data that was enough to nail anyone.'

'And what was that?' Kabir mock-asked him. They were clearly having fun.

'I'll come to that soon,' said Adrian and carried on. 'Gillian was a visiting faculty at Stanford, his alma mater. He'd been teaching there for the past decade. Though for the last six months, his appearances had become less frequent. That can be put down to senatorial duties.'

Everyone in the room seemed to be following.

'Four years ago, Gillian pulled out three top students and commissioned a secret, privately funded project without approval from the university. And what was the outcome of this project?' He looked at everyone, building the suspense. 'The entire plan, the paper documenting every minute detail about bitcoins, the operations, its issuance, market pricing methodology, transactions, verification of the transactions, the mining of bitcoins, etc. This project was where it all began. This group invented bitcoins.'

Everyone was shell-shocked.

'A cryptography expert in his younger days, Gillian Tan was

Satoshi Nakamoto.' Again he paused and looked around before continuing. 'He was the head of the classified committee on alternate currency, which was debating the value of currencies like bitcoins. We don't know if it was sheer coincidence or whether he lobbied for that position.'

Varun countered, 'Pardon me for saying this, but I don't understand completely. The data that was found could also have been on his computer because he was heading this committee for the US government.'

'Fair point,' Adrian agreed. 'This is where the Hooker comes in. There was something strange in the Hooker blog post that came out last week.' And he turned towards Aditya and pointed at him. 'Rather, he found something strange in the post.'

Varun nodded. Aditya was looking directly at him. Adrian continued, 'According to the blog, Gillian took time to warm up to her. The hooker had a pet name for Gillian—Frosty.' Seeing the blank look on the faces of those present, he added, 'Quite a strange pet name. Frosty is also the alias used by someone to promote Cotton Trail.'

'Cotton Trail?' Sundeep asked.

Aditya quickly detailed it out for him.

'As if cryptography and Frosty were not enough, the Hooker also explicitly described her rendezvous with Gillian and a third person, in the dorm at Stanford.'

'A threesome? Wow!' ACP Shome's eyes lit up.

Adrian looked around to see if there were any nervous faces in the crowd.

'Cotton Trail, cryptography, Stanford, Frosty . . . It was too much of a coincidence for us to ignore. We at the FBI believe that there are no coincidences. So we visited Stanford. It didn't take us long to figure out that Gillian Tan was a colourful man. His proximity to the President had protected him all his life. We discovered that he was particularly friendly with that one student, whose dorm he used to visit often. Even took the Hooker along with him. Of course, he took care to ensure that no one saw him enter or leave, but you know how college students are. They figured everything out. They are smart. But no one spoke about it, given his stature.'

Adrian turned to ACP Shome and said, 'Some coffee would be nice. Possible?'

'Of course! Let me organize it for you.' He looked at the others. 'Coffee anyone?' All hands went up. 'I should have asked earlier!' He smiled and went out, even as Adrian continued speaking.

'Coming back to the MacBook . . . There were names of three Stanford students on the encrypted report we found on Gillian's laptop. And guess what? Of the three, two are dead.'

# 95

# Mumbai

'One was a Japanese guy, found hanging in the dorm. Another, who was thrown out of Stanford, got into the line of fire. Decided to make love to a bullet fired by my man Tony. Eerie, isn't it?'

'You said there were three?' Kabir was now getting into the act.

'Yeah, that's correct.'

'One committed suicide.'

'That's what the official records say.'

'One you killed.'

'We didn't shoot to kill. He tried to murder Nikki Tan.'

'Where is the third?' Kabir asked.

'That's why we are here.'

'Meaning?' ACP Shome's face turned white. He turned and looked at the others in the room.

Adrian looked at him and nodded. 'Yeah, you are right.'

'Holy motherfucker!' ACP Shome exclaimed. 'Who?'

Everyone looked at each other. No one spoke.

'The Hooker's threesome with Gillian was in a dorm occupied by the third student. The only living person among the group of the four bitcoin founders. Someone who had 3 per cent attendance on days when Gillian was at Stanford but 99 per cent attendance otherwise. A person who, Gillian was in constant contact with even after leaving campus. A person who goes by the name of Altoids in cyberspace. And this is not speculation. Decrypting Gillian's laptop gave us all this information using which we were able to narrow down our list of suspects to one person who could possibly be Altoids.'

At that precise moment, the door flew open and Tony walked in. In his hand was a laptop. With him was a representative of the crime cell of Mumbai Police, who saluted when he saw ACP Shome. Tony went to Adrian and whispered something. The stress lines on Adrian's forehead relaxed. He smiled. When Tony was done, he looked at everyone in the room and spoke.

'Gentlemen and lady, we know who Altoids is. Until now we suspected one individual. Now we have evidence. Will the real Altoids please stand up?'

No one stood.

Adrian walked up to where all of them were seated. 'You want me to tell you? I have no problem with that.' He shrugged and stopped with Aditya to his right. He turned. It was like the elimination round of a reality show on TV. Then, he pointedly looked at the person sitting next to Aditya.

'Why?' he said. 'Why did you do all this? Was this just about bitcoins? Or was it something else?'

# 96

# Mumbai

'That's a lie!' Tanya yelled at the top of her voice.

Varun looked at Aditya, wondering what was going on.

'How can you accuse me of being involved in this bitcoin scam?' Tanya screamed. She was angry. And it showed.

'And more. You also killed your mother,' Kabir announced.

'Oh my God!' Her hands flew to her lips.

'Hmm, yes. If that means anything to you.'

'Nonsense. I loved my mom. Why would I kill her?'

'Your mother was only one of the people you killed, Tanya. We will come to that in a bit. First, let's examine how you killed her.'

Kabir looked straight at her.

'You are ruining my reputation without any evidence. I will haul your backside over burning coals!' Tanya was furious.

'Wait, wait, wait!' Kabir walked to his briefcase and pulled out another plastic pouch. Like earlier, he held it high up in the air and shook it for those present in the room to see.

'Wasabi,' Sundeep muttered. 'Wasabi-flavoured nuts?'

'Yes, wasabi nuts. What were they doing in your house, Tanya?'

'What kind of question is that? My mom loved everything wasabi-flavoured. And she always had it with her drink.'

'I know that. But how did this get into your house?' He pointed to the packet in his hand and asked her, 'These nuts? How did they get in? They were seized last week during the raid.'

'I told you. Mom must have brought them.'

Kabir held the packet out and asked, 'Would you like to eat one?'

'I don't like the smell of wasabi,' Tanya retorted.

'What? You don't like wasabi? Fair enough. But for our sake, won't you eat just one?'

'She doesn't eat wasabi. She is allergic to it,' said Varun.

'Doesn't matter. Won't do much harm, Mr Rao.' He offered the pouch to Tanya and said, 'One nut, Nightingale?'

Adrian too walked up to stand right next to her.

Tanya looked the other way. She said nothing.

'She won't,' Kabir said, looking at the others. 'She won't because these nuts are laced with poison from hemlock seeds. When Tanya went on to the terrace to give Malvika her drink, she offered her the nuts, knowing Malvika would never say no to them. The pungent smell of the wasabi masked the smell of the poison. Even small doses can be lethal. The poison would have begun to affect her within minutes. Malvika would have felt her legs giving way. Drunk as she was, she would have leaned against the wall for support. A combination of her being drunk and unstable along with a progressive paralytic attack would have made her trip on the parapet and fall to her death. Everyone would suspect suicide. Poisoning would not be on anyone's mind. Matter closed. What a fabulous cover you had! The finance minister. Tell the world of an affair with the minister. And just in case the suicide story didn't work, the world would think that the minister was responsible for the murder. Awesome, Tanya, awesome!'

'What rubbish! I did not kill my mom.'

'This small bottle of wasabi nuts was recovered from your kitchen. Forensic examination shows that this is laced with hemlock poison. The poison on just one nut is enough to kill a person.'

'I have no clue how it got there. I didn't even know that hemlock seeds are poisonous. And, for a minute, even if I believe that this is how mom died, where is the proof that I did it?'

Kabir laughed like a mad man. He walked back to his briefcase and pulled out a picture of Tanya getting into the ambulance. He showed it to everybody. Her bag was open. He pulled out another picture, 'This is the magnified image of the photo I just showed you.'

There was a buzz in the room. The second photograph was a close-up of Tanya's open bag. Inside the bag, they could clearly see a small bottle containing green-coloured nuts. It was obvious that they were the wasabi-flavoured nuts. He lifted the bottle that had been seized from Tanya's house and held it up for everyone to see.

'Same brand, shape, size, scratches, batch number . . . In essence the one in my hand is the bottle you are seeing in Ms Tanya Sehgal's bag.' He turned towards Tanya and asked, 'Can you please explain, Ms Tanya Sehgal, how that bottle came to be your bag? A bag that you were carrying on your person when you accompanied Malvika's body in the ambulance? And why would you carry wasabi nuts for your mother, especially at a time when the Four Seasons had been specifically told to ensure that wasabi nuts were served along with drinks?' He pulled out the confirmation mail from the Four Seasons and waved it at everyone present in the room.

Silence.

She had a faraway look in her eyes.

'Why would you suspect the wasabi nuts to be compromised, of all things?' Aditya spoke. The sole sensible voice in the room.

'Normally, we wouldn't but that night we found it in the kitchen. Right next to where the cleaning liquids are kept. Why would anyone keep wasabi nuts there? Not to say that we were sure something was amiss—it was just one of the things we decided to check. But our suspicion had been aroused for sure. After our tests found the poison in it, we asked to re-examine Malvika's viscera and found traces of the same poison. In quantities large enough to kill someone.'

'The initial post-mortem report didn't show it!' Aditya argued.

'It wouldn't. The problem with toxicology testing is that there is no one test that checks for all known poisons. The tests normally conducted in a post-mortem check for opiates and basic toxins. Only when someone suspects foul play or a specific toxin is forensic toxicology more useful. In this case, had we not found the wasabi nuts in the kitchen, we would never have figured out what could have caused her death.' Kabir was very forthcoming.

Aditya looked at Tanya with surprise. 'But this is unbelievable. There must be a mistake somewhere. Tanya couldn't have killed Malvika!'

'I have no idea what Mr Khan is talking about, Aditya uncle. I did not kill my mom!'

'That's for the courts to decide,' said Kabir.

'But, Mr Khan, even if we assume that Tanya killed Malvika, what could the motivation be? Why would she kill Malvika? The whole logic seems baseless!' Had anyone else said this, he would have had hell to pay. But Aditya had built a rapport with both Adrian and Kabir and that helped.

'It was not the wasabi alone, Mr Rao. If we carefully look at everything that Malvika had on her person at the time she died, it becomes clear we were wrong in concluding that Malvika committed suicide.'

Blank looks.

'In fact it was what she didn't have when she reached the hospital that made us wonder. We figured this out only a few days ago, when the CBI started re-examining the case.' Without waiting for responses, he pulled out another photograph. 'Here.'

It was a photograph of Malvika holding a wine glass. It was taken during the party. 'Look carefully at everything she is wearing.' He pulled out a few more pictures from his bag. 'Look at these pictures, taken before the ambulance arrived, and after she was taken to the hospital.'

Nothing seemed to be different. Adrian was not looking at the pictures. He was looking at the people in the room, gauging their expressions. 'And here is the list of items found on Malvika's body when she was taken in.'

'Notice anything amiss?' Kabir asked everyone.

No one responded. 'Tanya, do you notice anything amiss?'

'Let me tell you, since she won't,' Kabir continued. 'In the picture where Malvika is holding a wine glass, she is wearing a ring on her right hand. The next image is from when she was lying on the ground at the spot where she fell. The ring is still on her finger. In the third photo taken at the hospital . . . the ring is missing!'

'And here, look!' He passed around two more images. 'Tanya at the party. Tanya at the hospital.' Tanya was not even listening any more. 'Look at her fingers.' Kabir was persistent. 'No ring at the party. But mysteriously the ring appears when she steps out of the ambulance at the hospital!'

When everyone was done looking at the images, he added, 'Tanya is wearing the ring right now.'

'This was my mother's ring. I took it off her finger and wore it. How does that prove anything? What are you trying to insinuate?' She turned around. Everyone was looking at her. 'I haven't done anything wrong,' she cried out. And she walked towards Varun and hugged him, as if imploring him to take her away from there.

Varun pushed her back, just a bit. 'Then why, Tanya? Why did you lie to me about the ring?' He held her hand and pulled it up softly. Tanya tried to free herself. Varun's grip was stronger than she had thought.

'You are hurting me, Varun,' she squirmed.

Varun didn't bother. With his free hand, he held her fingers and tried to pull off the ring. Tanya's lucky charm. It came off very easily. It had come off easily that night too when it had scratched his finger while he was in bed with a drunk Tanya.

Varun walked up to Adrian and gave him the ring. He turned towards Tanya. 'Why did you pretend that day, when I proposed, that the ring was so tight that it wouldn't come off your finger?'

'I don't know, Varun, believe me! I don't know. It was tight that day. I couldn't take it off.'

By then, Adrian had pulled out a magnifying glass and was examining the ring. 'Perhaps you can then explain how a bitcoin private key made its way on to this ring?'

'I have no clue. What private key are you talking about?'

'As a bitcoin founder, you should not ask this question, sweetheart!' said Adrian. He looked at the others and explained what a private key of a bitcoin wallet is. After that, he turned to Tanya and said, 'So, sweetheart, now can you tell us if you killing your mom was all about bitcoins and nothing else?'

'If you are saying that Malvika was killed for the ring, then isn't it clear? It's about the money!' That was Sundeep. 'But Malvika couldn't have had so much money that anyone would want to kill her for it! And, in any case, Tanya is her only heir. Everything that was Malvika's would be Tanya's in any case.'

'She had enough money.' It was Aditya this time. 'She laundered the money by transferring it overseas for the finance minister. It was all to be in exchange for cash and the position of RBI governor. She moved roughly 500 crore rupees of his money overseas. In return, she received 50 crore rupees. She kept all of it in bitcoins and was paranoid that she would lose them. I told her she was mad to keep it all in bitcoins but she wouldn't listen to me. She maintained a record of everything, inaccessible to anyone else.'

'It's here,' announced Tony. 'All that is on this laptop. The details of her bitcoin holdings along with the transaction details are all here. Dan just sent in the contents in unencrypted form. There is just 1 GB of data on this 750 GB laptop. Clearly, this laptop had only one purpose—to manage her transactions. Rather, keep a record of her transactions. This laptop has never been used to log on to the Internet.'

Varun remembered the night he sent the mail to the FBI. He looked at Tanya. Fear was writ large in her eyes. She looked worried. Worried about being exposed? He wondered. He took two steps towards her. 'Is that why you stopped me from using that laptop on the net, Tanya?'

'When Varun? When did I ever stop you from doing anything?'

'That night, when I sent a message to the CBI detailing Swami uncle's deposition implicating the finance minister, you asked me to transfer the file to the other laptop. I thought you asked me to do so because the other laptop connected automatically to the wi-fi. I never imagined it was because it contained details of her finances, which could be stolen if anyone hacked into it. Like a fool, I believed you. Tanya, I believed every word you said.' Varun looked the other way, visibly upset.

Tanya stared at him. She was about to respond when Kabir stepped in. 'So how much money did your mother have in bitcoins, Tanya?'

'Enough!' she screamed. 'Enough! First you accuse me of killing my mom. Then you accuse me of stealing all her bitcoins. God knows what's gotten into you.'

'Hold it, hold it!' Adrian exclaimed. 'That's not the only thing you're being accused of. You also founded Cotton Trail, an anonymous underground haven for drugs, banned medicines, and criminal activities of all kinds. You got Gillian Tan killed because he was about to confess to the President about his involvement, and give it all up. You helped organize the 5-million-dollar ATM heist and you let loose a massive malware that infected millions of computers and smartphones worldwide.' Adrian had an angry look on his face.

Tanya's hands went up and covered her mouth. 'You can't be serious!'

'Can't get any more serious, miss . . .' and he paused, '. . . Nightingale.'

'And what's the evidence?' Tanya asked, her voice betraying fear and despair.

'Well, Gillian Tan's laptop has revealed trails of email conversations with you debating his decision to give it all up. Because this was becoming bigger than he had anticipated. The NSA has access to emails exchanged between you two. Even the one where you threatened him with dire consequences in case he didn't give up any such plans—that is on record. Twelve days before he died, you threatened to have him eliminated if he didn't listen to you. You will be given an opportunity to counter these allegations but chances of you being able to prove it are slim. Before I forget, traces of the communication you had with Gillian after he decided to speak to the President about his being the force behind bitcoins, have been found on your laptop. And the same have been matched with those found on Gillian's laptop. The reconstruction of the dialogue between you two, using the two laptops, has shown growing, rather extreme animosity between you and him. It's watertight, Tanya.'

'No, I didn't kill Gillian. He was such a gentleman. Why would I kill him?'

'Ah, finally one confession. So you knew Gillian Tan.'

No response.

'You needed money to keep Cotton Trail going, so you masterminded the ATM heist.'

'No, I didn't. This is a set-up. I do not know anything about the ATM heist. I need to speak to my lawyer.' Tanya was almost in tears.

'You will get a lawyer but only after we are done with you. The ATM heist in New York was carried out with five debit cards. All five belonged to senior employees of NYIB all of whom, in a strange coincidence, visited your house for a dinner four months ago. When a new CEO took over NYIB. The welcome party was at your house, wasn't it?'

'Yes, it was.'

'Under the guise of playing some stupid "know your family" game, you took away all their wallets, arranged them in a separate room, and asked the wives identify their husbands' wallets from a pile of wallets. While arranging the wallets in a different room, you managed to skim the data off five cards, and gave them to the mules in New York for execution. This morning, when we searched your apartment, we recovered the card skimming device from your closet. So confident were you of not getting caught, that the card skimmer still has the data containing those five cards on it. It clearly puts you at the centre of the ATM heist.' He held up the card skimmer for all to see. It was small and black, and looked like a battery charger.

'I have never seen this thing before,' Tanya protested.

'Your fingerprints are all over it,' said Kabir. 'The entire proceedings were videotaped just to avoid any complications. And here,' he handed her a piece of paper, 'is the list that details the items recovered from your home, today and on that night your house was raided. Both were done in the presence of panchas, and they have certified the findings.'

'It's a set-up!' Tanya was still protesting.

'Well, God only knows how many people you set up, Tanya,' Kabir said.

'No, it is a set-up,' Tanya insisted. 'I have never seen this in my house.'

'Who could have set you up, Nightingale?' Adrian asked her, sweetly.

'I don't know. I really don't know. You have to believe me!' Tanya spoke through tears.

'Who else has access to your house?'

'The maids. Who also come and go when I'm there, and . . .' She thought for a few seconds, trying to fight back the tears. '. . . and Varun. No one else!'

'Ah, Varun.'

'When did this party take place?' Varun asked Tanya.

'Four months ago.'

'I was in jail then, in Goa. Remember?' There was no way he was going to let Tanya turn the tables and make him the villain of the piece.

'That resolves it, Nightingale. You are the only one who has full access to your residence. Unless, of course, your mother was responsible for all this.'

Tanya had no answer.

'And now, coming to the last accusation against you,' said Adrian, taking over. 'A massive malware attack occurred in over a million computers across the world. This attack had its seeds in the Townsville game. Anyone who downloaded the game also downloaded a malware, which did two things . . .' He went on to elaborate.

'You guys have seriously lost it. If it is to do with Indiscape, you need to ask these three gentlemen.' She pointed towards Aditya, Sundeep and Varun. 'I don't have any contact with Indiscape. How can I influence anything?'

'Again a lie!'

'No, I'm telling the truth.'

'Who is Laksh Mathur?'

'Laksh who?'

'Laksh Mathur.'

'I've heard that name before,' said Tanya.

'Perhaps this will help you remember?' Adrian showed her and Varun a photograph. When she saw it, Tanya's head started to spin. 'What has he done?'

'Well, you got him a job in Indiscape, didn't you?'

'No, I didn't!' Tanya protested violently. 'I just forwarded his CV to Indiscape. He wanted a job.'

'Is that all?' Kabir asked. He had a dangerous look on his face. 'How did you meet him?'

'I met him at a party at the Otters Club in Bandra. He came up to me and started chatting. He dropped me home that night.'

Varun had a look of contempt on his face. 'Is that all, or was there more?'

'Varun, believe me, there is nothing more to it. While we were driving back, he told me that he had been laid off and wanted a job. He asked me if I had any contacts. I told him that I'd send his CV to you. I even mentioned that to you!'

'I'd have believed you had I not seen this guy walking into the apartment below yours. When I saw him that day, I couldn't connect the dots. But a few days ago, I saw him again on Sundeep uncle's floor, and I realized he was the same guy I had seen in your building. What am I to make of it, Tanya? You send me a CV saying he is a stranger when he actually lives in your apartment building. And then he fucks up my world-class product and soils our reputation. How do I believe you?'

'What, what did this guy do?' Tanya was visibly upset. 'I haven't done anything. I really haven't done anything.' She was crying now.

Varun had a distressed yet unrelenting look on his face. 'This man, Laksh Mathur, was the one who uploaded the game to the server. And while uploading, we believe he inserted a programming code, which was nothing but a virus. One that downloaded itself on all devices that played Townsville, scanned them for digital bitcoin Wallets and eventually transferred the bitcoins found to his personal bitcoin collection. It also made the computers and cellphones join a network of distributed bitcoin miners. The mining caused multiple computers across the world to collapse and overheat. Not to speak of injuries to the owners of these devices.'

Adrian added, 'I hope we arrest him soon. Until yesterday, 51894 bitcoins had allegedly been transferred into that wallet. That's a lot of money to swindle.'

Tanya turned towards Varun. Her eyes were fiery red. She looked angry. Insulted. Cheated. 'How the hell do you know that Laksh Mathur was the one who did all this, Varun? If you knew, why didn't you tell me earlier? Are you also one of them?' she pointed towards Kabir Khan and Adrian Scott as she yelled at Varun. 'All of you are playing games with me. I trusted you Varun. I . . .' She was getting hysterical now.

'Enough!' Adrian Scott raised his voice. It was sufficient to momentarily silence Tanya's outburst. 'Enough of this drama, Nightingale.'

Tanya glared at him.

'The only offence for which we do not have any material evidence against you—though we have more than enough circumstantial evidence—is Gillian's killing. However, we have enough to take you into custody for Malvika Sehgal's murder, for running Cotton Trail, for perpetrating the ATM heist, and for infecting millions of computers around the world. We have enough evidence to make sure you stay in jail for the rest of your life, Tanya.' Adrian was ruthless.

He had been sent on a wild goose chase for two-and–a-half months and he had hated every minute of it.

'I need to see my lawyer immediately. You people are talking a load of crap! I'm being falsely implicated in stuff I had no role in!'

Then Adrian dropped a bombshell. 'You are an American fugitive, hiding in India.'

He turned to Kabir and said, 'She holds an American passport.' Then, he took Kabir aside and whispered, 'Mr Khan, can we now produce her in court and seek permission to deport her back to the US to be tried for one of the worst and biggest cyber crimes in history? We will need permission from the President to make public anything concerning Gillian Tan's involvement. There is a diktat from his office. I can't disregard that.'

'The CBI is happy to support it. We can take it to court when it opens on Monday. But it may not be the best thing for me to do.'

'What do you mean, Mr Khan?' Adrian was surprised.

'Tanya is involved in Malvika Sehgal's murder. A crime for which most of the people of this country hold the finance minister responsible.'

'I know that.'

'We need to settle that issue first. We have to give the finance minister a clean chit. And we can only do that if we book Tanya for her mother's murder. Since the crime was committed in India, irrespective of the nationality of the criminal, we will have to book her here.'

'Ah . . . understood. Is there a way out?'

# 97

# Epilogue

The case against Tanya Sehgal was soon the talk of the town.

The FBI and the CBI carefully avoided any reference to bitcoins and her intimacy with Gillian Tan. The US government was worried that it might unnecessarily drag the President of the US into an unsavoury complication because of his close friendship with Gillian Tan. The only charge filed against her was for the murder of Malvika Sehgal, with the intent to steal her bitcoins.

The Indian finance minister was abdicated of any involvement in the murder of Malvika Sehgal. The connect between the minister and the laundering of 500 crore rupees didn't come out in the open. In any case, no one could link the finance minister with the laundering of the ill-gotten 500 crore rupees.

~

Nikki Tan's condition improved. When she regained consciousness, she gave a statement to the cops saying that Gillian was planning to confess to the President about being the brain behind bitcoins—that he was Satoshi Nakamoto. He was shaken up by the murders of two members of his secret team. Worried that he might be next in line. He wanted to make sure that the bitcoin project was in safe hands and was administered in line with the scale of the idea, and the infinite opportunities it presented. When confronted with the CCTV footage placing her at the site where the ATM heist plan was hatched, she had an explanation ready. She admitted to going there to meet an old friend and said that that's when Umar Farouk walked up to her to offer his condolences. Knowing Nikki's and Gloria's background, the FBI didn't pursue their interrogation.

The ring that Josh Connelly had tried to steal from Nikki was actually Gillian Tan's. Wary of losing his wealth, Gillian had had the private key engraved on the ring. He left out some elements of the key because he knew that without knowing how many and which characters were missing, neither Nikki nor anyone else would be able to steal his bitcoins. Josh, the third member of Gillian's secret team, had hoped to return the missing million dollars to the perpetrators of the ATM heist and also make a quick buck for himself by stealing Gillian's private key. Being one of the creators of bitcoins, he knew that even if the ring had missing characters, he would be able to recreate the key using code logic, which only he had access to.

～

Once the FBI identified Stan, Josh's roommate who was supposed to deliver the million dollars to the perpetrators in the Dominican Republic, as the American with the fake passport who molested the French woman in Pondicherry, they arrested him with help from the CBI and the local police. From the data on Stan's cell phone, the FBI was able to locate and round up the other people involved in the ATM heist. They also found the address in Santo Domingo where the cash and goods were supposed to have been delivered. It was not the same address they had obtained from Josh's laptop. Possibly the drop-point had been changed at the last minute as a precautionary measure. A SWAT team of joint operatives from the FBI and local law enforcement agencies raided the location and managed to take into custody a few of the perpetrators, who were nothing but pawns in the entire game. They were operators who did what they did for a cut. It was never meant to be their money in the first place.

Townsville, was withdrawn by Indiscape. This dramatically

affected Indiscape's standing in the world of gaming. Worried about the company's credibility and security systems, clients stopped playing their games. Revenues dried up and MAUs plummeted, taking the company's fortunes along. The company shut down within a few months.

eTIOS survived the hacking controversy. The joint audit committee formed by the regulators and a group of customers cleared them of any wrongdoing. Aditya's and Sundeep's personal relationships with their clients helped them regain confidence. The company has now consolidated its position as one of the best BPOs in India.

Aditya expressed his desire to hang up his boots. He handed over the reigns of his company to Sundeep, his confidant. Swami's wife, Kalpana, joined him. Together, they are taking the company ahead.

~

A few days after Tanya was arrested, Varun walked up to Aditya and said, 'Dad, we need to chat.'

'Yes, Varun?' Aditya sensed that something was bothering his son.

'I want to go back, Dad. When I came here, things were so good, it was fun. I met you, got a family—something I had sorely missed for many years. Now that I look back at it, Dad, I just feel that I was better off in the US. At least people don't pretend to be who they are not.'

'Who are you talking about, Varun?'

Varun struggled to look at Aditya. He was struggling to hold back his tears. 'Tanya, Dad. Why did she do this to me? I loved her. Why did she have to pretend? Why did she play with my emotions?' Varun was on the verge of breaking down. Aditya knew that more than Tanya's misdeeds, her cheating on him with Laksh had traumatized Varun. And he wanted to run away from these agonizing memories.

Varun promised Aditya that he would come back and settle

down in India once he got over the trauma. He planned to use the intervening time to pursue further studies in the US, which Aditya offered to fund. Varun declined any financial assistance. Aditya didn't have the heart to stop him. The only thing that has now changed for him is that he is closer to his son than ever before.

～

Dan Malloy retired and recommended Adrian as his replacement. The suggestion was accepted and Adrian succeeded Dan as head of the CRRU.

～

Mike Hendricks is slated to be the Republican candidate for the next US presidential elections. Possibly a reward for managing the public relations exercise surrounding the Gillian Tan episode and ensuring that the President's reputation was not tarnished by his close friendship with Satoshi Nakamoto. While Mike and Nikki continue to live apart, Gillian's death has made Gloria look up to Mike more than ever before.

～

One day, the mutilated body of a woman was found floating in the Hudson. It had been tied to a rock and dumped into the river. It had stayed there, at the bottom of the Hudson, for over a week, before the rope gave way and the body floated to the top. The *Sun* carried the story on the front page. The confessing hooker was gone for ever.

～

Swami's death is still being investigated by the crime cell of Mumbai Police. As with every sensational event, the incident was a media story for a few weeks, after which interest in it died down. He was relegated to the sixth page in the mainline dailies. With no evidence against the finance minister or anyone else, and given the fact that the person driving the dumper confessed to his crime, there was little that anyone could do. The driver of the dumper is free—out on bail. Given the slow legal process in India, he is expected to stay out of jail for a long time to come.

# 98

# A few months later

Dan was relaxing on a beach in Hawaii, enjoying his retirement, when his phone rang.

A call from Adrian.

'Hey, Adrian!' he exclaimed the moment he swiped the connect button. 'Why don't you get your ass down here and do what I am doing? Pina colada on the beach!'

'There's been an incident, Dan.'

'Go on. Am listening.'

'There's been a login. Under the name "Icebreakers".'

'Icebreakers?'

'A mint again, Dan. The mint Icebreakers.'

'Of course, of course. The one that comes in a round plastic box. Coloured base, white top?'

'That's not the point, Dan!'

'Then what is?'

'Someone logged in using this name and put up a post. It simply says: "I came across this website called Cotton Trail *Ver 2.0*. It's a TOR hidden service that claims to allow you to buy and sell anything online anonymously. I'm thinking of buying off it, but wanted to see if anyone here had heard of it and could recommend it. I found it through Cottontrail420.wordpress.com, which, if you have a TOR browser, directs you to the real site at blah blah blah. Let me know what you think . . .'

'You're kidding me!'

'Does it look like I am?'

'Does that mean that we were chasing a red herring all those months? That the real brain behind all this is free?'

'Maybe . . .'

'What's the choice?' Dan asked.

'Nothing. I don't intend to open it up again. We will look like idiots.'

'I agree. Let the world believe we got it right.'

# 99

# USA/India

Varun's cab stopped outside his townhouse in Seattle. He gave a fifty-dollar bill to the cabbie. It was twenty dollars over but he didn't bother. He was happy that day. He opened the door and walked in. The house was clean. What else did he expect? No one had lived there for over six months. There was a musty smell though.

Leaving the bag in the foyer, he walked up to the mezzanine. From there, he could step out into the garden at the back. It was a small but warm and comfortable house. He looked out through the window. Something caught his eye, alerting him to the presence of an intruder. Someone was on the swing, looking into the woods, away from the house. He pushed open the door leading to the backyard. Quietly, without making any noise, he tiptoed into the garden. Midway, he removed his shoes, lest he step on a pebble and make a sound.

As he neared the swing, he spread his hands, ready to pounce. The last few steps were difficult. He crouched, took one step at a time, carefully controlling his breathing so as not to be heard. And finally when he was within pouncing distance, he made the lunge. He jumped from behind, pushing the person off the swing, on to the grass. The two of them rolled down the lawn and went sliding for a few feet before friction brought them to a halt.

Varun looked at the person beneath him. His hands came up to her face, to move the few strands of hair away. He smiled. She beamed. They hugged.

'What took you so long?' she asked.

'I had to complete the job that I'd gone for, baby.'

'You are back for good?'

'Hmm . . . ' Varun nodded. 'For good. For ever.' And he hugged Gloria even tighter. She closed her eyes as his lips met hers. They kissed. Their first kiss in a long, long time. Varun's first honest kiss from the time he landed in Goa.

His thoughts went back to the days when he was in Stanford, pursuing a postgraduate degree in technology. Gloria was an undergrad. He had met her at a friend's party. And fallen for the innocence. The grace. She loved his aggression, his will to succeed, his sense of humour. They were made for each other. They had started seeing each after the party. Their life revolved around each other. They met every day, went on long drives, dinner dates, pub nights, movies . . . Gloria loved that one moment when they were watching *The Italian Job* at the drive-in theatre. In the movie John Bridger tells Charlie, 'Find someone you want to spend the rest of your life with and hold on to her forever.' At that very instant, Gloria felt Varun's hand snake into hers and hold hers tightly. She cried that day.

She also cried another day, when she came to Varun and told her heartrending story. A story of abuse. Of sexual assault by her own father. Gillian Tan, the beast. It had happened when Nikki was travelling. The day after Mike Hendricks was announced as the new chief of staff to the President of America, a furious Gillian Tan had returned home, drunk. Gillian was a contender for the post, but had lost out in the race. In Gloria he saw Mike Hendricks and was reminded of his personal and professional failures and poured out all his frustration and anger on her. He repeatedly raped her that night.

Varun was furious. He wanted to go to the cops. But Gloria talked him out of it. Gillian was too powerful. He was the senator who was the President's closest friend. She held Varun back from taking any rash steps. He then worked out a plan. A man who could violate his own stepdaughter was sure to have more skeletons in his cupboard.

He needed to know what those skeletons were.

Reprisal on his mind, he started following Gillian. Even all the way to Rio. That's where he learnt about Tanya. When he scraped the surface, it was not at all difficult to figure out that Tanya was Malvika's daughter. And Malvika was his estranged father's ex-colleague. Once back from Rio, he contacted the Hooker, who was then let loose on Gillian. His plan paid dividends. The Hooker was successful in seducing Gillian. They met a few times at a downtown hotel in California. That's when Gillian invited her to the Stanford dorm. It was not difficult to smuggle her in. It was in the dorm that Gillian's super-high libido came to the fore. The dorm played host to Gillian's rendezvous with the Hooker along with the one whose dorm it was—Tanya Sehgal. During the assignation, the Hooker dropped a bug in the room, allowing Varun to listen in to all conversations taking place in the room then on.

Once the room was bugged, it was just a matter of time before Varun discovered that Gillian was the creator of bitcoins, and went by the name of Satoshi Nakamoto in the virtual world. He also discovered that all was not well between Tanya and Gillian. They fought frequently and almost all the quarrels were on account of Gillian not sharing the gains from the bitcoin project with any of the project team. There was lot at stake, and Gillian kept promising but never delivered. From their conversation it was clear that Gillian had told Tanya about Gloria being his stepdaughter. Tanya repeatedly mentioned this to Gillian to poison his mind against Gloria and Nikki. She encouraged Gillian to sexually exploit Gloria when he lost the battle for the position of the President's chief of staff. Varun figured this out for Gillian brought it up a few times and even blamed her for his past actions when they clashed on the equitable distribution of wealth. Tanya probably wanted Nikki and Gloria to leave him. She believed that a baggage-free Gillian would be more committed to her. Irrespective of the rationale, in the eyes of Varun she was equally accountable for Gloria's plight, if not more.

Nikki played the waiting game. Once Varun had gathered all the evidence, a furious Nikki did confront Gillian, but she was more practical about it. She forced him to transfer his entire bitcoin wealth to her. She also threatened Gillian into agreeing to confess to his involvement in the bitcoin saga to the President. She didn't want to rake up the issue of Gillian and his stepdaughter publically, for she felt it would affect Gloria.

Once the bitcoins were transferred to her, Nikki approached Mike Hendricks. Though her romantic liaison with Mike was long over, he was Gloria's father had every right to know what had happened to his daughter. Mike decided to fix Gillian forever. He reached out to Islamic fundamentalists for help. Umar Farouk came forward but there was a cost attached to it. He had this grand plan of stealing money from ATMs using cloned cards and demanded support for that and free passage as compensation.

That's when Varun volunteered to help. His father, albeit estranged, ran a BPO which took care of cards processing for NYIB. His mother had convinced him that Aditya was the devil incarnate. This was a god-sent opportunity to get even with him. Mike looked the other way as Varun worked with Umar and chalked out a plan, which included stealing data from NYIB customers in India and hacking into their systems to increase their credit limits.

Once the plan was set, Umar was ready to roll. The attack on Gillian had to be a precision attack and needed serious logistic support. Umar contracted the Red Army Faction from Germany, a local militant organization known to use the Misznay-Schardin effect, to eliminate Gillian and they did so with precision. The payment made to the RAF was to be recovered from the ATM heist. This was the agreed modus operandi to make sure no fingers pointed back at Mike, Nikki, or Varun. Gillian was taken out on the very day he was to meet the President.

Everything went as per plan. Varun came to India. Befriended Leon D'Souza, the waiter who had access to drugs. Orchestrated a meeting between Leon and Tanya, met Tanya himself and then disappeared. Went to prison willingly, for a crime he did not commit.

The Nigeria-linked riots provided ample cover. He was prepared to give himself up in a drug fight, just to make sure he was imprisoned. He knew that if he called Aditya at an appropriate time, he would have Varun released and welcome him back into his life.

At an official party at Malvika's residence, organized to welcome Matt Metzger to India, Leon was the official caterer. He had also convinced Tanya to allow him to set up a festive kiosk on Malvika's terrace to sell Goan handicrafts. When the visitors (all senior management officials of NYIB) paid for the purchase, he skimmed the card information off the magnetic strip into the card skimmer he was carrying. It was a big risk; had he got caught, he would've had hell to pay. But Varun had paid him handsomely. Of the cards skimmed, Varun selected five and passed on the details to Umar to carry out the heist.

On Tanya's birthday, when she was drunk and fast asleep, in the guise of gifting her a life-size teddy bear, Varun managed to get her fingerprints on the card skimmer, which he dumped in her cupboard and was later recovered by the CBI. Tanya's fingerprints on the skimmer were enough to implicate her in the ATM scam.

In the meantime, Nikki decided to tackle Gillian's accomplices in the bitcoins project. She knew that one of them, the Japanese, was dead. Tanya was likely to be incapacitated, once Varun's plan in India was implemented. The only person left was Josh. She recommended to Umar that he use Josh to carry out the ATM heist. Evidence of Josh being involved in the heist would give her leverage over him if it ever came down to a conflict over Gillian's bitcoins. Umar met Josh and sealed the deal for half a million dollars. On the day of the heist, Nikki went to the café to gather photographic evidence of Josh's involvement in the heist. Even Mike Hendricks had recommended this. The heist went as per plan. Money was withdrawn from the ATMs as scheduled.

The ATM heist ran into rough weather when Stan ran away with the money that Josh had sent to the Dominican Republic. Confronted with Umar Farouk's ire, Josh panicked. He decided to do something which he had considered many times in the past but never followed through with. He decided to steal the private key of Gillian's bitcoin wallet.

Unfortunately, Nikki woke up and confronted him. During the confrontation, he saw the ring on Nikki's finger and recognized it as the ring Gillian had engraved with his bitcoin key. In the attempt to run away with the ring, he was shot at and killed by Adrian and Tony.

In India, at the first opportunity, Varun replaced Malvika's bottle of wasabi nuts with the hemlock-laced ones on the day of Malvika's party. At the party, once Malvika had picked up a few nuts, he took the plate away to make sure that no one else ate from it. When the same wasabi nuts were found in Tanya's house, the police made the connection as he had intended and implicated Tanya. When Kabir confronted her with the wasabi nuts, though she was genuinely surprised, she couldn't prove her innocence.

Varun's killer move was to bring in a long-time associate and ex-Microsoft programmer, Laksh. This smart programmer from suburban Bangalore knew how to get attention from women. He met Tanya at a party at the local club and approached her. Tanya found him interesting and they got talking. That night she brought him back to her house and after a steamy session in bed he told her that he had just come back from the US and was looking for a job. Tanya promised to help him out by referring him to Indiscape. When Laksh told Varun that he had slept with Tanya, it hurt his pride a bit, but he moved on quickly. He was on a mission.

The moment Tanya sent the CV to Varun, his objective was accomplished. Everything that Laksh did could be attributed in an indefensible manner to Tanya. Not that she was accountable for his actions simply because she had referred him, but it was enough to get people suspicious. Varun took extra care to make sure that people in office believed that he didn't know Laksh.

Finally, Varun hammered the last nail in the coffin by writing to Kabir and telling him the version of the story he wanted people to know. A version that suited the government and the CBI, and incriminated Tanya. At that time the bank CEO–finance minister saga was at a crescendo.

Malvika, who towards the end of her life, was quite depressed and worked up about the direction her life was taking, became an unsuspecting pawn in this deadly game.

By the time Tanya was taken away by the CBI—accused of the brutal murder of Malvika—the FBI was fully convinced that Tanya had not only masterminded the assassination of Gillian Tan and his project associates but was also the brain behind Cotton Trail and Satoshi Nakamoto's closest and only surviving associate in the bitcoins project. It was true that she was a part of Gillian's team. She was a sex maniac with a gigantic libido. She was Altoids. But that's all she was. She hadn't killed anyone. The Japanese student, who was a member of the project team was eliminated by Gillian because he had become a threat. He had started blackmailing him, threatening to expose his Satoshi Nakamoto identity to the world. Tanya is now paying the price, for sins she didn't commit. But life, as they say, is a big leveller. The crimes she committed were far more serious and far more heinous in nature. And given the FBI's interest in camouflaging those crimes, she would never have ended up in the dock for those.

For someone of Tanya's pedigree in the virtual world, she was very casual. Despite knowing that in the virtual world, everyone is naked, she did not even try to cover herself, for she thought she was alone. Unaware of the fact that the FBI and Varun were always watching her, for different reasons. Else the night Varun took her to the office, when he went back to check if the Townsville update had been uploaded or not, she wouldn't have logged in using Aditya's wi-fi network. Not only did she log on to the Internet, she also posted a message as Altoids, and asked the bitcoin community to help identify the missing alphanumerics in Malvika's private key. That night, Aditya had given her the wi-fi password as he was leaving for home. Even on the night of her birthday, when Varun left her in Aditya's room, after a passionate lovemaking session, she committed the cardinal mistake of logging in from there and posting another message as Altoids, agreeing to engage in order to get the missing alphanumerics.

~

Tanya has been denied bail by the high court and is housed in the Arthur Road jail in Mumbai, home to hardened criminals. When she comes out of jail, if she ever does, her life will be worse than death.

Nikki is happy that Gloria has found a loving partner in Varun. Someone who is willing to put his life and reputation on the line for her daughter. She is even happier to have all of Gillian's bitcoins, and more importantly, the entire blueprint of Cotton Trail.

Cotton Trail *Ver 2.0* is her latest passion. But this time around it is a Cotton Trail with a difference. A cleaner, genuine, well-meaning Cotton Trail *Ver 2.0*, trading in household goods, kitchen equipment, books and everything one can think of; except drugs, narcotics, banned pharmaceuticals and pornography of any kind. A site meant for clean libertarians who valued their online privacy and under no circumstances wanted that to be compromised. Though she never got back with Mike Hendricks, both of them knew that they were always there for each other.

A few months after Varun returned to the US, he and Gloria went away to New Zealand where they now run a small organic farm and live happily, taking care of each other.

The dry run paid off for Umar Farouk. In February 2014, he carried out the biggest ATM heist in the history of the world. In a coordinated operation lasting over twelve hours, using fifteen debit cards of a mid-eastern bank, a crew of cashers carried out 40,000 transactions across ATMs in two dozen countries and made away with 45 million dollars—the largest ATM heist ever. The Gillian Tan murder paid for itself ten times over.

The value of each bitcoin has soared to 1000 dollars, making Varun one of the world's youngest billionaires. He won't be seeing Aditya ever again.

BY THE SAME AUTHOR

*Bankerupt*

When an out-of-work banker joins his wife at MIT Boston in an attempt to salvage his marriage, he steps into a nightmare. MIT is a simmering volcano waiting to erupt. Accused of murder, the only way he can survive is to find the real culprits who will stop at nothing short of seeing him dead.

*Bankerupt* is Ravi Subramanian's most shocking and adrenalin-packed novel ever.

Penguin
Fiction/PB